RAZED

A Novel

Thatcher Carter

AN INLANDIA INSTITUTE PUBLICATION

RIVERSIDE, CALIFORNIA

Razed: A Novel by Thatcher Carter

Print ISBN: 978-1-955969-46-8

ePub ISBN: 978-1-955969-47-5

Library of Congress Control Number: 2025934643

Permissions
Inlandia Institute
4178 Chestnut Street
Riverside CA 92501

Printed and bound in the United States
Distributed by Ingram

Cover art: Carter Kustera
Book layout & design: Mark Givens
Publications Coordinator: Laura Villareal

Published by Inlandia Institute
Riverside, California
www.InlandiaInstitute.org
First Edition

I dedicate this book with much love to two sisters:
my mom, Harriet "Laurie" Keck Chamberlain
&
my aunt, Elizabeth "Betsey" Thatcher Keck

TABLE OF CONTENTS

CHAPTER ONE

Legacy

January 1973

If we'd had money for a taxi, we would have told the driver to take it slow, let us adjust to the change in atmosphere from one end of town to the other. But we were on a city transit bus, barreling toward my father's funeral faster than we could count the stops. The bus bounced over dips on Erie Boulevard, raising us above our vinyl seats and making our stomachs lurch.

Miranda and I sat in the back row and pressed our hands together, fingers intertwined. I needed her. She might have looked frail from the outside—thin shoulders and long red hair like a teenager at Woodstock or a diaphanous sprite from a Shakespeare play—but if you looked into her eyes, you would see a steeliness. I wished I could borrow it.

I hadn't slept the night before, thinking about my dress and shoes, trivial concerns. I'd insisted that Miranda and I buy new outfits. "Everyone will be dressed to the nines," I told her. "I'm not going to show up looking like a ragamuffin."

In the end, Miranda wore a black turtleneck dress with a crocheted vest, and I wore a wool dress that cinched uncomfortably at the waist. They had cost more than we could afford, but I'd insisted. And then I'd tried to sleep with my hair in curlers. Whoever thought of such a torture? I had tossed and turned and woken up with a crick in my neck.

And of course, the whole time, I was thinking about my father—memories and anxieties like home movies against the inside of my eyelids. He was gone. There would be no reconciliation, and everyone at the church would know what had happened.

"These people do not determine your worth," Miranda said in a hushed whisper across our tight, shared seat. "You don't have to talk if you don't want to."

"The bulletin lists me as a speaker," I said, looking out the window. Dirty snowplowed heaps on the side of the road blurred with the movement of the bus. "I don't have a choice."

My younger sister, Ginny, had left me out of the funeral planning. She'd picked the flower arrangements and hymns. And then almost as an afterthought, she'd asked if I would speak briefly and nicely. She emphasized the "nicely," pausing for me to understand her request. It wasn't like our mother's funeral when we were young. Then, we'd been whisked to the front of the church like celebrities, maids had fussed over what we wore, and the newspapers had taken pictures of us. Now, there was a risk I'd go off message. But Ginny must have trusted me to stay on the tracks. It was for reasons like this that I thought we could be close again someday.

"In twenty years, no one will remember if you spoke," Miranda said. "They'll pull their stupid bulletin out of a drawer and throw it away. They won't even remember who Herbert Wilson was." She said this slowly, soothingly, as if to speak her vision into existence.

I hadn't prepared anything. I felt dizzy with the pressure of what to say. I tried to take a breath, but it caught in my chest, and I realized I didn't have enough air. I gasped and squeezed Miranda's hand, then bent down and put my head between my knees.

"You're okay," she said.

"I can't breathe," I said in a ragged whisper.

"Take a small breath," she said, rubbing my back. "You don't need a big one. Small breaths. In through your nose, out through your mouth. Your body knows what to do."

"Sorry," I said. "It will be over in a minute." I fought for my breath and stared at the chewing gum and scuff marks on the bus floor. My mind swirled. Everyone else would arrive in a taxi or their fanciest car. We were the only ones arriving by bus, wearing dresses from the Salvation Army.

I counted to ten and then backward to one. I imagined myself on the porch swing in *To Kill a Mockingbird*, Scout's refuge. I imagined the gentle rocking motion, the humidity in the air, the sound of her father solving a problem at the kitchen table, his voice resonant and sure.

When I could breathe again, I leaned back on the seat and looked into Miranda's eyes, through her glasses and mine. I was grateful for her calm presence. I wished everyone could know this woman. She wasn't famous, but she should have been. She had been in *Life Magazine* when she was only seven years old. Not many people knew that.

At the corner of Cedar and Fifth, the bus lurched to our stop. The afternoon sun cut through the January clouds, spotlighting the Montgomery Ward window displays and the Singer sewing machine outlet. We walked toward the Old Southeast Church, the same downtown church my family had belonged to when my mother was alive. My father had given monthly donations until the day he died, but we'd never attended. I couldn't remember the minister's name.

Walking on the sidewalk, Miranda and I dropped each other's hands. Our town hadn't had its Stonewall moment. To the citizens of Carthage, we appeared to be two women headed for spinsterhood: in our early thirties, without the tell-tale look of the marriage-hungry. We encouraged their misunderstanding, but it was exhausting. We lived and ran Miranda's deli business together, but none of the customers knew we were a couple. We were like vampires, only able to show our love after dark.

As we crossed the street toward the church, my legs tried to stop me from moving forward. My brain was sending mixed signals. Walk. Don't walk. I dreaded seeing the executives from my father's bank. They knew what I had done. And the former police chief would be there. He and I shared the shame for not intervening when my father had crossed the line all those years ago.

The church bells rang. A collection of designer suits, knee-length dresses, and black wool coats from Bloomingdale's moved toward the open doors.

"Is that my Lucretia?" a woman called behind us. Only one person in town called me by my full name. Most people found it too formal, of another century. It reminded them of Lucretia Mott, the suffragette, or else, if they were well read, it conjured up the disturbing images of *The Rape of Lucretia*.

Freya, my father's former secretary, caught up to us, hurrying on her pointed heels. She was the most important adult from my childhood, but my rift with my father had put her in an uncomfortable position. I didn't know if my father had ever asked her to cut ties with me, but we hadn't seen each other in years.

"I was hoping to find you," she said, pulling me into a hug. "You poor girl, this must be so hard." She smelled of talcum powder and hairspray—a soft exterior to cover an iron will. In her early sixties, she was sturdy with strong shoulders and a low center of gravity. Freya had to be strong to survive and thrive as my father's secretary for almost three decades. She was unflappable.

"I'm hanging in there," I said to her. When my mother died in 1944, I was five years old, and it was Freya's job to get me out of the house. At the time, I called her Miss Hoffman. She would leave the bank, still on the clock as my father's secretary, and pick me up from our housekeeper. Most of the time, Freya would take me to the movies. We saw a decade of matinees. She started with *Snow White and the Seven Dwarves* and then moved on to musicals like *Meet Me in St. Louis*, but we bonded the most over dramas well beyond my years. Gangster films. Political thrillers. Intrigues.

"You look good," she told me. "You're all grown up."

"All grown out." I spread my hands to show how my hips and belly had grown outwards—more like my father's body than my mother's or sister's.

Freya shook her head and crinkled her eyes at me. "You'll always be my little girl."

She hugged me again, then turned to Miranda. "Good to see you, too—beautiful as always."

Miranda hugged her.

So, I had two bodyguards. I would need them for the ordeal ahead. Maybe I could hide behind them and no one would see me.

Freya leaned in close nd lowered her voice. "I have something for you. I'll give it to you inside."

"What could you have brought to a funeral for a father's less-favored daughter?" I asked.

"You weren't less favored." She brushed some loose hairs off the shoulders of my coat.

"I was definitely less favored," I said, nodding to emphasize each elongated syllable. "He cut me out of the will."

"It was complicated." Freya held my eye, trying to gauge my point of view on what had happened. "And you don't have to impress anyone in there. It's not your job to fit in with them or apologize for who you are. If you do that, you lose everything."

I nodded, but in my mind, I had already lost everything when

I'd challenged my family fourteen years ago. My father had never forgiven me. I had lost my close relationship with my sister. And I had lost my inheritance, not that I cared about that part.

At the front steps, I looked for an easy path into the church, a way to avoid the worst of the crowd. The men and women of Carthage always had something to prove at events like these. In other cities, they might relax on a Tuesday afternoon, but here, they had to show the world that they were as good as New York City. When people from other countries said "New York," they pictured the Empire State Building, the Statue of Liberty, the pulse of Manhattan. Upstate cities like Buffalo, Rochester, Syracuse, and Carthage didn't have that lure. In fact, we weren't even officially Carthage, though we called ourselves that. We were North Carthage, part of a disagreement with the other city of Carthage about who had legal rights to the name. We had orchestras and art museums, jazz clubs, and Jewish delis, but no one ever traveled halfway across the earth for those, not if they had a choice.

Most of the people parading into the church service knew about my relationship with my family. They knew that my sister Ginny and her husband had lived in the family home with my father, circulating with him at country club dances, civic events, and social hours. They knew that I had been relegated to the other side of the highway: not the side with the downtown sector, the university, or this stately church, but the other side of the elevated highway, past the underpasses of snow and trash—in the half-abandoned neighborhood that subsisted in the shadow of the highway. It used to be called "Jewtown" and "Blacktown," but after the highway had decimated it and the neighborhood no longer posed any threat, everyone called it "Old Ward Thirteen."

A Plymouth Satellite drove past with the loud baseline of Marvin Gaye's "What's Going On?" pulsing from the car speakers. Then a police cruiser pulled up in front of the church. The former police chief, Arnold Manley, climbed out of the back seat as if he were exiting a taxi. I couldn't look away. He wore his dress uniform with brass buttons and stars on the shoulders. The crowd parted for him to enter.

The sight of the cruiser gave me chills. I watched the eyes of the driver to see if he recognized me.

As we went up the stone steps, I shifted my gaze to my shoes, trembling even though I was wearing wool tights and a heavy coat. Inside, the church rumbled with small talk as people stood in the aisles and found their places. A faint thread of organ notes rose into the rafters. I held onto Freya and Miranda and moved slowly through the narthex, like an invalid with a pair of attendants.

Henry Sulliman, the former mayor and a close friend of my father's, stood in the aisle with his cane. Sycophants fawned over him and led him to an honorific seat in the front pew. His fluffy white hair and white skin gave him a ghost-like pallor, and the heavy black frames of his eyeglasses looked as if they were floating on that pale background. Mrs. Sulliman, a head shorter than her husband even when he hunched over his cane, wore a black hat with a lace overlay—an expensive choice, sure to be mentioned on the society page of *The North Carthage Register*.

As my eyes adjusted to the lighting in the church, my mind was consumed by my tights. The farther they sagged down my legs, the smaller my steps became. I wanted nothing more than to hike up my dress and re-arrange my underclothes. Instead, I tried to concentrate on the promise I'd made to my sister. I would give a brief remembrance, as the bulletin foretold, but I'd keep it short and not air my grievances. Our father was dead, and Ginny wanted to get through the funeral without additional grief. She wanted to paint a pretty picture of our family.

I wracked my brain trying to come up with a positive story to share. Since he'd cut me out of his will, my father and I had struggled to remain civil. He thought I had thrown my life away, and I thought he was a liar and a thief. If I thought back to the late fifties, all I could think about was the day he'd broken my heart, and I wasn't going to share that again. I'd gone to the newspapers with that story and the editors had run to my father to tell him. No, if I wanted a positive story, I'd have to go back to a time when I believed in him, a time when I still thought he was a good man.

Blocking our passage, the former president of Carthage Savings and Loan, Howard Kramer, stood with his head bent down to listen to a bevy of widows. He was unnaturally tall. He had a large head with slicked black hair, broad shoulders under a perfectly tailored suit. He had been president of the bank when my father was vice president, and they both had walked away with money far beyond their salaries.

Kramer spoke loudly, telling the widows that the stock market would reach new heights under the Nixon administration, and that 1973 was going to be a year of prosperity. They crinkled their eyes at him. They had reason to be grateful: Kramer and my father had lined bank accounts throughout the city, and as a result, these widows would never know a day of want or sacrifice.

Rather than push past him, I chose a pew near the back. Cousins from Pennsylvania, Brooklyn, and Manhattan filled the rows near the front—no one I really knew. A glance told me that my father's brother hadn't come. I didn't think he would.

In the front pew, with nothing between her feet and the minister, my sister, Ginny Tower, sat with a handkerchief under her nose. Her husband, Joseph Tower, stood next to her, flashing a broad Irish smile and shaking hands with a traffic jam of well-wishers.

I sat between Freya and Miranda. Freya arranged her heavy coat on her lap and pulled out a large accordion file, worn at the corners and creased along its folds.

"This is for you," she whispered. "It's everything you ever wanted to know about your father."

I looked at the bulging file. *Everything I ever wanted to know?* I doubted that.

"I saved every memo," Freya said, facing forward in the pew as if we were in a spy movie. "They asked me to destroy these, but I knew that wasn't right. I couldn't stand to let it happen a second time in my life."

I stared at Freya's face in profile—her eyes still blue, her skin creased with time, her dyed blonde hair curling around her ears.

I turned and exchanged a look with Miranda. She raised her eyebrows.

"I don't want this," I whispered to Freya, pushing the file back under her coat. "There was a time when I would have." I looked at her again. I didn't want to minimize what she was offering, what she must have gone through to put this file together, but I couldn't handle it. I was putting the past behind me. "I've moved on," I told her. "I'm not at war with him anymore."

Then, I looked past Miranda into the aisle. My sister Ginny had made her way back to our pew and was reaching out to me.

"Lucy," she said, pulling on my hand. She was in a black dress with a black lace collar, probably purchased at Lord & Taylor. On her blonde head, she wore a small hat, like one of Jackie Kennedy's. And of course, she wore our mother's pearls. They were her calling card even though they should have been mine. I know my eyes were clouded by resentment, but I thought my sister had become the worst sort of monster—a society lady. She went to the country club every day and sat on the Historical Preservation Committee. She threw tea parties and probably snuck gin into her teacup. She'd become everything we had maligned as teenagers.

I stood and hugged her awkwardly over Miranda's knees— I could feel Ginny's shoulder blades through the fabric of her dress.

"Come sit with us," Ginny said to me. She glanced at Miranda, as if weighing whether to invite her too.

I looked toward the front pew and saw Ginny's husband adjusting his coat and sighing. Their daughter, Sarah, was waving at me as she came down the aisle. She was the brightest light in Ginny's life, and for some reason, Sarah loved me. I wasn't sure why. Sometimes I thought Sarah was the only reason Ginny ever invited me to the house.

When Sarah reached us, she hugged me. "We went to the graveyard yesterday, Aunt Lucy, and you can't believe all the Wilsons there! I hardly knew who any of them were. We need to research them and make a chart."

Sarah and I were the researchers of the family, and on the rare times when Ginny let me take Sarah out on my own, she and I always headed to the library. I taught her everything I had learned in librarian school, and we studied whatever topic she could come up with—butterflies, teddy bears, daffodils. More recently, we had studied the Vietnam War and Civil Rights, but Ginny didn't know about her daughter's newer topics.

Ginny hugged Sarah close and whispered, "Not now. Go back and sit with Daddy."

Sarah walked back up the aisle, a dutiful daughter.

"Freya," Ginny said. "I'm glad you're here. My father—our father—would have loved that you came."

"My condolences," Freya said.

Ginny looked at me again, waiting for a reply.

"No," I said. "I'll stay here. There's not enough room up there for all of us."

She gauged my words, trying to spot resentment. Not finding any, she said, "Then, at least sit on the aisle." She patted Miranda on the shoulder and urged her to change places with me. To me, she said, "You'll speak after the first hymn."

I nodded. Ginny cared about such things. She didn't want any lag time during the ceremony; she needed to impress. She'd married our father's colleague to secure her place in Carthage society, and that brought its own little miseries. I didn't envy her glittering obligations. To me, she was still the little girl who had brought her dolls down during our father's cocktail parties. They would appear one by one, dressed in their finest finery, to be arranged at the foot of the fireplace hearth as if they were in a pageant. She needed all the guests to acknowledge both them and her. I'd always preferred to observe the crowd rather than garner its praise. This had made us well matched when we were growing up, each filling a different role, but it hadn't prepared us for the challenge to our relationship that was brewing in our yet unspoken eulogies.

I settled the side of my hip against the wooden pew and waited. I felt strangely blank about my father's death, but my heart was beating riotously at the thought of speaking from the pulpit.

A man directly behind us let out a series of wet coughs that turned my stomach.

A woman three pews ahead turned around to look at the coughing man, and she caught my eye. She smiled and then nudged the woman next to her. The first was Edna; she'd been a teller at my father's bank until the day she married one of the bank executives. She was nudging Sue, another former teller. The two of them waved at me as if I were a celebrity. They were probably wondering how much money I was going to inherit. Natural, at the funeral of a rich man, to wonder where all the money would go. But they must have heard the fact that I didn't get a cent.

Once the organ music started in earnest, the minister gave the benediction, and after that, the service moved quickly. We sang "Great Is His Faithfulness," and then it was my turn.

I gripped the edge of the pew and pulled myself up. My body felt stiff, and my stomach pressed against the tight waistband of my dress. My stockings had inched further down my thighs. My shoes pressed silently on the carpeted aisle while the congregation waited for me to reach the front of the church. They must have thought I was going to air some dirty laundry, and they wanted to hear every word.

In the pulpit, I straightened the microphone and decided to tell the only story I could honestly tell. "It was the morning of New Year's Eve when I was fifteen years old," I began.

All the white faces in the pews looked up at me.

"I had stayed up half the night," I said, "reading a translation of *The Diary of Anne Frank*. I was delirious with lack of sleep and a buzzing urge to make a difference. My father and sister were already at the breakfast table. I remember a platter of bacon and sausages, a covered dish with scrambled eggs, and a bowl of freshly cut oranges from Florida. Our housekeeper must have been there early." I paused for a small chuckle from the audience.

"I sat down with my plate and asked my father: 'What would we do if something like the Holocaust happened here? Would we save Anne Frank and her family?' I was always asking my father questions like this."

"At first, he rustled his newspaper as if to shut me out. I couldn't see his face. Then, Ginny asked who Anne Frank was." I rolled my eyes, knowing it would get a laugh. Even Ginny found it funny. I could see her face upturned toward me, proud that I was telling a nice story about our father, one she'd heard many times. I smiled at her and cleared my throat.

"I repeated my question to our father and he said we *had* saved Anne Frank, in a sense, or many people like her. He said that our American troops went to Europe and risked their lives, that Europe couldn't have won the war without us."

"But I wasn't asking him about soldiers and war. I was asking about us—who we were as a family. I looked around our house, thinking of places where people could hide. Ginny said we could hide someone in the closet under the staircase. But I had ears only for my father. He said, 'You'd have to look at it from all angles. You couldn't decide based on emotional or wishful thinking. You'd have to consider the risks.'"

"And then he changed my life. He gave me a looking glass onto our world. He handed me his newspaper, his sacred morning paper folded flat so I could read the front page above the fold."

I looked at the people in the pews. They were listening. I had more I wanted to tell them about how this fell apart in later years, how I lost my faith in both the newspaper and my father, but I had promised Ginny, so I stuck to the perspective I had had when I was fifteen.

"I remember staring at the words crammed onto the page, column after column, headline after headline. So much I didn't understand. I hunched over the paper like a jeweler. I remember wanting a dictionary next to me and a directory with the names listed in the articles." I looked out at the faces. "Some of your names, if I remember correctly." That got another laugh.

"I suddenly wanted to figure out how everything worked. I wanted to know the names of senators and governors and congressmen. I wanted to flick the paper like my father did. I wanted to wear pants, so I could cross my legs. Throw in a cigar, and I could figure it all out, I thought. I wanted to be like my father."

I looked up and saw Chief Manley smile and exchange a look with his wife. He knew the truth of what happened, why I was estranged from my family, and now, he was watching me cover it up as easily as he and my father had done. But what was the point of dragging it up again? My father was dead. We had to move on.

I swallowed and trained my eyes on the lectern. I didn't have any notes. I didn't need them—I could have told this story in my sleep. I continued, "Then, my father stood up and offered me his chair at the head of the table. 'Sit here,' he said. I settled myself into his chair, my elbows barely reaching the armrests. 'Clean your glasses,' he said. I wiped them on the hem of my dress. Then, he flicked the paper just right and placed it in my hands."

I took a deep breath. I looked at Miranda. My story ignored what my father had become, what she had urged me to expose about him. But I wasn't saying my father was right; I was saying my fifteen-year-old self had been fooled.

"Then he put his hat on my head. Ginny and I thought his hat to be the epitome of a debonair wardrobe. We thought it imbued him with gravitas and knowledge and importance. And here he was, lending it to his daughter. He said, 'This is what you need to do every morning before you decide to take a family into your home and protect them. You need to know the issues, the consequences, the background.' I nodded and asked if I could turn to him for help. 'Of course,' he said. 'And we don't have to agree.' He explained it was okay to disagree as long as it was an informed disagreement."

I turned back to the faces in the pews.

"And that's it. That moment formed my understanding of the world. I believed him. I believed that knowledge was obtainable, that newspapers printed all the news fit to print, that I could have some power over the world if I could understand it properly. I held onto that moment throughout my teen years. It was my secret weapon. Most fathers back then only wanted their daughters to be pretty. Mine wanted me to be smart."

That was my ending. I couldn't say another word. Telling that story had reminded me how much I'd lost. But I hadn't lost it this week when he died; I had lost it in 1958 when he turned against me.

Not another word, I thought. I stepped down from the pulpit and nodded to Ginny.

I sat down and let the breath out of my chest. I felt the pressure of my deflated lungs. Miranda patted my hand and then grasped my wrist. Freya laid her head on my shoulder for a moment, a sort of embrace. We stood for another hymn, and then we only had to endure the last of the eulogies.

Ginny and Joseph stepped up to the pulpit with barely enough room for their silk-lined outfits and coiffed hairdos. Once I listened to the litany of my father's accomplishments, I would be free. Tonight, Miranda and I would build a fire at home and have chicken pot pie with a biscuit crust.

Thinking of supper, I missed their opening salvo. If I had retreated into my brain, I might have happily missed the rest. But Joseph's words were hard to ignore:

He had the greatest foresight of any man in Upstate New York.
He was a friend to the people of this city.
His legacy will live on.
My life's greatest pleasure was to be his mentee and son-in-law.

And then it was Ginny's turn. It was even harder to ignore her voice. My heart had been trained to respond to it since I was three. I expected her to talk about visiting our father at his bank or how he loved his only grandchild, but she spoke in grandiose overstatements.

He came from one of the founding families of Carthage, New York.
He was a visionary of our city's future.
He was a self-made man.

Our father wasn't a self-made man. He was born with advantages. He didn't start at the bottom and move his way up. He never saw the basement where a damp chill might have gotten into his lungs or a rat's teeth could have infected him. From his starting point, he was given a team of supporters to help him find the staircase and eventually the elevator. At the top, he employed a team of artisans to expand the building upward. He paid carpenters, electricians, engineers, and plumbers to add to the dizzying heights—each story building upon the last. Then, he built a few levels himself, the penthouse, say, or the rooftop garden. The hammering and measuring became part of his origin story, part of the sweat equity he had invested that allowed him to tell future generations his success had come from concentrated hard work.

The city has immense gratitude for his work on the elevated highway and his clever securing of federal funds.

His work culminated in the best public works project in our city's history.

Then, suddenly, Ginny wasn't talking about the past anymore. She was talking about the future.

"Joe and I are happy to announce we have been working behind the scenes with the school board and have created a curriculum to celebrate Herbert Wilson's contributions to Carthage."

She paused as if the pews might applaud. Who wrote this speech for her? She couldn't have come up with this on her own.

Joseph leaned into the microphone from his cramped position in the pulpit. "The city deserves this," he said. Joseph Tower was a compact man with liquid energy running through his veins. He had bright blonde hair and cool blue eyes. You'd only notice the gray at his temples if he stayed still, which he never did. Even when he stood in one place, you could practically see the atoms in his body dividing and recreating themselves.

Ginny smiled from the pulpit but avoided my eye.

Miranda pressed her knee against mine. I understood her code. She was telling me not to worry. It may never come to pass. She was telling me to breathe.

"We've got a field trip planned with stops at the Carthage

Savings and Loan, the first stretch of the interstate highway at the edge of town, and the best part is they'll have their picnic lunch at the foot of the soon-to-be-built Herbert K. Wilson statue."

The murmurs from the pews practically rose to the level of applause. The man behind us let out a triumphant cough that must have landed a constellation of phlegm in his mouth. I tried not to picture it.

"The Historical Society will vote its approval this Thursday, and locations will be chosen for site studies as soon as possible."

I shook my head back and forth, back and forth. They hadn't even put him in the ground, and they were already raising him in molten metal. I pulled the inside of my bottom lip in between my teeth and applied as much pressure as I could to prevent my crying out. Goddamn you, Ginny, I wanted to say. Did our father have you on puppet strings even in death?

Of course he did. Our father would always be a wedge between me and Ginny. He would ostracize me from the grave. His power would rise up in front of me, no matter where I turned in this town. I closed my eyes and thought of places we could move to—Montreal, Manhattan, Minneapolis, Mexico City. All these cities—and these were just the ones with the first letter of Miranda's first name. I knew Miranda wanted to stay in Carthage forever, but I couldn't help dreaming of escaping the tight hold of this town. I couldn't live in a city that honored its criminals.

I folded my jacket and pulled my purse into my lap, ready to bolt as soon as the last words of the benediction faded into the final hymn. I glanced down at the space between Freya and me. Her accordion folder was still there. *Everything I ever wanted to know about my father.* Maybe the newspapers weren't interested, still cashing their checks from my father's advertising dollars. But certainly, the city would want to know. They wouldn't want children learning about a hero only to find him another flawed and venal man. Wouldn't they want to know the facts before having children build paper mâché replicas of the Empire Stateway?

But I didn't have the energy. If I took that folder, I would have to do something with it. I didn't want to. I was thirty-four years old. I couldn't continue to fight my father's sins. If I had learned anything as a child during all those matinees with Freya, it was that power was practically unstoppable. You had to have a gun or a blackmail scheme to stop it. You had to be a man. And you had to be willing to risk everything in pursuit of your goal.

After Ginny finished, I watched her settle back into her pew and hug her daughter Sarah. I thought about the bedtime stories poor Sarah would hear about her grandfather's accomplishments, and there would be no one to tell her the truth.

The minister rang out his benediction from Romans:

Neither death nor life, nor angels nor rulers,
nor things present nor things to come, nor powers, nor height nor depth,
nor anything else in all creation,
will be able to separate us…

Then, the triumphant organ music soared into the sanctuary. The man behind me tapped me on the shoulder. "Your father was a wonderful man," he said over the pounding notes of the doxology. "He gave me my first mortgage forty years ago and now I own five properties." He coughed into his handkerchief.

I turned away to avoid his touch. I saw Henry Sulliman being helped out of the pew with his cane and Howard Kramer pulling on his perfectly tailored suit jacket. Edna and Sue stepped over their husbands to get to the aisle. They were heading toward me. They were going to line up to tell me the stories of my father's brilliance, while privately marveling at how far I'd fallen from the tree.

I couldn't take it. These self-serving, hypocritical idiots in their custom-made suits and fashionable dresses, thinking they were so clever for beating the system—when the system was designed for them, run for them, the rules created for them. Laws were broken for them, and then the city looked the other way because they looked so nice showing up for Sunday services in their finery even as they coughed up their phlegm in church as if they were in their own bathrooms.

I closed my eyes and took a deep breath. What if I just took the folder and had a look? Taking it didn't commit me to any action, but leaving it might close a door.

"Thank you, Freya," I said, ignoring the man behind me. "I will take this."

We fumbled to conceal the bulging folder beneath my coat, and I held onto Miranda as we moved to the exit.

CHAPTER TWO

Inheritance

Miranda and I walked home from the bus stop. The afternoon air had a biting chill, and my nose was red and raw. I held Freya's thick accordion file under my arm. It was like carrying a foreign-made bomb. I didn't have the instructions, and it could go off in the wrong place as easily as the right one, and I had no idea what to do with it.

I calmed my overactive nervous system by repeating my wishes. If I exposed my father's sins, then I would feel like I had accomplished something with my life. I would be able to sleep at night. Ginny would hug me close and thank me for pulling the scales from her eyes. In my mind, if Ginny and I saw the past in the same way, we were bound to be closer in the future.

I listened to my boots crunch on the packed snow. We walked past the Salvation Army with its scratched mannequins and faded hats. It was already closed for the day. Then, we took the sidewalk past Amos's Appliance Repair with its dusty radios and sewing machines. Amos waved to us from his window—a hand above his head without his eyes leaving his table. He was a big man, but his thick fingers were dexterous, and he was able to fix any sort of appliance—crockpots, hair dryers, electric skillets. People came here to find resistors and transistors to make their radios work again. They came to replace power cords for their vacuum cleaners. Amos wore Coke-bottle glasses and left his home only for church and house calls. He was one of the

Black men in the neighborhood who had taken Miranda under his wing when her father had died. He was singlehandedly responsible for keeping our deli's refrigerators going every summer.

Our neighbor Lorraine was slowly sweeping snow off her painted front porch. Since her kids had grown up and moved away, she was on autopilot, and all conversations turned to the weather. She might have been curious why Miranda and I were dressed up, but she didn't ask.

"It's a cold one," Lorraine said. "Stay warm."

We nodded and kept walking.

Next door, Lorraine's husband, Speedy, ran a used car lot and car repair business. He had cars on blocks, a stack of used tires behind a fence, and a tight parking lot where he managed to fit ten cars—a jigsaw puzzle that only he could solve. They called him "Speedy" because he could fix an engine faster than anyone in town. He was always trying to get Miranda to buy a car or at least rent one occasionally.

After Speedy's, we walked past the only empty lot on our side of the street. It used to be Miranda's deli. It had been empty since 1958, snow piled in the corners and junk collecting against the chain-link fence.

Next to that was our home. George Pritchard came down from the front porch. He was a godsend—a hard worker and burgeoning young chef. He was also our business partner. He buttoned his heavy coat over his thin chest and walked toward us, his long-fingered hands without gloves or mittens.

His six-foot frame was tall, but he was dwarfed by the elevated highway. The Empire Stateway had stolen the four blocks in front of us and every building across the street from us, leaving us a "half street." On one side stood the buildings that hadn't been demolished, including Amos's repair shop, the Salvation Army, Speedy's used car lot, and Miranda's house, which had become the deli, and on the other side of the street was the ditch before the highway's concrete posts. In the mornings, we were on display to the passing cars, as if we were a Hollywood set instead of a real neighborhood. And in the afternoons, we were rendered invisible by its shadow. Throughout the day, we heard revving engines, screeching stops, and the steady hum of vehicles on their way to other towns. From the upstairs window, we could literally see the expressions on the motorists' faces.

Shoulders slouched, George lifted his head as he approached us. He kept his eyes on me, and he nodded. In that nod, I could decipher his condolences, his understanding of grief, and his sympathy for me. I couldn't have put that much into a nod myself.

He turned to Miranda and told her about the sales numbers, the inventory levels, and the roach problem. "Mrs. Rosenthal asked again if I was keeping kosher in the kitchen," he added. Mrs. Rosenthal trusted Miranda, but she loudly doubted George any time she caught him alone.

"I'll talk to her," Miranda said.

George had come to us fourteen years ago, looking for work right as the neighborhood was being dismantled for the Empire Stateway. Miranda had hired him to move the sales counter from the old store to its new location in Miranda's house. He had cut the cupboards to fit the room. He had sanded, painted, and smoothed the wood until it looked like it was born fresh in its new home.

Miranda was only twenty years old when her father Alexsander Fein died. He left her the deli business and a mortgaged house in Ward Thirteen. Next to each other on Sycamore Street these buildings were his pride and joy, his talismans of security and prosperity. When the deli was knocked down, Miranda moved the deli business into the house. It didn't meet the codes for a home-based business, but it made a living, and it was a testament to the thriving businesses that had been there before the highway. Jewish customers shopped here because they remembered the old candy shops, the many tailoring businesses, and the Jewish families who lived in the small clapboard houses. Black customers shopped here because they remembered the lumberyard, the jazz clubs, the barbershops, and the summertime barbecues that had spilled into the street.

Miranda paid George for his handiwork that day in 1958. He pocketed the money and asked if we had any more work. I remember the tentativeness in his voice and Miranda's quick response: "I have nothing but work. When can you come?"

George arrived the next day after school, put on a paper hat like the ones we wore in the kitchen, and never left. Even as most businesses regrouped on the South Side of Carthage, he still managed to drum up business for us and keep us in the minds of the Black community. The Jewish customers didn't accept him immediately, but they came around. It was unusual to have a Jewish deli staffed with gentile and Black workers, but Miranda said it was part of our mission—to show Carthage that intergroup alliances could thrive. She called me and George her "co-owners."

I never imagined being the co-owner of a Jewish deli—my father had never even allowed me to come to this neighborhood. Growing up, I subconsciously thought that everyone lived in basically the same circumstances as I did. It wasn't until I left home that I realized how divided our city was.

Before we stepped onto the porch, we heard a loud crash behind us. We looked up to the elevated highway, expecting a big rig truck to pitch over the concrete barrier. But the sound had come from our segment of Sycamore Street, and the offending red Volkswagen Beetle was still moving—erratically—from one dirty snow drift to the other—bouncing more than driving until it veered to a stop in front of the deli.

Miranda and I moved out of the way, but George rushed

toward the driver's side of the car. The young driver looked like she had been styled at a professional photography studio. Her dark hair swept away from her face in a bouffant, and her skin was smooth and glowing. Even with the grimace on her face from her automotive mishap, it was hard to ignore her beauty.

George opened the driver's side door, and she stepped out. She wore a blue tweed dress with a wide belt. Her shoes were unsuitable for the slush and mounds of snow on Sycamore Street, and she slipped as she bent back in the car to get her coat. He took her arm, and I watched their eyes meet. It wasn't often a classy, young, Black woman came into our neighborhood.

"I can change that tire for you, miss," he said. "I work at this deli here," he added. More words than I had heard him speak in a week.

The young woman nodded and looked down at her shoes. She was probably thinking it wasn't often that a six-foot-tall man arrived just when you needed him. But I doubted she had any trouble attracting men who wanted to help her with any little problem she might have.

In fact, she had attracted quite a crowd from our short block. George held up his hand to stop anyone from intervening. Speedy had come out of his car lot three doors down, wiping his hands on a grease rag.

George opened the back hatch and unscrewed the spare tire, as if he worked on automobiles all the time, as if he had a couple of German sports cars in his driveway at home.

I put my large file folder down on the closest porch ledge. "Let me help," I said.

Miranda nudged me and shook her head. "We've got work to do inside," she said pointedly.

He gave us a wave as if to say, *Nothing to worry about. I've got this under control.*

As we went inside, our two long-haired cats came in on our

heels. Emperor and Empress roamed the neighborhood when we went out, but they kept us in their sights when extra food was a possibility. I bent down and let my hand rest on Emperor's gray-and-brown head. His name contained his best quality: purring. He couldn't contain it. As soon as I pet his head or back or belly, he let out the raspiest, loudest purr, like an engine turning on.

I shook the cold from my coat and hung it up. I stamped the muck from my boots and arranged them on the floor under our coats. I pushed through the beaded curtain that marked off the back of the house, where we had the dining room table—my desk. Miranda went into the kitchen to fix supper, our favorite pot pie with chicken, carrots, onions, peas, and buttery biscuits covering the top. We had two sides to the kitchen—one kosher and one not. Miranda was not religious, but she was Jewish. Even though she didn't attend temple, she had a deep connection to her Jewish heritage. She kept kosher because she wanted to honor her father and our customers, but she didn't adhere to the rules when she and I had dinner alone, which was practically every night.

On my desk, *The Washington Post* lay open from the morning. The month had been abuzz with news. Nixon had claimed that the Paris Peace Accords ended the Vietnam War. The Supreme Court had overturned state bans on abortions in Roe v. Wade. But my eye, this morning, had turned to a story buried on page seven:

> **Last Two Guilty in Watergate Plot: Two former officials of President Nixon's re-election committee were convicted yesterday of conspiracy, burglary, and bugging the Democratic Party's Watergate headquarters.**

I was glad the jury had found them guilty—but I knew the real criminals would get off scot-free. Richard Nixon had been re-elected in a landslide. People in Carthage went on and on about the fantastic stock prices, but no one talked about Kent State or the Christmas bombings or what kind of lunatic was running our country. Nixon's nickname, Tricky Dick, had disappeared from the newspapers. The mantle of the presidency protected him.

I felt uncomfortable with the folder—I turned it upside down. I felt ashamed of how excited I was to see the contents, and I tried to re-direct my energy.

I went back into the front of the house. "Let me cut the carrots," I said.

"They're already cut," she said.

"I'll make the biscuits," I said, heading toward the pantry.

"I made the dough this morning," she said. "Stop stalling and see what's in that folder."

She knew me better than I knew myself.

I walked slowly through the front room, which served as our store, and stood at the store's bulletin board, staring at the advertisements: Handyman Available, Babysitter Needed, Hebrew School Now Enrolling.

I finally went back to my desk. I moved my typewriter and stacks of papers off the long table. I took a deep breath, unwound the string from the button at the top of the file, and opened it. It was packed tightly with papers of different sizes and textures, a tangled maze of incriminating evidence against my father. I lit a cigarette and sat back in my chair. This was the last moment I could savor before seeing what Freya wanted me to see. It was like the pause between the previews and the main feature in the movie theater. I didn't want to face anything too bad. I wanted to convince my sister that our father was wrong without having to expose anything that would shatter our family. We were fragile enough as it was.

The first paper was an internal memo about real estate

appraisals from 1956. I laid it at one end of the table. I could check it later against property records if I needed to. I was trained as a librarian and had taken all the classes. I was missing only the final project and exam. But I wasn't a journalist or a whistleblower. I didn't have the nerve for that anymore.

I pulled out a lunch receipt from 1957. I noted the names of the guests, marked in Freya's handwriting, in case I wanted to look them up later in the phone book. I pulled out paper-clipped copies of escrow papers and eviction notices and arranged them by date. I flipped through them, looking for the address of the property that used to be across the street. I tried to picture each address as it had existed before the highway. There had been houses, a church, apartments, and most importantly to me, the deli that Miranda's father had started.

"We were right," I yelled to her. "He demolished your father's deli, and look at this, it was long after he served eviction notices for the other properties. Almost four months." I could feel anger and frustration burning anew in my throat. I had always known what he'd done, but I'd been powerless to prove it. Even if I could have proven it, no one would've cared. I'd told my sister at the time that our father had demolished the deli to teach me a lesson, and she told me I was crazy. She didn't think our father could have been so vindictive. What good did it do to have more evidence now?

"We already knew that," Miranda yelled from the kitchen. On the kitchen radio, Roberta Flack slowly sang the lyrics to "The First Time Ever I Saw Your Face," a soothing contrast to the turmoil I was uncovering.

My father knew the proposed highway route long before the city did. That's why he'd bought most of the land and told his friends to buy the rest. That's why my father owned the most prosperous parts of Ward Thirteen: the Fremont Jazz Club, Washington Market, the movie theater, and the community center.

Then, he'd had them demolished—cutting the heart out of the community. My father sold each plot at an astronomical profit to the government. No one cared that it was unscrupulous because they had profited as well.

I muttered to myself, "I've already told Ginny this." I took a drag on my cigarette. This was old news. Since the Federal-Aid Highway Act of 1956, cities around the country had been tearing up minority communities, and rich men had been getting richer with every mile. It was common practice. It didn't stand out in the grand scheme of American corruption.

I thought, at one point, our father's corruption might matter to my sister and our town. Carthage wanted its heroes unsullied—they wanted them un-besmirchable—they wanted them better than they needed to be. Maybe Manhattan could celebrate its dodgy public figures, but in Upstate New York, we had a puritan streak that demanded both success and integrity—well, at least the appearance of integrity. We were the birthplace of the Mormons, Adventists, and a rushing river of other utopian and evangelical societies with charismatic leaders. We wanted to believe in people and worship them.

I looked up. Miranda stood in the doorframe, holding the doorway curtain of colored beads back with her shoulder, wiping her hands on her apron. The dough mixer whirred behind her. It kneaded challah, white, and rye bread doughs nonstop throughout the day.

"Is it good evidence?" she asked.

"It's good, but no one will care. I am not going to the newspapers again."

"That's okay—but it would be a shame to have that statue go up. It's a slap in the face."

She was right. I couldn't imagine a statue of my father in the very city where he had razed her neighborhood. I couldn't tolerate the idea of schoolchildren repeating his name and learning only about his accomplishments.

"I know," I said, "but they're voting this Thursday. They didn't give us much time to react. They're rushing it through." I pushed my glasses up the bridge of my nose. I felt put upon. Why should I be the one to do this? Wasn't it someone else's job to bird-dog the city?

"Does your sister even want this?" she asked.

"I don't think so," I said, shaking my head. "The statue probably isn't even her idea. I bet our father put her up to it. He probably had it all written out." I put a paperweight on the 1956 stack. My sister had many good qualities, but independent thought wasn't one of them. Growing up, I had always prided myself on being the independent thinker of our generation, but even as my thoughts remained independent, I noticed that, as I got older, I had gotten more cautious, and more dependent. Now, I rarely did anything alone. I hadn't finished school. I would only work in our house. I was practically a recluse.

Miranda sat down across from me as if she were one of my clients and pulled off her paper kitchen hat and ponytail holder. Her red hair escaped to her shoulders.

I pulled out a thick wad of mimeographed sheets—stapled together but taken from different sources.

"I'm not sure what these are. They're about the Empire Stateway Bond."

"Let me see." She read aloud: "The Committee shall convene and vote on the distribution of the bond funds until said bonds are paid in full."

"The bonds are the tolls on the highway," I said. "They were supposed to stop collecting them once the highway construction was paid for."

"It's been fourteen years," she said.

"Freya's showing us the small print," I said. "They haven't stopped collecting tolls because they keep rolling each bond over into a new one. And they use that money for whatever they want."

"How much are you talking about?" She was getting caught on the research trail with me, and I felt my adrenaline surge.

"It looks like it's hundreds of thousands of dollars every year—it's a perpetual source of income," I said, looking at the figures on a bank statement. "No wonder my father was so popular."

I pulled a contract out of the folder—employment for my father's services to the Empire Stateway Bond. My heart sank. It was one thing to use the money to grease the wheels, but here was proof that my father was skimming off the top.

"My father was taking a salary—from all those nickels and dimes in the toll booths."

Drivers had been putting coins in those slots from the very beginning, and my father had been tucking them away in his bank account, lining his already well-lined coffers. Robert Moses had done this in New York City as well with money pouring in from the Triborough Bridge. But Moses didn't use the money for his personal use. He used it to fund more projects.

Miranda hung her apron on the back of her chair. She looked at me, her hair curtaining the sides of her face. "This is huge."

"It's not enough. They're not going to care." I kept flipping through the papers. There had to be something more.

"Someone will care," she said. "He couldn't have given everyone a cut. They're not going to vote for a statue of your father once you show them this."

I thought of the mayor and the police chief and the Historical Society members getting richer and richer over the years, while Miranda and I struggled to pay our mortgage. Everyone was in on it—real estate appraisers, insurance adjusters, bank presidents. They each had dirt on each other, so no one ever blew the whistle.

"I'm not going to show anyone."

"Isn't Freya on the board?" she asked.

"She is—but she gave this to me. She doesn't want to do it herself." I shook my head. "I don't want to go down this road again. Remember what happened last time? I lost everything."

"Well, not everything," she said, smiling.

"Not everything," I agreed. "You know what I mean. I don't want to risk what we've built together. People get vindictive when you start messing with their money." I wanted to live a quiet life. We needed to live a quiet life if we wanted to keep what we had.

"Where's that salary going now?" she asked.

Good question. I thought about Ginny and Joseph traveling to Europe, paying for Sarah's private school tuition, and re-doing the house. That money didn't come from Joseph's salary alone.

But I didn't want to do it all over again.

Fourteen years ago, when I was twenty years old, I stood up to my father in his bank office. Miranda helped me gather the evidence. We were both in our early twenties and filled with idealistic verve. She had given me the confidence then to go against my father. I had stowed mimeographed sheets in my purse as if I was going to pull them out with a flourish and my family was going to submit to my demands. I thought it would be climactic. That's how my brain worked back then. Freya had taken me to far too many movies.

* * *

Back in 1958, I had been living with Miranda for only two weeks. Freya tracked me down and called me to a formal meeting with my father at his bank. I wore my best day dress: navy blue linen, white Peter Pan collar, smocked waistband. I wore my mother's pearls. I hadn't worn the pearls or my best dress since I had left home. I wore them now as a kind of camouflage—to fit back in. I opened the heavy brass doors.

"Good morning, Lucy," Sue said from her teller window. Her hair curled up at the ends.

"Good morning, Lucy Loo," Edna said with a wave. "Your father's in the back."

I cringed at the juvenile nickname. These same tellers used to give me lollipops, sit me on their metal stools, and let me pretend to hand out money—hard for them to adjust to my being an adult.

I forced a smile at Edna and Sue and waved—a noncommittal, adult sort of wave. My heels clicked on the marble floor through the lobby and then quieted on the carpeted hallway, past my father's office and into the conference room.

My father had summoned me to the bank to put his money and properties into my and Ginny's names. But I had decided that if he wanted anything in my name, then I had some conditions.

Looking back, I can laugh at my bravado.

I had studied public records in the library and knew why he had to get the holdings out of his name. The federal government was reviewing the books from the Highway Act grant. My father needed to cover some of his "below board" dealings. I had followed the real estate records and found the bank president, members of the bank's board of directors, the mayor, and of course, my father, Herbert Wilson, senior vice president of Carthage Savings and Loan, with their hands in the proverbial cookie jar. I had proof in an envelope in my purse.

Now I could finally see why this had amused my father, why he hadn't even flinched in the face of my evidence. I hadn't even scraped the surface of his corruption.

That day, my father had stood in front of a wall of windows, pouring a Scotch. He had opened his arms wide and beckoned me. "Lucy," he'd said. With that one word, he told me he was sorry, he loved me, and that my mother would be proud of me—the phrases he always said to me after our fights. I accepted his hug, but I kept my eyes on the floor.

My father had a booming voice, and he was always quick to offer a drink or a cigar. People described him as generous in size, offerings, and intelligence. He was a big man, taller than most, his chest like a barrel, but he had narrow shoulders. His tailors had to build his suits to accommodate the steep slope from his neck to his elbows, then quickly expand to contain his midsection that was filled with steaks and potatoes and Scotch.

"Lucy," Ginny said, waiting for my hug. She wore an elegant wrap dress and kitten heels. Her outfit was mature beyond her seventeen years, but her face was still her own. Her eyes glinted, sparkled, crinkled, and jumped the space between us. We hugged. She wiped away tears from both her eyes. We had so much to talk about. I felt like we had been away at separate summer camps and were bursting with stories to share.

"I've missed you so much," she said. We'd rarely gone an hour without talking, and now it had been a week since we'd talked. And so much had happened.

"I've missed you, too," I said. "I have so much to tell you." I wanted to bring Ginny to the deli and show her our new counter, our aprons, the cash register, and the box of paper hats. I wanted her to taste a knish and eat a smoked meat sandwich. I wanted her to meet Miranda.

I searched for the right words to invite her.

She grabbed my hand. Her finger drooped under the weight of a large diamond engagement ring—a roadblock between us. I had been learning how to run a deli out of a residential home, moving boxes and painting walls—all on the edge of an earth-shuddering construction site. The Empire Stateway was literally going up in front of Miranda's home. Dust covered everything, and the noise was practically unbearable: heaving, digging, grinding, cutting, screeching. In the meantime, it looked like

Ginny had been drinking champagne and accepting expensive gifts from a man twice her age. But I was sure she had stories. There was no way she didn't have funny stories to tell me about Joseph Tower.

Joseph walked into the conference room. He was shorter than I remembered, but he wore a well-cut suit with a thin tie and a silk pocket square. He practically spun Ginny away from me. Fred Astaire and Ginger Rogers. Maybe they were going to knock down the chairs and dance on the table. He had a lot to be happy about. Everything Ginny inherited would go into his bank account once they married, and they were moving fast toward their wedding day—a short engagement that would get the women at the country club speculating.

Surprisingly, Joseph wasn't moving Ginny to encircle her in his arms—he was moving her so he could embrace me.

"There she is," he said. "Back in the fold." He was charming if nothing else. His face still looked young even though his hair was graying around his temples. He looked genuinely glad to see me and held my hands longer than he needed to, trying to impart some message through a Morse code of squeezes and pats. He was saying, *Sorry things didn't work out between us. Sorry I've taken your sister. But we both knew I was going to be part of this family one way or another.*

"This shouldn't take long." Our father motioned for us to take our chairs. I smoothed my dress down before I sat, and Ginny did the same. We smiled at each other. Our mirrored gestures were always a source of amusement. We'd catch ourselves holding our hands in the same way or making the same face at someone's inane comment.

Joseph pushed in Ginny's chair and then rushed over to my chair to assist.

"If we have time afterward, we can go to Gallagher's for lunch," Joseph said. "My treat."

"Well, if this all goes well, then your treat will be my treat," my father said. "We're going to be family." He handed Joseph a cigar and lit one for himself. He laid out a map of Carthage and circled the properties he owned. Some were on the outskirts of town, but many were in Ward Thirteen: a cluster of circles sat next to the highway construction site.

I leaned over and saw the block of Sycamore between 22nd and 23rd—where Miranda lived—where I lived. Her house was the only one not circled. My father owned Speedy's used car lot and Amos's Appliance Repair. Miranda had refused to sell her home back when the offers had come in, but she had rented the deli building from a property management company, and she had no control over that.

"That's Miranda's deli. This one here." I pointed to one of the circles and looked at my father. "Did you tear it down?" I asked in a way that suggested I already knew and he might as well come clean.

"Who's Miranda?" he said.

"She's my friend. She's who I live with." I could smell the Scotch in his glass and it turned my stomach. "According to this, you own the land where her deli was. Did you tear it down?" I remembered the men in hard hats swarming over the building, using earth movers to take down her father's work. They didn't pause before they bulldozed the handwritten advertisements on the windows. They didn't shed a tear before sending a wrecking ball into the grease-stained walls. The smells alone should have given them pause: fresh bagels, smoked meat, grilled onions. The deli came down in less than an hour, Miranda shaking in my arms.

"I didn't tear anything down." He puffed on his cigar. "I have a developer who makes those decisions. Sometimes, buyers want a blank slate."

"But you never sold it. It's an empty lot. I see it every day. It shows here you still own it." My eyes flicked to the next-door lot. "You couldn't get this one," I said, pointing to Miranda's house.

"If I needed it, I could," he said. "That house is one condemnation away from forced eviction. I could have it in an hour if I wanted it."

"Did you knock down Miranda's deli to send me a message?" I held his eye. I wouldn't have blinked to save my life.

"And what message would you have gotten from that?" He sounded like he was teaching a school lesson, letting me figure it out on my own.

"That you can do whatever you want. That you can act with impunity." My vocabulary always went up a notch when I was angry.

Ginny jumped from her seat and put her arms out. "No, no, this isn't going to happen," she said. "We can talk about this another time. Let Daddy speak, Lucy. You haven't heard him out." She looked like she was shushing an audience, waiting for the best part of a movie, putting away the popcorn to give the scene her undivided attention.

Joseph collected two stacks of papers from the sideboard—fat stacks with large paper clips. "Get your John Hancocks ready," he said.

"I haven't discussed this with Ginny yet," I said, "but I want us to use this money to rehabilitate our town. Living in Ward Thirteen, I've seen some situations—" In truth, I had seen poverty on every corner—kids who were barefoot and not attending school, broken down cars, and men out of work. I had seen people living in squalor, their roofs decaying over their heads. If my father owned those properties, we could fix them up and give people a decent place to live.

"You're not living in Ward Thirteen—you're staying there while you get ready to come home," Herbert said. "We've kept your bedroom for you. Once these kids get married"—he gestured to Ginny and Joseph—"the house is big enough. You can move back and keep me company."

I could picture it. I hated my father for what he'd done, but I still loved him. If we could stop fighting for ten minutes, we could read books while Ginny and Joseph took care of the details. During their parties, we could sneak away to my father's study and talk about politics. I could be an old maid living with my sister and bypass the ridiculous sham of marriage. And the food. I could have a pantry filled with crackers and cookies and a refrigerator full of cheeses and jams. We could have roast beef and honeyed ham and oranges shipped from Florida. And there wouldn't be any rats. To live without the fear of rats behind every wall was a yearning dream of mine. But I couldn't give up my new life.

"I'm not moving home."

"You shouldn't be living there. It's not who you are," he said. This was what racism sounded like in my family: covert and polite. He reminded me I was different and suggested I was better.

I shook my head. "I'd like to put monetary parameters on the trust, like how much would go to charity. Miranda and I want to help the community, and there's an existential need for—"

"Yes, you should do that with your part of the money," Joseph said. "But it doesn't need to be written in."

"This isn't a negotiation," my father said. "I will maintain control over this money until my death. This is a change in name only." He paused and smiled at Joseph. "Though with my consent, you will have access to these funds, more than you have now."

I stared at Ginny. I needed her on my side. I needed her to flash her blue eyes at our father and get this train on the right track. One word from her and he'd be willing to put those good intentions into the contract. He'd commit to a series of scholarships or a food bank for Ward Thirteen or money for a new

YMCA. She owed me this, at least.

"I want to keep us honest," I said. "This money hasn't been acquired honestly, but we can at least give it away honestly."

"Honestly? Do you know what would keep me honest?" he asked. "Not listening to this drivel about how I earned my money. Do you know how much I've sacrificed to keep you and Ginny in knickers?"

He sat down, rested his cigar on his ashtray, rearranged some papers, and put a folder in his briefcase.

"These purchases were not completely honest," I said. "I looked at the public records."

I wanted to shift the conversation and show him I was serious. I thought of *Mr. Smith Goes to Washington,* a movie Freya and I had seen in the revival theater on Maple. I could hear the movie's triumphant brass band playing in my mind as I stepped up to make my case. "Yankee Doodle Dandy"—the hero's come to town.

I put three mimeographed sheets with the real estate records on the table. I had circled his name—our name. Ginny and Joseph recoiled, and Joseph leaned closer to my sister as if to protect her. My father stood up again, pulled my papers over to him with one strong index finger, and laughed.

"You don't like my real estate deals? Where in this research does it say I've broken any laws?" His voice echoed like he was trying to reach an audience in a half-empty auditorium.

My investigation seemed weak in the context of this office, its army of workers and filing cabinets. I felt like I was showing him a Girl Scout badge for investigative reporting.

"There is a law," I said, gathering my courage. "Against insider trading." I put my notes on the table about the 1934 law. All executives were barred from acting on advance knowledge regarding their holdings.

"There is a law against insider trading, but buying real estate is not trading," he said. "I took out a loan like anyone else and purchased the land. Some of that land was used for the highway. Some of it is still in my portfolio. I took a chance. I hedged a bet. I did what smart investors do. Do you find it morally reprehensible, Lucy? Does it not meet your smell test?"

I knew I had made him angry. I could see the set of his jaw and the veins in his neck. This was worse than when I'd challenged him about desegregation in the South or Eisenhower's second term. It was worse than when I'd brought up Eleanor Roosevelt and told Joseph, way back when he was a suitor to me instead of Ginny, that I considered Eleanor a superior diplomat to FDR, and that I appreciated her stand for racial justice.

"Then, why are you taking these holdings out of your name?" I asked. This was my kicker, my best logical evidence.

"I'm securing our family legacy. This isn't my money. It's Wilson money. My father's hard work is in here. My grandfather's hard work." He re-opened the folder tentatively. I could practically hear his brain clicking and clacking. His logic wasn't solid. He moved away from the question of how he had earned his money and turned it into an anthem to our ancestors.

"I surmise we are here today," I said, "because the federal government starts their investigation tomorrow."

I needed to be brave. I felt like I was Jimmy Stewart going up against the big guns, the novice politician challenging the Senate. I don't know why I had to be a man to be a hero, or a senator for that matter, but that's what the movies had taught me. If I could force him to admit his error, then he might agree to my stipulations. And he might even admire me for my initiative and cunning. To state it so baldly, however, was a mistake.

"If you're so sure, Lucy, then I suggest we take your name off these papers." He looked me in the eye, his final card.

"I want us to have a stipulation about—"

"You will not make stipulations." His voice rose so loudly on the last word that Joseph popped up from his chair and closed the door.

"Lucy," Joseph said. "Sign the papers and we can go to lunch."

"There will be no lunch," my father said. "If this is your stance, Lucy, there will be no lunch." He tore the papers into long strips. He pressed his finger on the intercom on the side table. "Freya, type up the deeds again with Ginny Wilson as the sole possessor." He looked at me.

I knew that was my last chance. I was giving up dividends, equity—money that might eventually be mine. I wouldn't be able to modernize Miranda's house or buy the foods I missed or hire an exterminator for the house. I wouldn't be able to invest in the neighborhood or start a foundation. I wouldn't be able to offset the damage my father had done. And we would never have enough money to escape Upstate New York. We'd never move to Chicago or Toronto or San Francisco, metropolises where women like Miranda and I could live openly.

Freya rushed into the room, closing the door quietly behind her. *Click.* "Mr. Wilson, I'm sure Lucy didn't intend for this to—" She didn't know what had happened, but she was going to bat for me. She had a pencil behind her ear, and her glasses hung from her neck by a chain. She had been in the middle of some other task, and now she was trying to figure out how best to help me.

"Why can't we discuss this like adults?" I asked.

My father threw his pen on the table. "The only discussion would be your apology."

I knew I was lying down on the wrong track, but I couldn't budge. It was every childhood battle rising in my chest—a lifetime of arguments with my father coming to a head: our fights about civil rights and politics and feminism and desegregation—our fights about excess and want. He might have conceded some of these arguments to appease me, but when they mattered, he would never back down. I had stormed away from enough dinner tables to know that there wouldn't be a plate waiting for me when I came down hungry in the night.

"If you give her a minute," Freya said.

"Type up the papers, Miss Hoffman. There'll be no more discussion."

"Yes, Mr. Wilson," Freya said.

Ginny started to cry. Even in her wrap dress, she looked like a little girl. Some of her tears were for me, I knew, but most of them were for the loss of her vision of a happy family. She would be willing to sacrifice any political position, any moral position, in order to have a happy family.

I didn't have that luxury. I had seen what our father had done. The curtain had been drawn back for me and me alone. I had seen the wizard and his machinery.

"I know what you did," I said to my father.

"I did what needed to be done," he said quickly, like he had been prepared for this line of attack. He looked away and shook the ice in his glass.

"Whatever gets in your way, you just remove it, even if it's a human being," I said. I knew this was not the time. I knew that I should be the good daughter, get my money, and spend it however I wanted. I knew I should be professing love instead of accusations, but I couldn't stand his smugness.

"Lucy, don't—" Ginny said.

"You think I'm selfish?" he asked. "Do you not see how you are being selfish? You're taking away from what should be a celebratory occasion. Your sister and Joe. This isn't about you."

"Joseph's only here for the money." I don't know why I said it. I didn't believe it one hundred percent, but he was standing there with the papers, itching for us to sign them, and if anyone benefited from this transfer of deeds, it was Joseph.

The room erupted. My father slammed his palm on the table.

Joseph yelled, "Now just a second."

"You're ruining everything," Ginny yelled. "How can you say Joe's here for the money when it's you? You never see us, but you show up to secure your inheritance."

"That's not why I'm here," I said.

"And you already took mom's pearls." Ginny held my eye.

Our father raised his eyes from the table and looked at me. There was no hiding the pearls. They were strung orb to orb around my neck.

"Give them back," he said. "How dare you steal from this family."

I reached up and touched the pearls. "She wanted me to have them."

"She wouldn't want you to have anything the way you're behaving," he said, like I was a child. He held his hand out. "She'd be disappointed in how you've turned out."

I pushed back my chair and shook my head back and forth. I unclasped the pearls with my trembling hands and laid them on the table. Each pearl made its clack against the polished table. I could have taken them and run out the door, but they had lost their value. The accusation had sullied them.

My heart pounded, pushing at my brassiere. I walked on shaky legs through the corridor. I felt the air conditioning on my neck. No one came running after me. No one called out "Lucy Loo" or "Lucretia."

Edna and Sue kept their eyes down as I walked back through the lobby. They shouldn't have averted their eyes for my sake—they should have averted their eyes because of the self-important, consequences-be-damned vice president of theirs who had written his daughter out of the family holdings.

I didn't know where to go. I had shut the door on my past

but hadn't secured the door to my future. I thought about the evidence in my purse and where I could go with it. I could show his colleagues. I could show the former property owners. I could take it to the editors at the newspaper. I imagined a headline that would make my father reconsider his dismissal of my claims. I pushed the big brass doors again, but they were heavier on the way out.

*   *   *

That had been 1959, and now it was 1973, and my father was gone.

"Let's focus." Miranda put her palm flat on top of the accordion file. Her hair hung almost to the table. She was breathing heavily. I looked past her to the macrame plant holders in our window and the crocheted pillowcases on our couch—the touches of home we had created together.

"You're right," I said. "We shouldn't go through everything tonight." I rearranged myself on my wooden chair, my thighs chafing against my tights.

She kept her eye on me. That wasn't what she'd meant.

"There's no rush," I said.

"The meeting is in two days. You have to decide what you want to do, either way." Miranda put her hand over her heart and took a deep breath.

"I can't do this," I said—and I meant it. We had spent fourteen years building a beautiful life together, and I wasn't going to risk it all to chase after the ghost of my father.

"Don't you want to?" she asked. She knew how much it meant to me to set the record straight. We had talked about it over our pillows more nights than I'd like to admit.

"I used to." It was a top priority for me when I was in my twenties, but now I didn't want to lose any part of my life. I didn't want to take risks.

"I feel the same way," she said, "but you should give this evidence to someone. Don't you think?"

I nodded. But whoever I gave it to would reveal their source. I would still be dragged into it. I felt weak and cowardly.

"I don't know what to do," I said.

"Can I show you something?" She pushed back from the table and went to the armoire. After opening its large doors and bending down to pull out the bottom drawer, she removed a cardboard box and placed it on the coffee table. She then moved the pillows on our couch and patted the space next to her.

I crushed out my cigarette.

"I've shown you most of this," she said, opening the box that held her father's papers.

I sat down next to her, my weight shifting the balance of the cushions.

She took a deep breath, and it caught in her chest.

"What is it?" I asked. "Your lungs?" Lately, Miranda had often been out of breath. She had been given a chest X-ray and a sputum culture—ruling out pneumonia and pleurisy.

"I don't know what it is. My shoulder hurts. I think it's all the baking."

"What did the doctor say?"

"He said it's a pulled muscle. He said to rest it." She smiled at me because we both knew she wasn't going to rest it. The deli required a full staff, and we ran it bare bones. She only rarely sat down and never took a day off.

Miranda exhaled and pulled out her father's items. Inside a faded envelope, there were typed letters, stamped visas, and faded passports. Her family history could be traced through these tiny, stamped papers. Her parents had fled Poland as soon as Germany had invaded, getting over the border before it closed, and from that moment, their Polish passports were a liability.

They had a large calligraphed "J" on the first page across from their photographs, covering their names and dates of birth. They traveled through Slovakia, Austria, and Northern Italy, painstakingly slow travel with stops for her father to earn money. They needed fake papers at every border. Her mother had died while they were hiding on a farm in Italy, but Miranda and her father had lived, and through an incredible stroke of luck and a sympathetic bureaucrat, they had been allowed passage on the *USS Henry Gibbins* troop transport ship. That's how they'd made it to New York in 1944. That's how Miranda had ended up in *Life Magazine*—one of the only refugees allowed into the United States during World War II without a visa. She had arrived with nothing, and she and her father had built a life here in Upstate New York.

She only opened this box on solemn occasions. Her father had been a paragon of perseverance. His goal had been to deliver his daughter Miranda, who he had named after the character in Shakespeare's *The Tempest*, to safety. In the same way that Prospero had worked to save his daughter through magic and deception, Alexsander Fein worked to save his daughter through fortitude and ingenuity.

She touched the black ribbon she had worn at her father's funeral, torn to express her grief. He had died over fifteen years ago, but Miranda's grief had not abated. It was the reason she worked so hard to maintain the deli. The store had been the community's gift to her father; they had given him money to outfit and stock his store in 1945. The community needed a Jewish deli, and they'd donated money to get it off the ground. Alexsander gave them twelve years of service, making recipes from the memory of his grandparent's kitchen and his father's kosher butcher shop. As part of the community agreement, he'd also collected recipes from the Jewish people in Carthage, originally from all over Europe, and re-created the tastes of their homelands.

"I've never shown you this." Miranda set aside her father's citizenship certificate and his autograph from Eleanor Roosevelt and took a handwritten letter out of a folded envelope, made ingeniously from the label of a large tin can of Italian tomatoes. She read it aloud to me:

> Dear Miranda, light of my life, I write this with a heavy heart after your mother's death. I write this in English because my hope for you is to know a life without German or Polish or even Italian. These languages have formed the sound environment of a life to which I do not wish to return.
>
> You came to us as a miracle late in our lives when I was a Latin and math teacher, and your mother sold vegetables from our farm. You were born with beautiful red hair, exactly like your mother's. We lived the life we always wanted, what God had prepared us for. Beyond what we read in the newspapers, we felt safe and secure in our future. Every step your mother took, she took for you. Every step I now take, however tentative, I take for you.
>
> My wish right now, grieving and cowering on this Italian farm (may God pour blessing upon this family for hiding us in their barn) is that you will see the other side of this inferno, that you will step lightly, that you will hold these memories in your heart but not hold them deeply in your bones. It is my life's work to see you delivered to safety. It is all your mother would have wanted. She will not rest until I have completed this commission.
>
> With my blessing and promise to you, your father, Alexsander Fein

I wished I had met her father. I wished I had known him. Miranda had said he was always a firm believer in improving the world, regardless of the cost to himself. Despite everything he had witnessed and lost in Europe, he believed it was his responsibility to heal society, to build something better from the ruins. Miranda's box of papers from her father was inspirational, while mine from my father was incriminating and dirty. Our fathers could have stood on opposite sides of almost every life circumstance. Alexsander was poor, while Herbert was rich. Alexsander was humble, while Herbert was proud. Alexsander was devoted to his daughter, while Herbert was willing to let me go.

"You had a wonderful father, Miranda." I took off my glasses and wiped my eyes.

"I still have him." She touched her heart again. "But that's not why I read this. I've been thinking about this letter all day. It's a call for freedom, a call for us to not live in the past. The atrocities should be remembered and documented, but we can't make them our lives. Otherwise, the inferno wins."

"What are you saying? That I should just let the statue go up?"

"We know what your father did. We should focus on not letting it happen again, but we shouldn't go back down this path. It's not good for you."

Miranda's logic made sense for her and her father. I wanted to take her advice. Lord knows, I wanted to lie down and not think of this ever again. But this decision was harder because my father was the perpetrator.

"I can't forget what he did," I said. That was the breaking point for me. His white-collar crimes could be swept under the rug, but when I saw his rage come out in his fists, it became my responsibility to bring his crimes to light. Or get someone else to do it. That would be the easier way.

"You don't have to forget."

"I wonder if David could take the evidence to the newspaper?" I threw it out there as a possibility. I needed to find a solution.

"He doesn't work with editors," she said. "He takes photographs for the writers."

"I'll ask him," I said. "He'll come over tonight, I'm sure." David was a childhood friend—Miranda's best friend. They had grown up in Temple Beth Israel, and he came over almost every night for a quiet cigarette on the back stoop before he went out for a drink at one of Carthage's underground gay bars. His parents thought he was courting Miranda. They thought he was going to be a dentist and have babies with her.

I held my eyeglasses and placed them in Miranda's lap, leaning my shoulder against hers. She took her glasses and placed them on top of mine. I smiled and moved mine on top. She pulled hers away and put them on top. Mine were thick with heavy frames—hers were light and horn-rimmed. My heart leaped, and I grinned with my lips pressed together, pushing the grin up into my eyes. I wondered how someone so slight could have such an outsized effect on me.

She reached over our glasses and clasped my hand. She put her other hand on my face, her palm light against my cheek. I could smell raw onions. I felt my tears make pathways around her palm. She kissed me and I pulled her face toward me and hugged her to my chest. We lay back on the sofa, adjusting our bodies to fit together. Empress walked lightly on the back of the sofa and looked down at us. She held her paw up and licked it luxuriously. She didn't have Emperor's purr, but she still let us know when she was content.

"I don't want to chase my father for the rest of my life," I said. "I feel like his death has opened a door for me to worry about other things. I could get my librarian degree finally. For real. An actual certificate. I feel like I can come out of the cave I've been hiding in, and he won't be waiting there for me."

"You do have a life to create for yourself. Let's pass this evidence on to David. I want you to be a librarian. And I want you not to be scared of your family anymore."

The research had stirred an excitement in me. I remembered

how much I loved fitting facts together into a coherent story, reading documents from the past, and trying to fill in the gaps. I wanted to research. I longed to research. But I wanted a different topic.

Miranda lay her head on my chest. I felt the warmth of her body against mine. Two black dresses, four feet tangled at the bottom of the sofa. Carly Simon sang "You're So Vain" on the kitchen radio. She sang about former lovers and what she saw in her coffee cup. The bass pumped through the thin walls.

"My stockings are a mess," I said. The fabric was cruel, unforgiving.

"Take them off," she said.

I shook my head. I didn't want to disrupt our positions.

She closed her eyes.

I closed mine too and took in the moment. The love of my life pressed against me, a hard day finished, and work still to do. I heard the roar of the elevated highway, the whir of the bread mixer, and the presence of Empress above our heads. Maybe we could just lay low and live our lives.

"What's that smell?" I asked.

"Oh hell, it's the pot pie," she said, pushing against the sofa and rising. "The biscuits are burning," she cried.

After supper, I washed the dishes, cast iron pan, and baking sheet. I kept my hands in the soapy water longer than I needed to, like a bubble bath.

Miranda dried the dishes, and then we changed our clothes upstairs. She called David to make sure he was coming, and then we sat on the couch in the back room. The accordion file sat on my desk like an orphan waiting for its adoptive parents.

"Anyone home?" David knocked as he opened the front door. "Yoohoo, I brought a friend."

David came through the beaded curtain. He was laughing

more than I'd ever seen him laugh. Maybe he'd been drinking already. I thought I might have to delay asking him to go to the newspaper.

"Announce me," a male voice said from behind the beads.

David laughed. "And ladies and gentlemen, we have with us tonight—ROGER."

Roger pulled the beads back to reveal only his face, a boyish, clean-shaven face with wrinkles around his eyes. Then he slid one leg through the curtain like he was doing a striptease.

"Hold that pose." David twisted a flashbulb onto his camera and snapped a picture of his friend entangled in the beads.

I sat up on the couch. Miranda got up and hugged David.

"This is Roger," David said. "Roger, this is Miranda."

I stood up awkwardly. This wasn't the post-funeral evening I'd had in mind.

"And Lucy," he added.

Roger shook our hands and laughed at the formality. Then, he kissed Miranda's hand with a flourish.

"I brought shredded potatoes," David said, holding up a paper grocery bag.

"Latkes?" she asked.

"Yes, I'm cooking," he said. "You're not to lift a finger."

"Hanukkah is over," I said, proud to know the main holidays on the Jewish calendar.

"Latkes aren't just for Hanukkah, my dear." He always reminded me I wasn't Jewish.

And I wasn't. I hadn't been raised with much religion at all. When I'd first met Miranda, I didn't know that the Torah contained five of the same books as the Old Testament or even that Jesus had been Jewish. But I was curious. She had told me about the miracle of the Hannukah oil lasting eight days and the tradition of keeping the light burning even through the darkest hours of the night. And she always cried on the high holidays, remembering the traditions her father had taught her.

"Do you have applesauce?" Miranda asked David.

"Of course." He put his arm around her shoulder and held her close. They were both petite and looked like the perfect couple. It was easy to imagine their wedding photos, under the chuppah, David's parents crying with joy.

"We're celebrating," David said.

"Celebrating what?" Miranda asked.

"Well, I don't know what you're celebrating, but I'm celebrating Roger." David kissed Roger on the cheek. Roger turned his head and kissed David on the lips.

I envied their openness, Roger's flamboyance. Miranda and I kept our relationship a secret. Half of our customers were part of Temple Beth Israel, and the other half went to the South Side Baptist Church. It wasn't our job to open their eyes. It was our job to sell sandwiches and pay the utility bills.

Roger was older than David, older than all of us. He wore eyeliner, face powder, and a tight-fitting shirt. He commanded attention. He made me want to sit up and arrange myself, maybe brush my hair and put on some lipstick—if only I wasn't so tired.

In the kitchen, Miranda sat on the countertop, and David put down his camera and donned an apron. Roger fiddled with the radio. I was exhausted, but I wanted to find an opening, a chance to hand over the accordion file and let David deliver it to the papers or the school board or wherever it needed to go.

Curtis Mayfield's "Superfly" came on. Roger let out a yell and bent his knees into a ready position. When the horns started, he pretended to hold a microphone and mouthed the words.

"Is this from the movie?" Miranda asked.

"Don't you know this song?" he asked.

"I try to keep up, but I was raised on polka music," she said.

"Klezmer bands. My family had an accordion." She laughed. She was as comfortable with her roots as Roger was with his sexuality.

"Well, let me introduce you to funk." Roger held out his hand to the radio like he was introducing a contestant on a game show.

David shook his head and laughed. He heated oil in a wide pan on the stove, the gas pilot burning blue. He took a plastic bag of shredded potatoes out of his grocery bag.

"Did your mom shred those for you?" Miranda asked him with a grin.

"She did not. I did it myself." He smiled broadly. He took an egg from our refrigerator and whisked it in a bowl.

Miranda jumped down from the counter and got him some flour, baking soda, salt, and pepper. She looked over his shoulder at how he was coating the potatoes.

"No, no," he said, shaking his finger at her. "I'm the chef tonight."

I always had trouble getting Miranda to relax or let me take the lead on household or deli-related tasks, but David was able to deflate her over-eager work ethic, at least temporarily.

Miranda took a bottle of wine from the pantry and four juice cups from the cupboard.

Emperor hid behind my chair. I patted him on the head as he arched his back. I had found Emperor and Press when they were kittens, abandoned. I lured them in with tuna fish. For weeks, they didn't trust me unless my hands smelled like food. Miranda teased me about how much time and energy I spent on them. People in other countries didn't bring cats into their homes, she told me.

"Too late for wine?" she asked me.

"Never too late," David answered for me.

"Why would it be too late?" Roger asked. "Who tells you what time to do anything?" Miranda's question had struck a chord with him, and I could see he was prepared with an entire concert in response. "You've got to release yourself into your own life." He said it like a pronouncement.

"Got to let it go," David agreed. That was rich coming from him—as if he hadn't spent years cocooned with me and Miranda. His repression was as legendary as his devotion to his mother.

"Okay, I got it," Miranda said. She poured wine into each of the cups.

"There's something I actually do want to let go of—" I said.

"You can't keep it bottled up," Roger interrupted. "Every norm we break makes it easier for those who come after us." He turned down the radio. "I'm serious. This is important."

Miranda and I exchanged a glance. Apparently, this was the Roger Show, and we were tonight's spectators.

"Two years ago," he said, "I lost my job in the school system because someone reported me as a homosexual. I thought I had lost everything, but now I'm living out loud. I've never been happier." He sounded like an Amway salesman making a pitch. But his words rang true for me. I wanted to live out loud. I wanted to escape the constraints that had been put on me since I was a child. I wanted to confront my father's sins and tell the world what I knew. If I didn't, then a new generation of crimes would be built on the back of these unpunished crimes. But it was hard to take the risk, especially without any guarantee of safety.

"The police used to patrol public bathrooms looking for us," Roger said. "They don't do that anymore. They only did it when we were afraid to be outed. Our fear was their power."

Roger wasn't wrong. But we all knew that the first people out the door had the hardest time of it—billy clubs and prison sentences and lost jobs.

Roger's words sparked a vision for me. I imagined a middle ground. Miranda and I could live together quietly, and instead of bringing down the wrath of the city upon our shoulders by revealing this evidence about my father, what if I could get my sister to do it? I only needed her to cancel her plan for the statue—we didn't need to go fully public. It would be like blackmail but nicer. I felt, not for the first time, that I had some of my father's ruthlessness inside me.

David laid latkes out on plates and spooned applesauce on top. The crisp edges of the potatoes were sprinkled with salt. The applesauce was sweet and tart. I savored each bite.

"Come out with us tonight," Roger said. "We're going to King Tut's."

"I'm not going to a bar," Miranda said, holding her fork above her plate.

"There are never any women there," I added.

"It's not called Queen of Sheba's," Roger said.

"Even if it was, it would still be for us," David said with a laugh. "The Queens of Sheba."

"I wish we had our own place to go," I said.

"But you'd never go," David said. He knew our quiet ways. "King Tut's would be yours if you went."

"I want to know," Miranda said. "What does a bar have that we don't have here?"

"It's public," Roger said. "If it happens in private, does it even count?"

I thought it did. The private conversations and private relationships were the richest. This was who I was. This was helping me make my decision. I didn't need to go public with the evidence about my father. I needed to go private.

"That reminds me, David," Miranda said. "Lucy wanted to ask you a favor."

"Hit me," he said.

"I don't know," I said. "Roger's got me thinking. Maybe I can do this on my own."

Miranda looked at me with a question in her eyes.

"Your choice," David said.

"I'm serious, Roger," I said. "You opened my eyes. I've been told all my life—be feminine, be straight, be married, be quiet, listen to my elders. It's like a cult. I don't have to play by those rules." I said these words without a hint of emotion. My brain was moving ahead, but my body was still too tired to put any oomph behind my words.

"Go, sister," Roger said. He took the last bit of his latke and licked his plate.

"I've never known you to be feminine or straight or married or quiet," David said with a smile.

I laughed. "But in front of my family, I'm all of those—except married. Oh, how they wish I was married. But I always wear a dress. I follow the rules." My family never stood around the kitchen and ate latkes, dancing to songs on the radio. We never had guests in our house who felt comfortable enough to change the radio station. We never felt comfortable enough ourselves. I couldn't remember Ginny or me ever changing the radio station if our father was home. Now that he was gone, couldn't Ginny and I redefine the rules? What if I took a bit of this world and inserted it into their world? I could make a difference.

I remembered the way my father had laughed me out of the bank, scoffing at my mimeographed sheets. I would never forget his vast sense of impunity—impregnable protection provided by his status and power. What if Ginny and I embraced the freedom of our generation and put an end to the secrets and lies? What if we stopped caring what other people thought? I didn't need another scandal or disappointment—I just needed my sister and I to stand together like we couldn't do that day at the bank. We needed to see that it was our responsibility to build the world anew. Surely, we had changed enough in the past fourteen years that we could start fresh.

"I believe in you," Miranda said. She smiled at me even though she wasn't sure what I had decided to do.

CHAPTER THREE

Exhumation

I woke up the next morning humming TV sitcom lyrics, letting them bubble up from my chest—not an entirely appropriate response to my father's funeral, but I wasn't going to deny my good mood.

"You were sound asleep, I couldn't bear to wake you," Miranda said, sitting on the bed. She was already dressed, her hair pulled back in a plump red bun.

"I haven't slept that hard in years." I rubbed my eyes and touched her elbow, rough with winter skin. "What time is it? Have you already done everything?" Miranda and I prepared food every morning for the deli. Then, she and George ran the store while I met with clients at my desk.

"You needed the sleep," she said. "I brought you coffee." On our bedside table sat a steaming mug, pale with milk, just the way I liked it.

"Do I even need coffee after that much sleep? I feel like a superhero." I sat up in our soft bed and pushed aside our faded quilts. I gave her a kiss—not as extravagant as the kiss between David and Roger the night before, but it was a kiss to welcome more joy into our lives.

I wanted us to change. Miranda and I were practical to a fault, especially Miranda. Punch lists. Customer orders. Prep work. Bills. I wanted us to be more romantic. I thought about the single vacation we'd ever taken together. We borrowed a car from Speedy's and traveled to historical sites in Upstate New York: Seneca Falls, stops on the Underground Railroad, and an emotional visit to Fort Ontario, the grounds in Oswego, New York that had served as a refugee camp when Miranda and her father arrived from Europe. She and I stayed in motels and ate in restaurants. It was way beyond our budget, but I treasured every moment.

"It's time we took another trip," I said, tapping her hip. It was exactly what we needed.

"Let me get this shoulder thing figured out," she said, touching her chest, "and we'll pay some bills. But, then we should go."

She stood up and smiled at me, still rumpled on our bed.

"Where?" I asked. Planning was half the fun, imagining all the different trips we could take.

"Niagara Falls?" She raised her eyebrows.

"Cross into Canada," I added.

"I've always wanted to go to Montreal," she said. "I need to compare those famed Montreal bagels to ours."

She straightened her apron and kissed my cheek. "Let's talk about it in the kitchen," she said. She wasn't going to let some fantasy trip planning get in the way of her prep work.

I went to my dresser and pulled open the top drawer. I had worn my best tights to the funeral yesterday. I looked through my remaining pairs. Something to go with my brown dress, but there was a hole in one pair, a run in another. I thought about the pain of my tights yesterday at the funeral—constricting and uncomfortable. And even with the tights, my legs were freezing in the January wind. Without thinking about it further, I gathered all my tights and stockings and pantyhose: the blue and black, nude and tan. I molded them into a ball and placed them in our bedroom wastebasket. They didn't fit, so I shoved them. See how you feel, I thought, being shoved in a space you can hardly fit.

Those tights had cost me probably thirty dollars over the years, if not more, but I didn't care. I was done with them. I took off my nightgown and spun around in front of my dresser. Take a woman who has been frightened of her father her entire life, put him in the graveyard, give her a good night's rest, stir, and this is what comes out.

I went to our closet and flipped through my dresses. If I wasn't wearing pantyhose, then I also wasn't going to be wearing any dresses. I could fetch a few dollars for them at the thrift store. I flipped through my pants, clicking the hangers over the wooden rod. At the back, double hung on a bent wire hanger, was a nubbly coral pantsuit—thick wool blended. I'd bought it when I thought I was going to be a librarian, but it had been too big. I'd always meant to take it to the tailor.

I pulled the jacket off the hanger and released the pants from their decade-long crease. I pulled on the pants. They fit. I pulled on the jacket. *Voilà*. A new me. No shirt, but hey, when you're looking good, you don't need all the pieces. I smiled and tiptoed into the bathroom to look in the mirror. I buttoned the large, cloth-covered buttons on my jacket. I had forgotten how fabulous they were, arranged in a "T" across the front of the jacket with two buttons holding down flaps from the shoulders.

I wanted to go downstairs and show Miranda, but George would be here any minute, and he didn't need the surprise of his life when he saw me half-undressed.

I found a shirt and put some socks on the radiator to warm up. I pulled out my boots. I was going to see my sister, and every bone in my body told me this was the start of a new era. Without our father in the house, Ginny and I would be free to talk and giggle and be sisters again. We wouldn't feel stiff and awkward and worry if our father could overhear us.

Yesterday was a fake ceremony, I decided. I had said things to the pews that I no longer believed about our father, and Ginny had talked about statues and accolades. Today, we could have a real conversation about our father's death and legacy. We were the only two people who knew him as a father. We didn't need an audience to get on the same page.

I looked out the window at the elevated highway: motorists on their way to specific destinations. They each had a goal in mind, and they didn't pause to look from side to side—they kept their eyes on the road ahead.

I came down the stairs, holding my coffee cup and quietly singing the theme song to *The Mary Tyler Moore Show*.

I could see someone through our beaded curtains, standing near the bulletin board. I thought it was George. I came through with more drama than usual, holding the beads in my fist. I sang the refrain, hitting each syllable with a nod of my head.

I thought I'd get an awkward smile out of him, but it wasn't George. It was the woman with the red Volkswagen from yesterday—the blown-out tire.

"I'm so sorry," I said, covering my mouth.

"I'm sorry." She emphasized the "I'm" part, and we both smiled.

"I don't usually sing like that," I said.

"That's okay, I sing to myself all the time. I'm Alma," she said and stuck out her hand.

"I'm Lucretia." We shook hands.

"I'm just putting up a flyer," she said. "George said I could."

I looked at her neat three-by-five card, offering her typing services.

"Just until I get a real job," she added.

I laughed and pointed to my own flyer. *Need help with your paperwork? Ask for Lucretia. Reasonable prices.* For a fee, I helped people fill out welfare applications, rental agreements, court documents—any bureaucratic paperwork that made them feel disconnected and powerless. My customers didn't pay much, but I helped them buck the system—one paper transaction at a time.

"I haven't had a real job in ten years, and somehow I've been perfectly fine," I said with a laugh.

* * *

Later that morning, the bus engine rumbled through the heels of my boots. A rhythm played in my mind as a chant: *I was right about my father. Always right about my father.* The research and the talk with Roger had invigorated me.

From the closest stop, I walked past the Victorian mansions on Erie Boulevard and the country estates on Oneida Drive. My father had overseen the re-branding of this neighborhood in the fifties. He had stone pillars built at the entrance to the tangle of winding roads: Algonquin Road, Iroquois Way, Montauk Lane, Oneida Drive, and Onondaga Way. My father had gotten the city to change all the street names to Native American names. He called the neighborhood Hiawatha Heights. Hiawatha had been one of the great Onondaga leaders, honored for his ability to join tribes into a strong alliance. But according to my father, just having an official name, any sort of name, added ten percent to the property values.

When I got to the house on Onondaga Way, I took a deep breath. The stone-front design stood proudly on its raised lot. Stained glass windows shone in deep jewel tones, and a trio of peaked rooftops each rose to a different height. The middle peak alone was enough for two families. The wings on each side were bonuses. The house looked different to me, mostly because our father didn't live there anymore.

"You're late." Ginny opened the door before I started up the flagstone steps. She smiled down at me.

"You knew I was coming?"

"You're late from yesterday. Why didn't you come to the reception?" She leaned on the doorframe, dwarfed by the mansion's facade. She wore her typical outfit—pencil skirt, silk shirt, patent leather belt. She had belts in every color to emphasize her small waist. "You left the church like it was on fire," she added.

"I kept my promise," I said. "I gave a remembrance." Normally, I'd already be annoyed with my sister's criticisms. I'd have set my jaw and blurted out a cutting response. But now, I could take her barbs. I had my coral pantsuit as protection.

"It's freezing out here," Ginny said, rubbing her arms.

Sarah, my niece, came up next to her mother. She wore a striped T-shirt and a pair of high-waisted pants. Her stomach popped over the top in a way only a twelve-year-old can pull off.

"Sarah, why aren't you in school?" I asked as I climbed the steps. The January wind gusted, giving me a boost.

"We stayed home," Ginny inserted for her daughter. She ran her fingers over Sarah's bangs. She had an idea where each hair on her daughter's head should go.

Sarah came outside in her bare feet and down a few steps to hug me. I could practically feel the cold stone against the soles of her feet.

"I want to make a chart of the gravestones," she said, skipping the pleasantries. I loved this girl. She was me but better. "We have to research each name," she added. "I took pictures, and Mom is going to get them developed."

"I know a librarian who can help us."

"Mrs. Caravaggio?"

"The one and only." I had done my university hours with Mrs. Caravaggio, and she was a marvel. Sarah and I worked with her at the public library whenever we were there.

"I liked what you said about Anne Frank yesterday," Sarah said.

"You did? Then, I'm glad I said it." I hadn't told the story for her, but I was glad she'd been there to hear it. I put my arm around her, and we climbed the final few steps together.

Ginny stepped back and gestured for us to enter—as if we were in a silent movie with broad, stylized movements. The front foyer, paneled in mahogany, was streaked in color with the light streaming through the stained-glass windows. The built-in sideboard overflowed with flower arrangements: roses, carnations, and baby's breath. Two extravagant wreaths leaned against the cabinetry, blocking the door to the hidden coat closet.

When we were children, I had shared the secret nooks of our house with Ginny—the dumbwaiter from the kitchen to the basement, the maid's quarters with the sloping ceilings, the window seat in the study with its thick, velvet curtains, the ladders in the library to reach the highest shelves. I thought about the days she and I had gotten to stay home alone when we were children, how free we felt to roam the house without the watchful eye of our father. We'd listen to Buck Rogers and The Lone Ranger on the radio. We'd raid the kitchen cupboard and set up picnics in the library. We'd yell for no reason. We'd bring our bedcovers down to the living room and make forts. Back then, Ginny would play whatever games I proposed and let me make the rules.

"We're resting after yesterday," Ginny said. "Even our creator had a day of rest." She smiled like she'd been repeating that phrase all morning. Her blue eyes shone, but the skin around them sagged. She seemed tired and relieved, in a perfect mood to hear my proposal.

"We need a day to eat all the leftover food," Sarah said. She rubbed her hands together after standing in the wind.

I took off my coat and gloves. My face was raw from the cold air, but the house's heat was roaring. I kept my coral jacket on with its smart buttons and rearranged my shirt around my middle. Static electricity popped in my fingers.

In the inner foyer, portraits of my parents presided at the base of the stairs, above the fireplace mantel. My father was presented as he had been—overweight and overstuffed into his three-piece suit. The painter had captured the twinkle of intelligence and humor in his eyes. My mother was young in the painting, younger than I was now, her face without wrinkles, her hair pulled back loosely in a low bun—her profile in a quarter turn. I wished I had had more time with her. I had never asked her enough questions about her childhood or what she was like in school or what drew her to my father. I never knew what it was like for her to move into this big house when she married. I shook my head—too late now.

"That was quite a service yesterday," I said. "Nice turnout." I couldn't think of any other small talk.

"Coffee?" Ginny asked.

"I knew you'd have a pot on." I caught her eye. Even with our differences, I still knew my sister better than anyone. She always wanted a warm cup of something in her hands, and she couldn't turn down a sweet even if she had to say a million times how "bad" she was being. We both knew food and drink were the cornerstones of any conversation.

I followed her into the kitchen—a large space with double ovens, a kitchen island, and a cozy breakfast nook for the kitchen table. I took one of the chairs at the kitchen table, and Sarah took the one next to me. This is how family stories got passed down, I thought. The women sat around drinking tea or coffee—the kids listened in. Ginny and I had missed that with our mother dying so young. We'd only heard our father's soliloquies.

Ginny reached into the cupboard for a cup and saucer. She'd had the cupboards stained dark brown and purchased new appliances in avocado green. Our father had given her free rein to decorate the house after she'd married Joseph.

"I miss Daddy so much," she said.

I hadn't expected Ginny to be grieving. To me, his death was only a formality. I had done my grieving fourteen years ago after that day at the bank.

"I'm sorry for your loss. You, too, Sarah."

"It's your loss, too," Ginny said sharply. "Everyone wondered where you were yesterday."

I nodded. I didn't want to explain how my brain had short-circuited at the end of the service. I wasn't ready to talk about the accordion file.

"You looked good," Ginny conceded. "I loved that dress. And your hair is so thick. You should get one of those bob cuts."

I nodded. I tugged my long hair over my shoulders on both sides and straightened the buttons on my jacket. If I got a bob, I would look like Thelma from Scooby-Doo with my big eyeglasses and thick hair.

"I love your hair," Sarah said. "It's the same color as mine." Hers had more highlights, but there was no denying we looked alike.

"I'm just saying—when you make a little effort—" Ginny started.

I ignored my sister and smiled at Sarah. We were both subject to Ginny's eternal makeovers. Ginny's goal was to make everything look nice on the surface even if it was roiling underneath.

"If you want to find a husband—" Ginny said.

"I don't want to find a husband," I interrupted her. We'd had this conversation enough times it was like reading lines off a script. This was normally where I'd get red in the face and start using my big vocabulary to make Ginny feel small. But I wasn't going to do that anymore.

"The whole time you were up in the pulpit talking, I was thinking about eligible bachelors," she said. "We'll find you someone. You're not too old. We had a cousin who got married in her thirties." She shook her finger at me like I should hold onto stories like that to keep my hopes alive.

"I remember," I said.

"You're not going to find anyone if you spend all your time at the deli. There's not an eligible bachelor in all of Old Ward Thirteen. Not one. You've proven your point, Lucy. I know our world isn't perfect, but it's time to come home."

I smiled at her. I couldn't imagine going back to the country club and making nice. And I would never give up Miranda.

"Honestly," Ginny went on, "Joe and I have talked about this. If you do get married, we'll pay for everything. Sarah can be the flower girl." Ginny bustled around the kitchen while Sarah and I sat patiently at the table.

I smiled at her enthusiasm. She meant well. She did.

"What's a flower girl?" Sarah asked, bemused that she had been volunteered.

"I want you to be happy." Ginny talked over her daughter.

"I'm happy," I said. "I've never told you, b—" I paused. I didn't come here to tell Ginny about my relationship with Miranda, but it seemed possible. There was an opening.

Ginny handed me coffee with milk and a spoonful of sugar, how I used to take it when I was younger. I stirred it and set the spoon in the saucer. I could set the conversation afire by telling her about Miranda. I wanted to be like Roger coming through the beaded curtain without knowing what he'd find on the other side. Maybe someday I'd come out like that. But for now, I only wanted to talk about our father.

"What were you going to say?" Ginny pulled platters out of the refrigerator. She put cold canapés—mini cheese balls, deviled eggs—on a round plate. And hot savories—prawn *vol au vents*, sausage rolls, lobster tartlets, mushroom canapés—on a metal baking sheet. She had another plate for sweets—ambrosia salad, pecan tarts, petit fours.

"Nothing," I said.

"Tell us," Sarah said.

Ginny opened her shiny avocado oven and slid in the tray of canapés. She placed the plate of cold sweets in front of me. The cakes had pink, white, and brown icing, with tiny silver balls around the edges. How much did it cost to have someone make these tiny, perfect cakes? I dreamed of having enough money for such things. I wanted a bank account that wasn't in jeopardy, with money to travel beyond the confines of our state. I wanted to travel to Poland to see where Miranda was born. I wanted to pay to fix up her house. I wanted a refrigerator that didn't have a fraying plug at the back. I took a deep breath, trying not to resent Ginny's good fortune and not forgetting that half of this could have been mine. I let a petty thought escape: if Ginny could pay for my imaginary wedding, why couldn't she give me the money? Our father had cut me out of the will, but nothing was stopping her from sharing.

"Remember our beach house?" I asked, changing the subject.

"Of course," Ginny said.

"You would've loved it, Sarah," I said. "We'd go for the whole summer. Our dad came up on the weekends. We'd have the place to ourselves with just a nanny to watch over us."

"It was on an island," Ginny said. "We could only get there by boat."

"It wasn't fancy, though," I added. "Your mom and I shared a room. We had these little iron beds."

"That's when Daddy was at his best," Ginny said.

"It was on one of the Thousand Islands," I told Sarah. "Between New York and Canada. Perched on a hill with a long wooden staircase down to the water. When we were little, I had to help your mom down the stairs. She had to keep one hand on my shoulder and one hand on the railing the whole way down. It was a rule. She followed all the rules."

"You did, Mom?" Sarah bit her bottom lip and smiled.

Ginny nodded and sat down with us. Her blue eyes caught the

light and looked livelier than they had at the front door.

"I remember swimming out to the wooden raft," I said. "To get in, you had to run into the water until you couldn't stand it, the St. Lawrence water pushing the chill up to your waist, and then when your toes went numb, you had to run back to the beach, slapping your thighs to get the blood flowing. We must have looked so funny."

"Granddaddy didn't always come down to the water," Ginny said to Sarah. "He'd have his coffee on the patio and yell down to us when breakfast was ready. 'Rinse your feet.' 'Wash your hands.' I guess I did like all the rules. They were part of the ritual. When Daddy came for his weekend trips, he was relaxed and funny. He'd bring candy. He'd give the nanny a day off and an envelope with money in it."

"He read us stories," I said.

"He told us stories," Ginny corrected me. "Every night."

"That's right. I had forgotten. We loved his made-up character."

"Boy extraordinaire," Ginny said, smiling.

I remembered stories of lost pets and scary noises, and his made-up character would find all the pets and solve all the mysteries.

"That's how I remember him," Sarah said. "He was the nicest grandfather alive. He bought me books. He talked to me about everything. He played backgammon with me."

I knew what Sarah was talking about. When my father turned on the charm, he was as endearing as Frank Morgan in *The Wizard of Oz*. Ingratiating. When he gave you his full attention, it was like a spotlight that confirmed your very existence.

"He could be nice," I said. "And everyone knew him as generous."

"That's why everyone's in favor of this statue," Ginny said.

I coughed. "Your proposal took me by surprise," I said.

"It took us by surprise. The city really wants it." She nibbled on a pecan tart and smiled at me. "I really shouldn't have this," she said, covering her mouth as she talked. "I had three yesterday."

"Ginny, the statue's not right." I tried to keep my tone light. I used her nickname Ginny instead of her formal name Virginia. "Our father should not have a statue."

"Why?" Sarah asked.

"Because he was complicated," I said to Sarah, "and not everything he did was good for the community." I didn't want to go into too much detail.

"We need something positive to hold onto," Ginny said. "This statue will be good for everyone. Why did our father do so much work if he wasn't going to be recognized for it? He got the federal money to build the highway, created jobs, put Carthage on the map, literally. Have you seen how much bigger our city is in the AAA map? His work fed the university's reputation, made downtown more vibrant. He gave us a chance."

"Everyone at the funeral said how much they loved him." Sarah shrugged as if that was unusual at a funeral.

"The world needs positive role models," Ginny added.

I let the flurry of their arguments settle around me. I took a sip of my coffee. I wasn't here to fight. Ginny was right about the world. We had been on a bender of division and upheaval, a historic roller coaster. We had the highs of the Civil Rights and Voting Rights acts and the lows of assassinations and burning cities and Vietnam. Our country was divided and Nixon, divider extraordinaire, had taken the helm for a second term. Our hearts couldn't take anymore.

"We could spend the money on improving our city rather than celebrating our father. The highway did damage. Why not repair some of it instead of building a statue?"

"It's not our money," Ginny said. "The city's paying for it."

I took another sip of coffee and held the cup in front of my mouth. Why would the city pay for it? If Ginny was paying for it, I could see why they would agree. But why would they want to use taxpayer dollars to honor my father? They knew he wasn't entirely above board.

"Was the statue Dad's idea?"

"No—but he hinted at it. We both know he would have loved it." She smiled at me like we might share a laugh. Whenever our father Herbert was featured in a newspaper or magazine, he saved a copy. He would show them to us, smoothing them out on the dining room table. He collected his public recognitions as insurance against obscurity. He told us over and over again that his daughters had killed the Wilson family line. There was no son to carry on the name. In the face of his dying family tree branch, Herbert wanted to complete his to-do list and shout his accomplishments from every hilltop. A statue was an accolade he wouldn't have to pull out of a drawer.

I took a deep breath and lowered my voice. "I was given a stack of memos and confidential papers from the bank," I said. "I think if you look at them, you'll see that this statue idea could back-fire—if any of this information comes out."

"What information?" Sarah asked.

"Lucy, please, let's not do this again," Ginny interrupted her daughter. "What does it matter if he made a few mistakes? No one's perfect." She pushed the plate of sweets closer to me.

This was where we divided. I had seen our father's other side. I knew what he was capable of. Ginny had only seen our father at home. She couldn't imagine that someone as generous and witty and fun as our father could also be a cheat and a bully.

"I'm not asking for perfection," I said with a grunt.

"You've never gotten along with him." She got up and prepared another pot of coffee though we hadn't finished the first.

"That's not true," I said, pushing back my chair. "Dad and I were perfectly suited. We were the serious ones. If anything, I got along with him better than you did." I sounded like a toddler arguing about who was the favorite child.

"What did he do that was so bad?" Sarah asked.

"He tore down the colored neighborhood," I said. "The Jewish neighborhood. He didn't touch the white neighborhoods."

Sarah looked at me. I saw a glimmer of interest behind her horn-rimmed glasses.

"Is that what this is all about?" Ginny asked. "Civil rights? You're going to give up your family for a concept?"

"It's not a concept. It's personal. He razed Miranda's business. You weren't there that day, Ginny. You were supposed to be. If you had been, I don't think we'd have trouble agreeing right now."

"I had a reason for not being there," she said.

"Sleeping in after your engagement party?" I asked.

Sarah turned her head to look at her mother.

"No," Ginny said. "I talked to Daddy after we went to that club. You'd gone to bed. You don't know as much as you think you know."

"I know he could talk you out of anything," I said, "because you'd believe anything he said." The conversation was getting away from me. We were going over well-trod territory instead of branching out into a new era. My coral pantsuit was losing its power.

"That's not what happened." Ginny took a nut covered cheese ball and bit into it tentatively. "It's like when we found those bodies in the backyard."

"What?" Sarah asked. She shook her head back and forth and widened her eyes comically.

"Aunt Lucy thought it was a big scandal," Ginny told Sarah. "But it ended up being an innocent misunderstanding."

"How do you misunderstand bodies in your backyard?" Sarah looked at me and then her mother.

"I never believed the explanation we were given," I said. "To me, it was another example of our father covering up the past."

"He wasn't even alive when those people died." Ginny held up her hands like she couldn't conceive how I could find fault with our father.

"But he was alive when we found them," I said.

* * *

Fourteen years ago, Ginny had cried on my shoulder about two skeletons in our backyard. They had been uncovered during a landscape remodel before she and Joseph were married. Everything had moved so quickly that summer. After the day of the highway protests, I had left home in a rage, Miranda had lost her deli, and Joe had proposed to Ginny. Boom. Boom. Boom. Those events had each changed my life, and they all happened within a week of each other in 1958.

George, Miranda, and I were unloading boxes of kosher meat from a delivery van when the phone rang.

"Fein Foods, Lucretia speaking." I held the phone under my chin and wiped my hands on my apron.

"Lucy, I'm so glad you answered. I didn't know if I had the right number. You can't believe what's happened." Ginny broke down in tears.

"Ginny? What is it?" I hated to hear her cry. It sparked adrenaline in my body like a fire alarm.

"They're landscaping the backyard—for the wedding. Daddy has earth movers flattening it—for the guests." She gasped for air after every sentence. "And they stopped because they found bones—human bones in our yard."

I wasn't expecting this. I couldn't process it. How did they get there? I held the phone and watched George carry a box of beef into the kitchen.

"Is this a bad omen?" Ginny asked, her nose stuffed with

crying. Typical of Ginny to think how this would affect her rather than how it had affected the people who were buried in the yard. And typical of her not to address what had happened at the bank, just jump right into what was bothering her.

"Maybe," I said. I didn't believe in omens, but if there was anything that could get Ginny to call off her wedding, I was happy to entertain it.

"Lucy, don't say that. Will you come over? I need you to see this. I need you to come," she said.

Even as I was deciding, I was taking off my apron. My body had decided for me.

"I'll be back in an hour," I told Miranda and George. They both held heavy boxes and looked at me without comment.

I ran to the number 32 bus, past the empty jazz clubs and the closed corner stores. They looked like they had shrunk since their customers moved away. The buildings were covered in dust from the highway construction—a thick layer like the houses in Pompeii after Vesuvius erupted.

I rode the bus, bouncing my legs with impatience. If Ginny needed me to come in a real emergency, I would hate the thirty minutes it took to get across town. I was still Ginny's big sister even if I had moved out of the house, even if she was marrying the man who had first been offered to me.

At the stop closest to Hiawatha Heights, thick-leaved trees created a dark shade. It was twenty degrees cooler than Ward Thirteen. At the house, I went to the side gate. No reason to see my father if I didn't have to. When I got past the stone carriage house, I saw the magnitude of their project. It looked like Daddy was building another highway right through his own backyard.

Two earth movers sat atop mounds of freshly turned dirt. Men stood in clusters, wearing overalls and caps, smoking and gesticulating. They didn't find human bones every day—they would tell this story over dinner.

"Lucy," Ginny said. She fell into my arms, letting her body collapse against mine, and started to cry again.

"Show me," I said. I needed to know what she was making into such a catastrophe.

We walked over the dirt, what used to be a sloped and grassy retreat, and peered into a long, deep pit. The men's shovels were resting against the trunk of the old oak tree. They had done enough digging to reveal two human skulls side by side and torsos down to their elbows.

It took me aback. My skin tingled despite the heat in the air. Who could they be? Two human beings. Why were they in our yard? When were they buried? They'd been there long enough to turn from corpses into skeletons. I felt like I was in a movie. I pictured it in film noir, black and white, a fog over the earth movers and mounds of dirt, a man in a trench coat stepping out from behind the oak tree.

I grabbed Ginny's elbow and she nodded through her tears.

"It's awful," she whispered. The workers were close to the pit, smoking cigarettes in the brisk air, watching Ginny as she clung to me. "How could these bodies have been here through our whole childhood?" she cried. "I keep thinking we played out here. We ran over their bodies. We had no idea."

I leaned down to look closer. Dirt was caked on the bones. I wanted to clean them, give them a proper burial. "It's not a bad omen, Ginny," I said. As much as I wanted her to call off her wedding to Joseph, I couldn't lie to her. "It's just something that happened."

"I know, but I hate it," she said.

"They probably hate it even more," I said, gesturing to the two skeletons.

"Daddy's making this wedding into something enormous," Ginny said under her breath. "He's inviting everyone in Carthage."

"It's not until the fall."

"That's why this has started." She gestured again to the yard, and we instinctively turned away from the skeletons. "Daddy wants to flatten the backyard so he can have two hundred guests."

"Could we make it two hundred and one?"

"Who do you want to invite? A boy?" She took my arm and held it close. We were almost whispering—it felt sacrilegious to talk about anything but skeletons in the presence of skeletons.

"No. Miranda."

"Miranda's the girl you live with?"

"Yes, I want you to meet her." I looked Ginny in the eyes. I wanted to tell her about my kiss. About Miranda's red hair. About her acumen for dealing with life's obstacles.

"She can come. Remind me to send another invitation." She smiled at me and tucked her arms around my arm, pulling me close.

"I will," I said.

"And I wanted to give you something from Mom's jewelry box. To wear the day of the wedding. You can even keep it. We'll look upstairs if you want."

"Not the pearls?" I asked.

"Daddy was adamant I keep those." She avoided my eye.

I sighed and shook my head. What kind of rules did our father make? *If you took the item that meant the most to you and nothing else, then you couldn't have that or anything else.* He didn't even know why I loved the pearls. Not because of my mother. I could barely remember her wearing them, but I did remember my high school graduation when my father had brought the pearls downstairs and clasped them around my neck. He said my mom would have been proud of me and he wanted a piece of her at the ceremony. I could see how much he loved me at that moment, and that's why I cherished the pearls. I never asked about anything else in our mother's jewelry box.

But now, with sentimentality off the table, I felt angry that my father was conspiring with my sister to cut me out of the will.

"You should split everything with me," I said in a low growl of a whisper. "I don't see how you get everything and I get nothing."

"It's just, last week at the bank. If you apologize—"

"Daddy wouldn't respect me if I apologized," I said. "That's the whole point." I couldn't explain this to Ginny. My stance was my worth. I couldn't compete with Ginny in adorableness or charming naïveté. If I apologized just to get the pearls, then the pearls would lose their meaning.

"We can figure it out later," Ginny said, closing the subject. "What am I going to tell Joe when he gets here? Who has skeletons in their backyard? I don't want him having second thoughts about our family."

"He won't. But are you having second thoughts about him? You know you don't have to go through with this." I was furious with the situation, but I wasn't furious with Ginny. She was my little sister, and I would do anything for her.

"I want to marry him, Lucy. My life is leading nowhere. I can't trust myself to navigate everything."

"You're only seventeen," I said. "This is all happening too fast. You're supposed to navigate and mis-navigate. That's how you figure it out."

"I messed up that night we went out."

"We were just being young," I said.

"And I don't want to go to college," she said in a softer voice. "This is safe. I'm safe. They showed me what could happen if I played with fire and I don't want to play anymore."

"What do you mean?"

"Nothing," she said, shaking her head.

"What?" I asked.

She tried to laugh it off. "Well, I felt safe here before we found these bodies."

I looked behind my shoulder to see if our father was there. This house had always been in our family. Our family must know something about these bodies. Was it a Jimmy Hoffa situation—bodies buried with the hopes they would be forgotten? Was this a crime of passion? I couldn't help my mind from twirling through the scenarios—a late-night burial, smoking guns, shovels wielded by armed men.

"There's probably an explanation," I said. "What did Daddy say?"

"He said not to worry about it. But then the bulldozer operator said he had to call it in."

"The police are coming?" I asked.

"They're on their way," said our father, stepping up behind us. I practically fell into the pit with the skulls. I let out a yell.

"Did I scare you, Lucy?" He laughed. His body looked enormous, standing on higher ground.

"Daddy, don't!" Ginny yelled. "My nerves are already shot."

I froze with fear. I hadn't talked to him since the day at the bank. I had taken my mimeographed evidence to the newspaper, but they hadn't printed anything. I didn't want my guilt to show. I kept my eyes on his feet and felt sweat pooling in my armpits.

"Who do you think the bodies are?" I asked him, trying to keep my voice level and cool.

"They're before our time." Our dad stood with his feet in a wide stance. "But the police want to have a look. They'll take them for evidence."

"Evidence in a crime?" I asked.

"Not everything's a crime, dear girl. You've watched too many movies. I imagine they're relatives."

"But why would they be buried here and not in our family plot?" I asked.

"Maybe the cemetery was closed during the war."

"The first war?" I asked.

He nodded.

"Or during the Spanish flu," he said.

"Then, why aren't there any grave markers?"

"That's a good question." He looked at me with a mixture of pride and pity. He always called me his smart girl. "But it's nothing to worry about. What we should worry about is how much time we're losing. Right now, I'm paying this crew to stand around, smoke cigarettes, and ogle Ginny."

He went over to the crew leader and gave him instructions to be back in the morning. He stepped back over the bodies in the pit. He looked at me again.

"If there was ever a time to bury something," he said, "tonight would be the time."

"That's a terrible thing to say," Ginny said.

"Everything's an opportunity," he said. "If you want to get rid of something, or someone," he added with drama in his voice, "you could do it tonight after the police left." I felt like he was saying this for my benefit. I had seen my father in a new light since the day at the protest, and I didn't know if he was pretending to be evil or if he was sending me a message. What was he going to bury in his backyard? What did he want to hide from the police? He was responsible for a man disappearing that day at the Sycamore Street March, the man in the Army uniform. Miranda and I had looked for him and asked around the neighborhood, but none of the Black neighbors would talk to us about him.

"Daddy, stop," Ginny said, hitting him on the shoulder. Their relationship had always been based on teasing and joking while my relationship with him was based on matching wits and standing our ground.

I took a deep breath and decided to focus on the bodies at hand.

"Have you looked in our Bible," I asked him, "to see if there was a time two Wilsons died at the same time?"

"We can do that—may be a nice piece of evidence for the police." He looked at me keenly when he said the word "evidence."

Even Ginny heard that innuendo.

Our father couldn't have been happy with the real estate evidence I had presented at the bank, but he didn't know that after that, I had gone to the newspaper office. I had talked to a reporter, who put his finger up while he got his editor. Back in 1958, I had laid it all out for them: the real estate deals, the federal money. The editor looked at me for a long time when I was finished and asked me only one question: *Why would you provide this evidence against your father?* I told him: *Because it's wrong. What he's doing is wrong, and he's the one who taught me right from wrong. And the whole system just watched him do it. There aren't any checks and balances. The system is relying on everyone to have their own moral compass, or it's assuming that they don't need one if they're in power. I don't know how he can sleep at night.* The editor only nodded and tucked my evidence into a folder. Nothing had come out in the paper.

Freya and I had seen *The Big Combo* in 1955—its black and white shadows creeping into my dreams. The main character, Mr. Brown, had an outsized influence on his city. Even the police chief wouldn't pursue him for fear of repercussions. The only way Brown ever came to justice was because of one righteous man—Detective Diamond. *The Big Combo* was the first time I had ever seen a polygraph test, and I had longed for one ever since. Imagine being able to detect any lie. If it was possible, I would carry one around with me and use it on everyone. Keep them honest. I would use it on my father. *What were you doing the day of the protest? What crimes have you committed? What happened to that man?*

We stepped carefully over the mounds of dirt and went back into the house through the service door. I followed him through the cool air of the kitchen and dining room to the other wing where his study was. The house was solid, quiet, protective. You couldn't hear anything through the thick walls. I thought of the years I'd spent here. My room upstairs—a cocoon of comfort. I thought of my closet filled with shoes and dresses and coats and hats. I'd barely taken anything when I left home the week before. My long camel haircoat, my black scarf and hat, my leather gloves, they were still up in my bedroom. I could feel the lure of the house Ginny must have felt when she agreed to marry Joe. She could be taken care of instead of taking care of herself.

In the study, our father pulled the family Bible off its podium, the same podium that had housed it for his father and his father before him. This study had been inhabited by the patriarch of the family for almost a hundred years. As the oldest son, Herbert had inherited the house outright, and his brother had not gotten anything.

Herbert looked at the names in the front—births and deaths. Agnes Marie Wilson, 1729. Godfrey George Wilson, 1754. Catherine Marie Wilson, 1789. All the people who had lived in this house and the houses that had come before this. Our family lineage in fading ink.

Ginny looped her arms around my arm while we watched him read. The radio was broadcasting the BBC newscast at a low volume, the British accents covering the world news without a hint of emotion—two German-designed rockets had hit the upper atmosphere and the University of New Orleans had become the first integrated public university in the United States.

Herbert's finger stopped at Cordelia Anne Wilson, 1918. That was the year of the influenza outbreak, but there was no other name for that year. He closed the Bible.

"Dead end," he said. This was always the phrase he used when he wanted to challenge me. To us, there was never a dead end—only a signal that we hadn't searched long enough or asked the right questions. There was always another encyclopedia to consult, a different word to look up, and often there was a trip to the library to enlist the help of a professional researcher. That's why I had wanted to be a librarian. Librarian school taught me to investigate public questions about history or finance or politics, but how could we research our own family? Especially if it was a secret no one wanted told.

"It's one piece of the puzzle," I said. "We can show it to the police."

"I'll put it in the foyer," Ginny said, taking the Bible, walking with a lighter step.

"You're not going to go to the paper with this, are you, Lucy?" he asked in a low voice that wouldn't carry out of the room.

I froze. How did he know about the newspaper? I checked every day, and they never printed it. I looked him in the eye. He'd known all along. How stupid I must have looked to the newspaper folks. Of course, they wouldn't print it. They probably brought it right to him. They were all connected. The bank and the newspaper and the police. Everyone who mattered had been bought into the scheme.

I thought about the polygraph test and one more question for my father. *Why did you string me along?* He had spent a lifetime telling me what I wanted to hear—that I could think for myself, that it was okay to disagree. But boom, when it mattered, my voice meant nothing. It was his way or the highway. And in this case, his way was the highway, and I couldn't do anything but live my days beneath it wondering if I'd ever convince Ginny of what he'd done.

*   *   *

From the kitchen table, I watched Ginny putter around. I

could feel Sarah watching me. The clock on the avocado stove ticked. The canapés smelled overdone. Miranda had taught me to bake with an olfactory timer. You could smell when baked goods needed to come out of the oven; Ginny had missed that time.

"So, who were the bodies?" Sarah asked, impatient with our slow narrative.

"Don't call them bodies," Ginny said. "Daddy said they were two servants who died during the influenza outbreak. None of the public cemeteries were open, so they had to be buried here."

"That's what the book claimed," I said. "Someone wrote a book about our great-grandfather, the one who buried the bodies, and they told that story. Daddy certainly didn't tell that story before or even when we found the bodies."

Ginny gave me a sharp look.

"What else can I call them? Corpses?"

The coffee pot gurgled, and Ginny filled our cups again.

"I don't know why they would publish something if it wasn't true," Ginny said. "We have the book if you want to see it."

"I would actually," I said. We had changed the subject from our father to our great-grandfather, but in my mind, they were connected. If I could get Ginny to stop believing even an iota of family lore, I might gain some traction to talk about our father.

We left our cups and saucers. I turned off the oven. No need to have the *vol au vents* turning black while we were in the other wing.

We took the back hallway and came into the library from its hidden door in the wood paneling. I felt a reluctant surge of delight before I passed over the threshold. My father's library never failed to enchant me. Walls of books from floor to ceiling. Thin books, thick books, faded tomes of philosophy, shiny bestsellers. My father had arranged the books loosely by complexity, with the children's books near the floor, and the more obscure and academic texts high on the shelves. Large ladders were secured to each wall. Book spines stood erect on every shelf. Maroons and browns and blues created a beautiful, haphazard mosaic on the shelves. You could reach the second-story balcony by climbing an iron spiral staircase in the corner. On the balcony, more books stood sentry over plush reading chairs. The effect was a two-story library with books from its head down to its toes. This is the room where I practiced being a librarian.

Ginny pushed open the hidden door, and I heard Joseph before I saw him. "Oh, you gave me a start," he said to Ginny. "What in the world?"

I was disappointed to find Joe there—I thought he had gone to work. I had been enjoying my time with the ladies of the house, and I knew he would change the dynamic.

"I'm sorry," Ginny said to him with a laugh.

Joseph sat in what used to be my father's chair. "Lucy, my goodness, you can't let my wife scare me that way. You're supposed to be the sensible one." He was charming even when he'd been startled from his morning paper and coffee. Our father would have bellowed for silence and sent us to our rooms.

Joseph put his newspaper aside and gave me a hug. He had grown a thin set of blonde sideburns, carefully shaved against his pale Irish skin. I wondered if he had waited to grow them until after my father had died.

After an eternity of small talk about the funeral and careful avoidance of the topic of the statue, Sarah asked him if they had the book "about the bodies in the backyard."

"What? Oh—the book about your mom's great-grandfather? His name was Chester Wilson, and he did a lot more than bury a couple of bodies. Let's see, it's right over here." He went over to the western wall and ran his finger along the book spines. "I thought it was here."

"Maybe Daddy lent it out?" Ginny suggested.

"What did it say about the bodies?" Sarah said.

Ginny tightened her jaw, and I chuckled to myself. I wouldn't overtly influence Sarah to disobey her, but I was happy that the word "bodies" had been allowed.

"I can't remember the details, but it was a couple of servants. Influenza, I think," Joseph said.

I hadn't read the book. It had come out shortly after Ginny and Joseph's wedding. I was barely speaking to them at that point even though Miranda and I had attended their wedding, and I had stood up as her maid of honor.

"Did you read it?" I asked Joseph.

"I did. Your father said not to—he said that it was just a puff piece by a non-academic historian, but I found it interesting. A lot of detail about the architecture of this house. This library got a whole chapter."

"Isn't it weird that the bodies weren't given back to their families?" I asked. I thought about them trapped in our backyard for so many decades.

"They were given back," Joseph said. "The police released the bodies after the investigation. The families had them re-buried."

"Weren't they angry about the book?" I asked.

"They might have been," he said. "You can never make everyone happy." He returned to his chair and took a sip of coffee. I thought of him as our father's colleague—strange to see him sitting in my father's chair.

I took a deep breath and sat down in the chair next to his—a lamp shade on the low table blocked us from seeing each other's faces. "Speaking of opposition, I was telling Ginny that the statue you're planning might have some as well. It might not be the right time to hold our father up to new scrutiny."

"We thought about that," Joseph said with a dismissive wave. "Not everyone is going to like every statue, but your father deserves this."

Ginny pulled Sarah over to the bookshelves to continue looking for the book about Chester Wilson.

"Was the statue your idea?" I asked him.

"No," Joseph said, letting the word become its own sentence. I leaned around the lampshade to see his smile. "They came to us. The Historical Society has been wanting to do this for years. People loved your father, Lucy."

"Do they know everything he did?" I sat back in my chair and held my hands together in a clasp as if I were a priest in a confessional.

"I think they know," he said. "They know the good outweighs the bad."

"For whom?" I asked. "I know that the good doesn't outweigh the bad for the people in Ward Thirteen. And I'm not sure I want them to discover my father's role in all that. Right now, everyone says that the demolition orders came from 'the bank,' but if you put up this statue, all of our father's dealings will come to light."

"I know." Joseph un-crossed and re-crossed his legs. He had started at Carthage Savings and Loan before he even had a college degree. He had been a delivery boy, taking college courses at night. Our father took him under his wing, groomed him, marched him through a month of being a bank teller and then right into the back rooms with the executives. Joseph was the son our father never had. He knew about everything in my accordion file. He'd seen those memos as they were going out.

"I've seen some documents that suggest my father was taking a salary from the toll roads, that the tolls should have stopped years ago, but the money kept getting deposited into his account." I kept my face out of his line of vision and closed my eyes. Confrontation was easier without eye contact.

"I'm glad you brought that up." Joseph folded the newspaper neatly in his lap. "Your father was a great banker and a terrific planner, but he did have some flaws."

"I know," I said. I thought about his temper and his inability to apologize.

"Did you know about his gambling?"

My eyes shot open. Gambling? I could not picture my father playing cards in a smoky room in someone's basement.

"What are you talking about?" Ginny asked, turning away from the bookshelves.

"Now, now." Joseph held up his hand. "Your father got it under control, but before that, he did some damage to his accounts. He had a bookie. He liked to bet on sporting events—everything from the World Series down to the log sawing competitions up north."

"What do you mean?" Ginny asked, coming to stand in front of her husband. "Did he have debts?" I had to laugh to myself. Ginny wasn't concerned about whether or not our father had knocked down Miranda's deli out of spite, but if his bank accounts weren't in order, she wanted to know about it.

"It's complicated," Joseph told her. "We're going to have to make some adjustments to his portfolio."

Our father had taught Ginny and me to write checks and balance a checkbook when we were young. Now, she seemed oblivious as to how credits and debits worked.

"Is that where the money from the tolls went?" I asked quietly. I wanted to confront them. I wanted them to take back their petition for the statue, but I needed to tread carefully.

"No," Joseph said, disdain in his voice. "He earned that money from his work, his expertise, doing the books, filling out grant reports."

"But where did it go?" I asked.

"Lucy, you did this same routine with your father when he was alive." He leaned forward and looked at me around the lamp. "In the bank, you accused him of crimes you didn't understand.

Insider trading, did you call it? I can see from the outside it might look like your father was breaking the law, but this is common practice."

"Gambling is common practice?" I asked. "Taking people's homes so you can bet on a football team?"

"Let me explain something," Joseph said, keeping his voice low and steady. "Your father was vice-president of the bank. Not president. The vice-president is the henchman—he does the dirty work. Your father had to make sure we got in front of other states and cities for that federal money. He had to order demolitions. He had to engage in some questionable practices."

"I saw what he did," I said, leaning forward as much as Joseph had. We were both perched on the edges of our chairs. I felt tears sparkling in my eyes. I did not want to go back over our entire past, but it was tangled. One event linked to another like chapters in a book.

"What did he do?" Sarah pushed on her father's knee with the side of her leg, leaning in with all her weight.

"Ginny," Joseph said, motioning for her to take Sarah out of the room.

"I want to know," Sarah said, looking back and forth between her parents. Her T-shirt slid up her tummy, and she pulled it back down with a rough tug.

"There's nothing to know," Joseph said to his daughter. He waved his hands as if that would make Sarah disappear.

Then he turned his back to them and looked only at me. His hands were clenched. "Lucy, you always come back to this. I know it's upsetting to you, but we didn't do anything illegal."

"I'm not accusing you," I said, emphasizing *you*. I wasn't interested in what blood Joseph had on his hands. I was only interested in what my father had done. "I came across a damning paper trail. The Historical Society won't like what I have. They won't want evidence of our father's corruption. They won't want even rumors or innuendos. They will want the Wilson name to shine bright, and my father did not shine bright in all areas of his life. We don't even know the half of it yet—like what he buried under the oak tree."

Joseph guffawed, but his hands were still clenched. I could see he was frustrated.

"Oh, Lucy, you can't possibly think—" Ginny started.

"What's under the oak tree?" Sarah cried. "More bodies?" She came around to the other side of my chair, out of the reach of her parents, but she addressed the question to them.

"You'll be laughed out of town with this half-baked idea. It's scuttlebutt," Joseph said. He stood up and towered over me—he reminded me of my father. I could see a store of rage under his skin, roiling. He would be pleasant as long as he got his own way, but if he was backed into a corner, he wouldn't hesitate to use force. He didn't know how to back down to a woman. He didn't know how to save his pride except through winning.

"It's not scuttlebutt if I can prove it." I bit the inside of my lip. I had nothing to prove—I was grasping at straws. And I was making him angrier. He turned away from me. I could practically see steam coming out of his ears, like a Bugs Bunny cartoon.

Ginny interceded on his behalf. "Prove what?" she asked me. "What do you think is under the tree?" Her shoulders slumped as if I had worn her down, and now it was time for a nap.

"It's what he said when we found the bodies," I said. "He said it after I saw him at that protest. You must remember."

So much had happened since that day. So many words. It was hard to untangle what I heard and what I'd imagined. I was curious if Ginny remembered it the same way I did.

"He was trying to scare you," Ginny said.

I paused—she could be right. Our father loved to push my buttons, and he could have been teasing me.

"And what about that book?" I asked. "Where did it go?" Even as I said it, I knew I sounded hysterical. I could never be a lawyer—I couldn't stick to a single argument.

"You should have been a detective," Joseph said. He moved across the room and opened the hidden door. It looked like he was disappearing into a wall.

"Or a librarian," I called after him.

We sat in his wake for a moment. His presence had given the conversation its focus. He and I had information to exchange in barbs. Without him, I had only accusations. As a man, he was able to end any conversation by just leaving the room—women had to stay for politeness. Maybe that's why women covered more topics than men did—they had to stay past the point where it got uncomfortable.

"Maybe the book's at the library," Sarah said. "Can we go and see?" She was the perfect investigator. She could sense the tension among the adults, but she saw the truth as the only way out. If we had all the information, we'd all get along. I felt the same way.

"Not today," Ginny said. "We're remembering your grandfather today." She looked shaken, as if she needed a drink. She sat in the chair Joseph had vacated.

"Please, Mom, this would be remembering him." Sarah sat in her mother's lap, her long legs dangling. "You can't tell these stories and then not let me see the book."

"No, we need to rest." Ginny closed her eyes.

I suppose, in my fantasies, Ginny would have heard my accusations and immediately withdrawn the petition for the Herbert Wilson statue. We would have fallen into each other's arms and vowed to never grow estranged again. But instead, I was sitting here with my heart racing and no more moves to make. Every project that he funded, for which he was so beloved, had been paid for with toll money. The toll money was probably paying for the statue. I closed my eyes like Ginny. Maybe a nap was a good idea.

"Mom, I have books to return," Sarah said.

"Since when?" Ginny asked, unable to mask her exasperation.

"Since before Granddaddy got sick," Sarah said.

The two of them sat together in silence for a moment. There was some unspoken communication happening between them that I could not decipher. It was all eye contact and facial tics.

"They're upstairs," Sarah added.

Ginny nodded, and Sarah leaped from her lap and made for the door in the wall paneling.

"We'll be quick," Sarah said over her shoulder. "I'm sure they have a copy. Mrs. Caravaggio has everything."

*   *   *

"Where should I park?" Ginny steered our father's Oldsmobile toward the library on Erie Boulevard. The North Carthage Public Library was a long, low building, structured like a warehouse rather than a paean to knowledge. Our city had been in the running for a Carnegie library at the turn of the century, but Syracuse had won the bid, and in an almost spiteful burst of architectural pettiness, Carthage had built our nondescript library on the edge of town. You never would have guessed it was two stories the way it clung to the ground—none of the soaring ceilings or intricate details of the Carnegie libraries—no stairs leading to the front door—just a rectangular, featureless box.

"I've never driven a car to the library," I said. In truth, I had never driven a car at all. I had a fancy pantsuit on, but I was basically a teenager in terms of life skills. I had never rented an apartment, applied for a job, or gone on a date. I looked at my sister behind the wheel of the car and realized, besides getting her driver's license, she had never done any of these things either.

Inside, the ceilings were covered with acoustical tiles, and the furniture was a slew of generic chairs and small couches, seat cushions covered in vinyl. To offset the bland decor, the librarians had splurged on colorful pillows, probably bought with their own money, and inspiring book displays. This month, the main book display was in celebration of NASA's Space Shuttle Program. On a round table, they had arranged hardcover children's books with astronauts and planets: *The Little Prince* by Antoine de Saint-Exupéry, *2001: A Space Odyssey* by Arthur C. Clarke, enormous reference books, and coffee table books whose covers were graced with intriguing images of outer space.

I saw Mrs. Caravaggio, the head librarian, bent over a card catalog with a box of empty cards and a stack of new books. She had dyed brown hair, set in place by a hair hood dryer and at least half a can of hairspray. Her hair didn't move as she sped around the library, up and down the stairs, in and out of the stacks. It kept its shape and order in the same way that Mrs. Caravaggio kept the library intact.

As soon as she saw us, she put down her box and came around the counter to give me a hug. We had shared so many afternoons together at the library, and she had urged me to finish my librarian degree. She had wanted me to follow in her footsteps. I had every intention of doing so, but then life intervened. And by life, I mean my father.

"And Sarah!" she cried. She gave her a hug, like the grandmother Sarah never had. Mrs. Caravaggio's gaze fell on Ginny. "And you must be Sarah's mother?"

"This is Ginny, my sister," I said quickly. "Yes, Sarah's mother."

"A hug for you as well," Mrs. Caravaggio said. She was nothing if not magnanimous.

"We're here to find a book about my great-grandfather," Sarah said.

"Your great-great-grandfather," Ginny corrected her.

"The Vantage Press book?" Mrs. Caravaggio knew every book

in the building and could recall authors and publishers with mind-tingling accuracy. "We have it under history, but it's up for you to decide if that's where it belongs. It was donated by your father." She held her tongue on opinions she might have about the book or my father's donation, but mentioning the Vantage Press was a death toll for the book's historical value. It was basically a vanity press where anyone could publish anything.

Ginny and I exchanged glances. This explained where our family copy had gone.

We followed Mrs. Caravaggio, her hair keeping its own direction as her body turned the corner into local history in the 900 section. She recited the call numbers as she got closer to the book.

"Here it is." Mrs. Caravaggio handed me a shiny hardcover book, half the size of the bestsellers. It had a portrait of our great-grandfather on its front cover and the title *Chester A. Wilson: A Gentleman's Gentleman.* The author's name was at the bottom in small print—Amos Pendleton—it sounded familiar.

I sat on a round step stool in the aisle and opened the book to its index. Its spine cracked.

What would it be under? Corpses? Graves? Scandal? I kept going and tried "Servants." I flipped to page ninety-seven and there was a congratulatory paragraph about Chester A. Wilson coming to the rescue of two families whose children had lost their lives to the influenza pandemic.

"That's what I told you," Ginny said, overly proud of herself.

"Let me see." Sarah held out her hand for the book. I gave it to her, and she turned to the photographs in the middle section.

"Who's that author? That name sounds familiar," I said to no one in particular. I thought through family members and friends and local writers.

"Look, it's a picture of our backyard," Sarah said.

Ginny took the book from her. "I remember this. The police

took this picture. We were standing right behind them. What a mess the yard was. Remember how upset I was, Lucy?"

"I do remember, but I can't remember where I've heard of this author," I said. Once I had a puzzle before me, I had trouble letting it go.

I stared at the cover: a painting of my great-grandfather, done in the same style as my parents' portraits: flattering realism. Chester A. Wilson's hair was white and fluffy, softening the shape of his head. He wore spectacles and a notched collar shirt—a man of means.

"Come with me." I led Ginny and Sarah back downstairs to the reference area. Sarah walked and took the stairs without ever taking her eyes off the book. She must've inherited that skill from me.

Downstairs, Ginny and Sarah settled into two of the waiting room chairs, and I used the microfiche catalog to search for the name—nothing. I looked in *Who's Who* 1958, 1959, 1960—nothing. I sat in one of the chairs—flummoxed.

"Dead end?" Ginny asked.

I looked at her. Did she know the joke I had with our father?

Mrs. Caravaggio overheard Ginny and came over. "Not a dead end yet," she said, and smiled at me. "Amos Pendleton was the pen name of a local. That's how I remember it."

Then, it hit me. Amos Pendleton was the name our father used when he told stories. Amos was the boy who shot rabbits and got in trouble with his father. He was the Huckleberry Finn of our childhood tales. He was imaginary. Our father was his creator—so he must also be the author of this book. How had he ever kept this from us? Our father loved a mystery or a teasing riddle, but he also loved to get credit for his accomplishments.

"Amos Pendleton, boy hero extraordinaire," I said, catching Ginny's eye.

I smiled at Sarah. She was smart to get us to come to the

library. This was a perfect way to convince Ginny of our father's double nature. What could be more perfect than an alias, right here on a hardcover book?

"Didn't the families protest the release of this book?" I asked Mrs. Caravaggio. It was all coming back to me. So much had happened that year, but I did remember a small picket line outside the library.

"They did protest in 1960," Mrs. Caravaggio said. "I have some boxes in the archives—interviews with the rural residents outside Carthage. It was right around that time. It's a long shot, but I'll let you know what I can find." I trusted her to find more than anyone else could find on the subject. She had been working at this library since she was a young woman, hired to assist the main librarian, a man who wore only suits. Mrs. Caravaggio had shown gumption, smarts, and a nearly photographic memory. When the fussy old man had retired, she'd stepped in as his replacement. She brought the Dewey Decimal System to Carthage, redid all the call numbers and card catalogs. For that enormous project, she'd used an army of female workers from the university program. That's how I'd met her—long nights carting books down from the stacks, into the labeling area, and then back upstairs into their new homes.

I watched Mrs. Caravaggio disappear behind the counter again. I could almost see the wheels in her head turning underneath her halo of hair-sprayed hair.

"It must be our father," I said to Ginny. "Don't you think? Don't you remember his Amos Pendleton stories?"

"I do. But why would he lie about it?" Ginny opened her eyes wide. She looked like the same little girl who used to sit at our father's feet as he spun his tales of adventure.

CHAPTER FOUR

Old Ward Thirteen

The next morning, I put on my faded apron and large oven mitts, pulled my thick hair back in a net. I heaved a pot of water onto the back burner and set the gas flames on high. I tried to concentrate on the task, but my mind was elsewhere. My father was a gambler, I had learned. He had written the book about our great-grandfather, it seemed. The bodies in our yard may not have died from natural causes. Was it enough to change Ginny's mind? I'd seen her faith in our father flicker at the library.

When the water boiled, I used rubberized tongs to transport the mason jars from the counter into the pot. They clanged together as they settled at the bottom, surging in the strong boil.

George was off on Thursdays and Fridays, but many of our customers needed their shopping done before the Sabbath, so every week, Miranda and I filled the shelves with options—every delicacy a displaced European Jew could want and all the snack food the locals craved. I was behind schedule and had a counter full of jars to seal—Scotch-soaked prunes, jellied striped bass, goose lard, stewed cherries. These weren't foods I had ever eaten as a child, and most of them, to be honest, I didn't want to eat, even as an adult.

Yesterday, when I got home, Miranda asked how my visit with my sister had gone, but I didn't have words. I sat in front of the television, watching whatever came on until the broadcast ended at midnight and the national anthem played. I threw my coral pantsuit in the hamper and wondered what I had been so excited about. "New Day—New Me" had turned into "Old Days—Old Ways."

The deli phone rang.

"Fein Foods, this is Lucretia," I said, gripping the long spiral cord in my fingers.

"I was hoping to catch you." I recognized Freya's voice, still as strong as it was when she was my father's secretary. "Do you have a minute?" she asked.

"I do." I looked back in the kitchen at the stove. Each batch needed ten minutes at a hard boil.

"I got a phone call from your sister," Freya said. "She wanted to know if she had my support for her petition. We're voting on it tonight." Freya's German accent had faded over the years, but I could still hear it in the way she pronounced "wanted" and enunciated longer words.

"She called you?" I thought Ginny might pull the petition after discovering our father had lied to us—at least postpone it. But instead, she was campaigning for votes?

"I called the chairman and put you on the agenda for a rebuttal," Freya said.

"No, no," I said. "I can't do that. I can't speak in front of those people." I could submit the evidence if she didn't want to, but I wasn't going to be there.

"It wouldn't be fair if you didn't get a chance to speak," Freya said in her clipped accent. She didn't use unnecessary words, an efficiency of language.

"None of this has been fair." I didn't want to have a corrupt father or a deluded sister. I didn't want to talk in front of an audience. I wiped my hands on my apron and felt my throat tense. I didn't know if I was going to cry or scream.

"I'll look for you there," Freya said. "It starts at 7 p.m."

I heard the dial tone but stood holding the phone, the long cord wrapped around my hips. I had turned several times as I spoke and inadvertently trapped myself.

Miranda stared at me through the opening to the kitchen. "What's not fair?" she asked.

"My sister's going ahead with the petition. Freya wants me there."

"Tonight?" she asked.

I nodded.

"You don't have to do it. It's not written anywhere that you have to fight this battle." She leaned against the door frame.

"I know." I nodded but looked at the floor.

"You could still give the evidence to David," she said.

I nodded again with a sigh.

"Standing up to them publicly is a lot different than standing up to them privately." Miranda wasn't afraid of much in this world, so her trepidation gave me reason for pause.

"What are they going to do to me that they haven't already done?" I asked, playing devil's advocate.

"Your family owns this whole block." She went back to the kitchen, but we continued talking.

"Except this house," I said to her back. A win for our side— Miranda owned her property outright.

"Your father said he could take our house down in an hour with a single call to the city," she called out from the kitchen.

"That was years ago. And that was my father. Ginny and Joseph don't have a grudge against me." I didn't think they did. I had kept everything civil. I had spoken nicely at the funeral.

The front door opened, tripping the small bell we had hung with a ribbon.

"Good morning, Miranda," one of our regular customers yelled, ignoring me.

"Good morning, Mrs. Rosenthal," Miranda yelled from the kitchen.

Lida Rosenthal came every week. She was the social butterfly of the local synagogue. If she had ordered one platter of bagels and lox from Fein Foods, she had ordered a thousand. I stood at the counter as she shopped with her back to me. For her age, she was the most fashionable woman in Carthage. She wore a suede wrap dress with nude pantyhose and heels. She had a fur coat over her arm and gold earrings to match her necklaces, rings, and eye shadow. This was her outfit for a Thursday morning.

"It's a cold one," she yelled.

"Hot in here," Miranda yelled back from the kitchen.

She and Miranda communicated with a steady volley of yelling.

Lida Rosenthal never yelled to me. She barely said my name. She resented me because she wanted Miranda to attend Temple Beth Israel, and she suspected I was preventing her. Of all our customers, Lida came closest to knowing the extent of my relationship with Miranda. Everyone else was clueless.

"I'm taking two jars of cherries," Lida yelled. "Put them on my tab."

Miranda could have four orders yelled at her and get them all in the book with New York State tax calculated and any discounts applied, all while prepping the food for the afternoon rush.

I was helpless with customer service and the preparations in the kitchen. I had tried to learn the whipping, sautéing, proofing, and tempering that Miranda had mastered over the years, but it remained a form of alchemy to me. I grew up with a housekeeper who shooed me out of the kitchen and a mother who had died before I could help with the baking. I was better at inventory and taste testing. And even with that, I failed on many occasions. Miranda couldn't trust my palate or my attention span.

I didn't know why anyone trusted me to do anything. Why did Freya give me all those papers? What if I dumped them in the garbage, tore them to shreds, threw them in with the orange peels, fish guts, and rotting cabbage? Who would ever know? I didn't want to go to the Historical Society. Miranda was right—this confrontation of my family was dangerous, reckless, pointless. I didn't want to parade these facts before anyone but Ginny. I wanted to sleep for a week.

Our radio sat on the kitchen counter, its antennae reaching for the ceiling. The deejay announced that the Committee to Reelect the President had pleaded no contest to eight violations of campaign finance law. They were fined eight thousand dollars. Watergate was basically over, and Nixon was not implicated. Of course not, I thought.

"David's here," Lida yelled.

Miranda looked at me over her shoulder. She kept chopping prunes. I took up my station in front of the boiling jars. As I leaned over, my glasses fogged up.

"David Tull," Lida added at a higher volume.

We knew who David was. Lida knew that we knew who David was, but she announced him like she was the herald at a society ballroom. She had matchmaker lodged into every pore of her body. She didn't know he visited us at night or had a boyfriend named Roger. To Lida and their synagogue, David was a quiet young man who brought his camera everywhere. He came from a good family, and horrors of all horrors, he was single at age thirty-five. Daytime David wore bell-bottom corduroys and a shy smile. I wondered if he'd ever come out of the closet like Roger.

Over the radio, I heard Lida talking to David. She used the same volume with him as with everyone else, so there were no secrets: her grandchildren were in town, they were going to a matinée on Sunday.

She told David about an old friend of hers from Pennsylvania, who was visiting from her new home in Toronto. "She's very famous," Lida told him. "Her name is Jane Jacobs, and I knew her when."

I didn't hear David's response, but Lida's voice came back loud and clear. "You haven't heard of her? What is happening to the American education system? She is a published author and a city planning celebrity."

"Miranda's heard of her. Haven't you, Miranda?"

Miranda and I exchanged a glance in the kitchen.

"Miranda's going to come out and say good morning to David," Lida added. "Aren't you, Miranda?"

Miranda wiped her hands on her dish towel and took off her paper hat.

"Should I ask him about the newspaper?" she asked me. "If they want to see the evidence against your father? Anonymously submitted, of course."

"It's too late," I said. "The vote is tonight."

She gave me a hug and looked me in the eye, sending me the energy needed to make my decision. Then she went into the front room. A few pleasantries, a smile for David, and Lida would be satisfied for the week.

I reached into the boiling pot with my tongs and pulled out the first jar of prunes. I set it on a dishtowel and went in for the others. Sweat dripped down the sides of my face.

Karen Carpenter sang from the radio. "Every sha-la-la-la… Every wo-a-wo-wo…"

A few minutes later, Miranda came back into the kitchen with the mail, absentmindedly singing along with the radio.

"How's David?" I asked, lengthening the syllables in his name as a joke.

She shook her head.

He wasn't courting Miranda, but we couldn't ignore his attraction. A small part of my brain worried he was a fallback position for her and that she was a fallback position for him. Since Miranda and I couldn't have a formal announcement of our commitment, it felt precarious. We couldn't call each other anything beyond "best friends" or "business partners" or "roommates." If we did, we could go to jail according to the local ordinances, and if not that, we could lose customers, lose our business. Miranda could lose her standing at the synagogue. She didn't attend services, but she belonged.

She flipped through the letters from our mailbox and tucked one in her apron pocket.

"What's that?" I asked.

"The county." She pulled it out and ripped it open. "Twelve cases of botulism in Onondaga County," she read. "New codes for canned food, effective immediately." She folded the letter back into its envelope.

"Do we meet the codes?"

"We follow every precaution. That's why we boil the jars. But we don't have the capital to keep up with every requirement." She tucked it back in her apron. "They send notices to every food business. It covers them legally if someone gets sick."

The deejay talked about the weather front coming in. Clear skies until the afternoon, storm clouds in the evening. High of thirty degrees.

The bell on the front door rang again.

"Is anyone here? I've never seen such an empty store," a familiar voice said. Henrik Neubauer came to the deli almost every day. He was a second father to Miranda—a weighty role since she had lost her dad. He'd known her since she was a girl. He was a thin, stooped man in threadbare clothes, but he packed the intensity of a giant into his small frame, mostly through the blaze of his eyes.

I set a timer for the second set of jars and went to greet him. Henrik stood amidst our crowded shelves. I looked forward to seeing him. No other customer accepted me the way he did.

"Good morning, Lucy. How's your family?" It was the same question he asked me every day.

"They're good." I stood behind the counter, and he took my hands in his.

"Have you seen them?" he asked, as he always did. My relationship with my family was a constant worry for him.

"I have," I said. "I went to my father's funeral."

"Your father's funeral. Oy, Lucy. Why are you working? You should be mourning." Henrik moved toward me as if to remove my apron.

I wanted to tell him everything that had happened, lay my family conundrum at his feet and let him guide me through the mess: the stand-off with my sister, the evidence I had against my father. Henrik had been on the refugee ship with Miranda and her father. If I borrowed his life vision for even a moment, I would run to Ginny and apologize. He always told me, *Nothing is more important than family.*

"It's complicated," I said.

"Never too complicated." He shook his head back and forth as if to dislodge the thought from entering his ears. Henrik had a gag reflex for family excuses. "There's nothing more important than family."

He went to Miranda and gave her a hug and then held her head in his hands. She had to bend down, but he had been doing it since she was a child, so the ritual was seamless. He kissed her on the top of her head, the longest kiss he could muster.

"Our families are gone," he said to me. "We've lost the most precious thing, so we hold onto each other."

She nodded.

"You have to protect your family."

"I know." I had heard this before. I understood the depth of their loss, but it didn't translate into forgiving my family. Henrik would want me to pull my family close, forgive them for their trespasses. He'd be happy if I avoided the Historical Society tonight. He was right. Why air my dirty laundry? Why fight a statue of my father? I wasn't going to set anything right by blocking this statue. And what was the point of fighting one arm of an octopus?

"You know here that you love your family," Henrik said as he touched my forehead. "But you have to know here," and he touched my heart.

My heart was torn. I wanted to forgive my family, sit around the kitchen table with matching teacups and petit fours. I wanted to tell family stories and go to the library with Sarah. But every time I did, I came up against this grudge of mine. It wasn't a grudge—that's what they wrongly called it—it was knowledge. How could I pretend we were family when we couldn't even see the facts the same way?

I turned away from Henrik and wiped a tear from my cheek. My timer went off and I went back to the canning. I lowered the heat and reached in for the jars. I could barely see through the fog on my glasses.

Botulism bacteria existed in the world without our notice. They were generally harmless if left to their own devices. However, once you sealed them into an airtight container, cut off contact with the regular world, they became dangerous. I sealed the jars, thinking that my attempts to preserve the contents were the exact actions that could activate the deadly bacteria. I had to trust that I had sanitized them correctly.

The front bell rattled again. I took off my oven mitts and went into the store. George and his mother, Ida Mae, maneuvered past our crowded rows of shelves—slow-going because Ida Mae carried a large basket.

"Hello, Mrs. Pritchard," I said. Ida Mae Pritchard had been as loyal to our business as George said she would be—she came every week for bagels and schmear and brought a steady stream of Black customers to our store.

"Morning," she said. Ida Mae was tall and solid, made taller by her thick heels. She wore a heavy wool coat over a matching skirt and jacket. Her hair was pulled back from her wide forehead and commandeered in a low bun.

"Isn't it your day off?" I asked George.

"A day off means a day of helping my mother." George shook his head. He was competent in our store, often completing the day's punch list before noon and then prepping food, running the cash register, scrubbing counters, and fighting the building's decay. Over the years, he had become indispensable, mastering the ins and outs of running a Jewish deli on the wrong side of town. He had even taken over the business for a week during the summer of 1971, when Miranda and I had taken our only vacation.

But with his mother, George was a little boy, questioning himself and checking his mother's face for signs of disapproval.

"It's his job to help his mother." Ida Mae was no-nonsense. George sometimes mentioned his confrontations with her—he never mentioned any victories on his part. He was twenty-six years old, and his mother still told him what shoes to wear.

"I wanted to get an early start, so I could watch the—" he started.

"As soon as you get yourself a wife," Ida Mae said to George, "she can take me shopping, and you can stay home and watch whatever sporting event you want." This was an on-going conversation. According to Ida Mae, any problem in George's life could be solved with a wife.

Miranda came out of the kitchen. "What if George and his imaginary wife have a baby? Who's going to help with your shopping then?" she asked with a smile.

"Well, that would change everything, I imagine," Ida Mae said. "I'd have to turn around and help them." Her face was plain, almost severe, until she smiled, and then it was like sunshine itself. "Lord, grant me the opportunity to care for a grandchild," she sang.

"Let me find a wife first." George drifted over to our community bulletin board and straightened the flyers and index cards: job notices, advertisements for concerts, babysitting offers. He straightened the job notices. If he hadn't seen me watching him, I swear he might have kissed the one Alma had placed there.

I joined him in the corner and whispered to him. He stooped down to hear me. His height was often at odds with the small store. He bumped his head on the door frames and had to bend over the stove like a praying mantis. He was all elbows and shoulders.

"I met her yesterday," I whispered again. George caught my eye and turned his back to his mother. "Don't mention her," he whispered. "My mother has scared away every woman I have ever met." His eyes were deep pools of the softest brown, but once he focused them on a task, they were anything but soft. He didn't offer up conversation. He didn't joke around. He got his work done, and if we ever had a slow day and the weather was nice, he would pull a kitchen chair onto the back stoop and sit in a patch of sun. He would pet Emperor and Empress as they gathered around his feet, and more than once, I found him with one of the cats in his lap, absentmindedly petting their backs. He was satisfied to spend time in his own company. I didn't know what his imagination conjured up for him out there on the stoop, but I felt a kinship with anyone who didn't need other people for entertainment. And he loved our cats. That spoke well for his character, in my opinion.

"My lips are sealed." I wanted to ask him a million questions, but I allowed myself only one. "Did you know Alma before her tire blew out in front of the deli?"

He caught my eye, his face holding in a smile. "For almost six months," he said.

I was practically lip-reading because he was only mouthing the syllables. My eyebrows raised at his long-kept secret.

"Not a word," he reminded me.

George had secrets from his family as I had from mine. When you have a parent who's larger than life and powerful, you learn to dole out information, anticipating how it might come across. Powerful parents can lock their children into patterns nearly impossible to break, like handcuffs we hardly notice until our wrists have grown. Both George and I had our reasons for hiding, and we each felt safe in the shadows.

"I have a proposition for you," Ida Mae said to Miranda over the counter.

Miranda looked at George. Usually, it was him coming up with ideas for the store, not his mother. He was interested in the business side of the deli. He paid attention to the ordering trends and had learned to balance the books. He wanted to manage a store someday, and this was his training ground. He'd already created a discount shelf that he named "Going, Going, Gone," and he copied McDonald's to come up with some sandwich deals that came with chips, a pickle, and a drink. He wanted Miranda to hold cooking classes at night to bring in another stream of income.

But George held both his palms open as if to present his mother as evidence in a courtroom drama. "This was her idea," he said.

We joined them at the counter.

Ida Mae laughed at George's gesture and put her basket on the counter. "I have here my famous Alabama barbecue sauce and a dozen homemade sweet beet biscuits," she said. "I know you have mostly Jewish recipes in here—old world. But as an old-time resident of Old Ward Thirteen, I think my recipes will fit right in. I'd love for you to sell this sauce in your store."

"Our recipes come from the neighbors who started my father in this deli," Miranda said as an explanation for why they didn't carry other local products. "They taught my father the recipes that they learned from their grandparents."

"I can teach you this recipe," Ida Mae said.

"They were refugees," Miranda said, "desperate for a taste of home." The Fein Foods menu honored each family for their recipe and country of origin: Lida Rosenthal's stewed cherries from Yugoslavia, Gitla Bercowicz's gefilte fish from Austria, Margit Friedmann's potato dumplings from Czechoslovakia, Ester Salzstein's beef goulash from Poland. They gave the recipes to Miranda's father for free, but the deal was that part of the proceeds would always go back into the community. Miranda donated to the synagogue every month, even when money was tight.

"We're refugees as well," Ida Mae said. "That why I thought you could expand the tradition."

"I thought you were born in the States," Miranda said.

"I'm a refugee from the South," Ida Mae said. "I left with two sons—one under each arm."

"Wait. You have a brother?" I asked George.

"In a sense," he said.

"What do you mean?"

"We haven't seen Ells in a long time," Ida Mae said.

"He served in the Army," George said, "and he never really came back."

"He's in Germany, still stationed there. It's been over fifteen years now." Ida Mae set her jar of barbecue sauce on the counter.

"I'm sure you miss him." Miranda lifted the barbecue jar to guide the conversation back to food.

"We *think* he's in Germany," George corrected his mom.

I looked at George, trying to understand what he was saying, but his mother shut down George's doubts.

"He is in Germany. He writes to us, but he feels more comfortable in Europe," Ida Mae said. "He's older than George—moving up here was harder on him. We were desperate to leave Alabama. I didn't have all my ducks in a row. We had some lean years. We stopped in Queens before we made it up here." This was more about George's family history than I'd ever heard.

"He left Carthage and never looked back," George said. "We weren't enough for him."

"That's not fair," Ida Mae said, as if she had gone over this countless times before. "He had a vision of what our family should stand for and when we didn't come through—he found another place to live."

"Sounds like someone I know," Miranda said, looking at me.

Ida Mae looked at me but did not wait for elaboration.

"It wasn't just us," Ida Mae said. "Millions of families left—went to the big cities. We left behind our okra and grits and ham hocks and corn," she said. It was like she could taste each word.

Ida Mae was a local hero to the Black community. She was a seamstress, and her house had been the heart of the community before the highway came through. She tailored suits and designed dresses for every wedding, every funeral, and every baptism. The Pritchard house and the AME Zion Church were the two places everyone went for any major event in their lives. When the highway came, Ida Mae was one of the only people who found a new house to rent, so she stayed, but the rest of the community, including the church, had to re-start on the South Side of the city. Except our block. We still had the Black-owned businesses with Speedy and Amos.

"It's been hard to re-create our recipes up here," Ida Mae said. "But this barbecue sauce is something else." She took the jar from Miranda and opened it with a pop. She knew how to seal a mason jar.

"Smells good," Miranda said. The barbecue tang mingled with the strong cheeses in our front cases. Ida Mae's biscuits were red and flaky. Sweet beet biscuits—I'd never seen such a thing.

"With George working here for so long now, a few of us thought—"

Miranda put a spoonful of sauce on a beet biscuit and took a bite. She nodded up and down.

"I knew you'd love it," Ida Mae said. "Just imagine it on some beef ribs, slow cooked. I've always said that home is wherever I can taste this flavor."

"My father used to say that home was wherever God let him lay his head," Miranda said.

"I remember your father, dear child—Alexsander Fein," Ida Mae said. "How do you think I got a taste for bagels and schmear?"

"I don't remember you coming into the store," Miranda said.

"You always had your nose in that recipe book, but your father, he checked in with every customer, trying to find out what they might want to try," Ida Mae said.

I wondered what Ida Mae had thought of Alexsander: a tall, thin man, fresh out of a refugee camp when he arrived in Carthage, his English tinged with a Polish accent and absurdly formal grammatical sentences.

"He knew how to get people to try new things," Miranda said. "That was the teacher in him." Miranda always told me he was a fast talker, a born salesman. That's why he had been such a good teacher in Poland—he sold ideas to his students. In Carthage, he sold food instead.

"We didn't know where we'd end up," Ida Mae said. "And when we landed in Carthage, we thought we had arrived at the promised land. We had a real community here."

"It's what I think of every Passover," Miranda said. "The Exodus was made real for us." At every Passover, Miranda would recite the four questions, and she never failed to cry. She had taught me the questions and answers: *On this night, why do we eat only unleavened matzah?* To remind us of the haste with which our ancestors left Egypt. *On this night, why do we eat only bitter herbs?* To remind us of the bitterness of slavery. *On this night, why do we dip the herbs twice?* To remind us of our coming and going from Egypt. *On all other nights we eat sometimes sitting and sometimes reclining. On this night, why do we all recline?* To remind us of how free people relax.

"Now, your people have moved to higher ground." Ida Mae meant the parts of Carthage up near the university—most Jewish business owners, landlords, and tenants had moved there when the highway had come through. The Black community had moved to the other side of town. The highway had broken their kinship.

"That's true," Miranda said. "But they still have a few store-fronts here. And they come here to shop all the time."

"It was different back then," Ida Mae said. "We never imagined our neighborhood would be torn down. They took almost fourteen hundred homes."

I walked behind the counter and wished my timer would go off again. So far, no one had connected me with my father. Nobody ever asked my last name, except Henrik, but it was a small city, and there weren't a lot of white women in Old Ward Thirteen. I kept staring at the counter, following the grooves of old scratches as if they were the latest novel. If I didn't move, maybe I could disappear entirely.

"The one thing that kept us going was that we got to stay in the neighborhood. We found another house to rent," Ida Mae said.

"And your business," Miranda said.

Ida Mae nodded. She still ran her business out of her front room, like we did with the deli.

"A good reminder we can never know the future," Miranda said. She was saying this for my sake. I couldn't tell if she meant to encourage me or warn me. Was she telling me we couldn't know if the statue would ever go up or we couldn't know how my family would react to a public rebuttal?

I grimaced. I knew the shape of the future if not the details. Old Ward Thirteen was a sliver of its former self. We had only one square block left with some raggedy edges on both sides. The sewing machine factory cut us off at one end, and the highway curved and cut us off at the other end. Meanwhile, my sister lived in a neighborhood that sprawled and stretched, as if each property were a cat after a nap. My father had put Ward Thirteen residents at risk, their businesses in jeopardy. They didn't know his name, but a statue to him would be a slap in their face. And all the hoopla around the statue would bring his name to the forefront, and everyone would know he was my father.

I felt frantic with the idea that the statue was going to expose me. It wouldn't be long before they figured out that I had been there when he did his worst crime—the one that still woke me up in a sweat, the one I didn't have any way to prove. Freya's folder didn't have videotapes or photographs, and the eyewitnesses didn't yet know I was his daughter. They never connected the dots, but if that statue went up, this might come out. They'd ask me the one question I couldn't answer: *Why didn't you do more at the time?*

"The difference for you, Miranda," Ida Mae said, "is that you were a child when you left your world behind—same with George here. You had to go along. You didn't even know where that ship was going when you got on it. But your father did. He had his eyes on the future, the promised land. He had to deliver you. He had a completely different experience than you did."

I thought about the letter Miranda's father had written to her. Ida Mae might have written the same letter to George—to both her sons. They took the future and molded it for their children.

My father also took the future into his own hands. But he throttled its neck—he stamped it down. He turned people out of their homes in Old Ward Thirteen. Did he know that the neighborhood was filled with refugees from the war and from the South? Maybe every single person in Old Ward Thirteen was a refugee of sorts. A family doesn't end up in an apartment with sagging floors and leaking windows and call it the promised land unless they've left something much worse behind.

And I had it in my power to do something. What was I afraid of? My father was dead. He wasn't going to rise from his grave and destroy this neighborhood again. He wasn't going to build another highway. I was an adult, bringing relevant information to a meeting.

I half-listened to Ida Mae and Miranda talk about the possibilities for her new line of offerings. There were other people from the South who wanted to offer their own recipes: sweet tea and collard greens and corn fritters. It would be an enormous change to our store, and space was already tight. But Miranda was listening carefully, and when she pulled out her yellow legal pad to take notes, I knew she would consider it.

After George and Ida Mae left, I turned off the burners on the stove and leaned against the counter. Ida Mae's strength and courage had inspired me, but I felt stuck.

"What do you think?" Miranda asked. She could have been asking about the barbecue sauce, the historical society, or the war in Vietnam.

"I think I'm very lucky to have met you," I said.

"Thank you," she said, eyeing me curiously. "Same to you."

I meant it. She inspired me. I loved knowing that this capable, confident, courageous person found me tolerable. More than tolerable. She had welcomed me into her life with open arms. But I also felt envious. She knew what she wanted—she had a purpose. I felt like I was tagging along. When customers asked me a question about our stock or order schedule, I could answer them. We'll have more bagels in the morning. The meat truck comes on Wednesday. But if anyone asked me about the culinary vision of the deli or the cost-profit analysis, I would have been dumbfounded.

"I don't know what I offer to this relationship," I said. "I'm freeloading on your goodwill."

"That's not true. You bring that big brain of yours to the table every time you help someone with their paperwork. You bring a great, open heart. And you give me free rein to try out my recipes, and you're a willing taste tester."

I held in a smile, pushing my lips together. I loved to see myself though her eyes. When I looked in the mirror, I could only see someone blubbering along, never good enough to make it in my sister's world and completely ill-equipped to make it here. I felt like my life had a jagged line—a deep, dangerous fault line between where I'd come from and where I'd gone.

My personal drama over my father was never going to make it into the history books, but I couldn't live with myself if I let them revise history, making my father out to be a hero. I knew I had to go to the meeting.

I felt my throat tighten. My palms began to sweat.

"I should show them what I have," I said quietly.

"Then, get prepared." She put her hand out to take my oven mitts. She never wasted time waffling on her decisions, so she assumed I wasn't going to waffle on mine.

"But I'm scared." I couldn't imagine how I could force myself to talk to the board. Everyone would be shocked I was speaking against my father, and someone would be taking minutes. I couldn't hide, and it might prompt them to look more closely at me and my life.

"It's a risk," I said.

"We know that," she said.

"Even if I go," I said, "they'll probably still get their statue." I pictured it as the Colossus of Rhodes, my father straddling the entrance to our city.

"Who knows when they'll build it—if they'll build it—" She rearranged the jars on the counter, straightening the rows. "And even if it does go up, we'll just avoid that part of town. There's no way to know what the future holds."

I wiped some stray tears out of my eyes and nodded. I didn't like where this conversation was leading me.

"Would it help if I went with you?" she asked.

I couldn't believe it. "Yes," I said. "That would help." I knew it caused her distress to be anywhere near my family, especially when I was confronting them, but with her by my side, the process seemed doable.

The radio deejay spun another record. The bass line came through. The horns. The Staple Singers. They would take us there, and no one was crying about that.

CHAPTER FIVE

The Other Society

Erie Boulevard used to be a wide, quiet avenue with a streetcar track down the middle and plenty of room for horses and carriages on either side. Now it was a crowded, four-lane thoroughfare with traffic lights swinging and horns blaring.

Miranda and I stood near the bus driver, holding the straphangers tightly as the bus settled in front of the Historical Society. Their meetings were held in a city-owned Victorian mansion, one of the faded beauties from the 19th century. The first two floors held municipal offices, and the third floor, a former ballroom, was used for large public meetings.

We walked toward the elaborate, gingerbread entrance with a stream of Carthaginians. Near the front door, we log-jammed with another flow of people coming from the parking lot in the back. We moved slowly up the staircase with a murmur of polite chatter swirling around us.

In the stairwell, we saw framed photographs of black-and-white vignettes. The city's first ice truck. A driver standing on the running board. Carthage University's football team from their state championship run in 1920. The first convening of the Historical Society in 1965. The framed pictures directed the eye toward the parts of history they wanted us to remember, missing a large section of the population. As I looked at each picture, I saw white person after white person. Where were the pictures of the lumberyard workers? The first Black professor at the university? The jazz greats who had visited Ward Thirteen in its heyday?

At the top of the stairs, women handed their long wool jackets and fur coats to the coat check. They wore wrap dresses and pearls. Their heels clicked on the marble floor into the ballroom.

Through the crush of people, I saw that most of the folding chairs were taken. I touched Miranda's arm and pointed. Neither of us wanted to stand after working all day on our feet.

In front of a wall of arched windows, I saw two chairs in the middle of a row, and we made our way awkwardly past knees and boots to claim them. I couldn't pull off my jacket fast enough. The room was overcrowded and overheated. I stuffed my hat and gloves into my coat pockets.

I saw Howard Kramer from Carthage Savings and Loan. A row of widows sat behind him in a cloud of perfume, here to protect my father's legacy. I could feel my father's hand in this, even from the grave. His power had spread, and these people were united in the face of a common enemy. That enemy was me.

I could hear voices behind me: "The bombings were necessary. That's how we got to peace."

Another man said, "It went on too long, but at least he ended it without losing. He'll always be remembered for that."

They sounded confident that Vietnam was a game the U.S. had won. Nixon was their quarterback. Nothing could shake their confidence in him or in themselves.

I sat on the too-small folding chair and pushed the tangle of my coat and scarf between my feet. Miranda did the same. We exchanged a glance. Neither of us had expected such a spectacle. I tried to take a deep breath, but my chest was tight. I took shallow breaths and pictured myself back at home. A bottle of wine, strong cheese, Ida Mae's leftover biscuits. A mantra played in my mind, a soothing list of foods to come.

I looked up. Freya was on the dais. Her gray-blonde curls were hair-sprayed into place, and she wore an oversized, neutral suit. Nearby, Ginny stood with Joseph and Sarah, a family portrait for the ages. Sarah wore a velvet dress with a tortured bow on the front. Ginny straightened the bow, fixed Sarah's bangs, and pointed her toward a set of chairs on the side of the dais, reserved for family of the Historical Society's executive board.

Ginny sat down in her appointed chair on the dais. She studied the agenda on the table and didn't look up. I wondered if she felt pressured by our father to push the statue idea forward. When we were teenagers, we would've laughed at this sort of self-congratulatory display. Now, Ginny seemed to be as stuck in her position as I was in mine.

The chairman, Patrick Doyle, took his seat and banged his gavel. "Ladies and gentlemen," he said. "Please take your seats. We have a full agenda tonight, and I know many of you have tables waiting at Gallagher's."

The audience laughed. I took another look at the people around us—all white, well-to-do. I realized I should have brought my own crowd. I should have brought George and Ida Mae. I should have brought the Ward Thirteen Neighborhood Group and the members of the synagogue who'd been moved out of Ward Thirteen. I should have contacted the AME Church on the South Side and asked Speedy and his wife, Lorraine. I should have asked Amos to come. They should know about this vote. How were they going to feel to see a statue of the man who had razed their neighborhood?

"I call this meeting to order," the chairman said. "If you don't have a seat, please wait in the vestibule, and more chairs will be brought out for you. The proceedings will be broadcast over the speakers." He was puffed with delight at having such a large audience. His argyle sweater vest strained to keep him contained.

I looked at the doorway—a wall of people between me and the exit. Legs and coats and elbows and flesh stood between me and the vestibule, also full. Only one staircase to get outside. Sweat swam down my back. I looked at Miranda. Her face was pale.

"Are you okay?" I whispered.

She shook her head. She took off her sweater and pressed her shoulder with her opposite hand. With the heat being pumped into the room, I thought we might both pass out before the meeting started.

"We start with an action item. Item 1A," the chairman said into his microphone. "May I have a motion on the floor?"

"I move to approve the petition for the Herbert K. Wilson statue and park, location to be determined," a woman on the dais said.

"I second," a bald man said.

"And for discussion, we have one speaker in opposition and one speaker in favor, and then we will open the microphone to public comment. First, Lucy Wilson."

My last name rang through the ballroom—Wilson. It would've been worth getting married just to avoid this glaring conflict of interest. A daughter speaking out against her father did not carry clout. I climbed over Miranda's knees and struggled past the rest of the row. I walked up the aisle to the standing microphone and podium. I faced the dais, while the audience watched the sweat soak through the back of my shirt.

"I'm not here today to denounce my father," I said. "I want only to provide facts that'll make you reconsider a statue in his name. He was a great man in many ways, and I regret bringing this evidence forward so shortly after his death."

I arranged my papers on the podium and went through the evidence quickly and calmly. I hadn't studied everything in Freya's folder, but I had organized much of it into a coherent narrative. My father had personally profited from the highway; he had redirected federal funds into his own pocket. I spoke clearly and checked with the woman taking minutes to make sure she had each piece of evidence recorded before I moved onto the next. I gave a general economic analysis of the highway: according to tax records and property evaluations, the highway hadn't provided the sort of income it had promised.

I purposefully didn't widen my accusations to include Joseph or the bank. They weren't on trial here, and even though I had memos from Joseph's office, and even though his signature was on some of the deeds, I left him out of it.

"As if that were not enough," I said, "I will provide one more argument why you should reconsider a statue to Herbert Wilson." I looked at Ginny. "In 1958, I lived in Old Ward Thirteen. I saw people kicked out of their homes without compensation. I saw them turned down for federal aid when they applied. I saw them move in with family members who didn't have enough rooms or food to go around. They lost their homes and their places of work. And when they protested this treatment, my father had them arrested. They were sent to jail. I saw them in the police station, having to pay bail with money they didn't have."

"And all the while, my father was using the toll money from the highway to line his own pockets. It's a matter of character, isn't it? That's what we're voting on today," I said. "A man who could do something like that shouldn't be memorialized in iron or bronze."

The chairman nodded at me. I collected my papers and made my way back down the aisle. The audience was quiet. I could hear my shoes' muffled strides on the marble floor.

"Thank you, Miss Wilson," the chairman said. "And now as a representative from the Tower family, we have someone who may be our youngest public participant, a moment for the history books indeed—Sarah Tower." The audience clapped.

I turned back to the stage. I couldn't believe it wasn't Joseph who was speaking. Sarah was a well-chosen secret weapon. Who was going to vote against a child and her grandfather? I looked for my chair, but the path to it had closed.

I caught Miranda's eye, pointed to the back of the room, and took a place standing among the latecomers and the men smoking along the back wall.

Sarah read from a typewritten speech, eyes close to the page. She needed her glasses. I wondered if Ginny hadn't let her wear them. One of the audience members got up and lowered the microphone for her.

"My grandfather was a great man. I am proud to be his granddaughter," she said haltingly. "He made a difference for the city of Carthage, and I believe he should have a statue. My grandfather taught me how to read and how to use an encyclopedia. He taught me backgammon. He always said, 'Protect your pieces.'" Sarah stopped there, staring at the words on the page.

I knew what she wasn't saying. I knew what my father had said to Sarah about backgammon because he had also taught me how to play. "Protect your pieces and send the other guys to jail." We always called the bar at the center of the board "the jail" because if you were sent to the bar, you had to roll the right numbers to get back in the game. Sending the other guys to jail was a good strategy for backgammon, but it sounded cruel after the allegations I had made.

Sarah didn't read that part of her speech. She put the paper down and spoke directly to the people on the dais, including her mother. "I listened to my Aunt Lucy. If what she said is true, then I would like to know: Did he take houses away from poor people? Did he have people sent to jail? I want my grandfather to have a statue, but not if all that is true."

I stared at Sarah's velvet back. I could see Ginny's face as she tried to comprehend what her daughter was doing. Ginny pulled in the sides of her mouth in a pained expression.

Sarah had listened to me. I wanted to yelp aloud. I wanted to spin the room's suited gentlemen around their brass ashtrays like we were in a musical. It was possible—I could have the truth and my family—both of them. Ginny would have to forgive me if Sarah was on my side.

Joseph moved toward Sarah with one hand in his pocket and one hand in the air, as if he were calling for a timeout in a basketball game. He probably wished he had a whistle. Sarah saw him and started crying. He corralled her back to their seats.

The audience was dead silent. Miranda looked back and caught my eye. This was why movie directors didn't like working with animals or children. They were too unpredictable.

"Okay, thank you, Sarah Tower," the chairman said. He looked up and down the dais as if he might find a signal as to how to proceed.

Freya raised her hand, and he passed the microphone down to her.

"I move that we table the vote until further information can be provided. This is not the right situation for making a final decision, and we haven't had time to study the facts. Given enough time, we could conduct our own investigation and come back to the issue at our next meeting."

Ginny's blue eyes were wide. She exchanged a look with Joseph. He shook his head.

Freya passed the microphone back to the chairman.

"Thank you, Miss Hoffman. There's a first for this amendment," he said to the rest of the executive board. "Do we have a second?"

No one said a word.

"Then, we proceed with the only motion on the floor: to approve a statue of Herbert Wilson in recognition of his contributions to the city of Carthage. For public comment, please line up in the aisle. You each get one minute."

I exhaled through my puffed-out cheeks. The noise drew the attention of the men standing near me. I figured my audible sigh might make it into their dinner conversation. *I was standing right next to her when they moved forward with the public comment*, they might say after their salad course, wiping their mouths with white linen napkins. I wanted a cigarette, but there weren't any other women smoking, and I didn't want to add to the scandal of my behavior.

Henry Sulliman, the former mayor of Carthage, was elderly and slow to the podium, but out of deference, the other speakers let him go first. His white hair rose with the static electricity in the air. He settled his cane against the podium and waited until everyone on the dais had given him their full attention. "Overshadowed by Manhattan," he said. "Second fiddle to Albany. How did we get ourselves on the map? It was Herbert Wilson." He coughed lightly, and his hair trembled. He adjusted his black-framed eyeglasses and leaned slightly against the podium before he continued. He listed some of my father's most notable achievements and gave his signature phrase: "Let's move forward with this." The audience clapped uproariously.

They'd fall over themselves to say something nice about my father. Then, they'd fight each other to be the first at Gallagher's to order their steaks and swill their wine. Steak after steak would be delivered to their tables, and they'd never see the slaughter that had taken place to make it possible.

I didn't know where to put my hands. I had left my jacket and purse with Miranda. I realized how hungry I was. I hadn't eaten lunch.

Next, one of the city engineers spoke. Tall as a basketball player, he bent down to speak into the microphone, his wide, striped tie brushing the podium. "Manhattan had to throw garbage in the river to get more land," he said, "but we can expand indefinitely. And where do we get that workforce and population?

We get it from the Empire Stateway delivering people right to our downtown." He listed some of his own accomplishments just to round out his minute with the microphone, and he also got a hearty dose of applause.

These people would believe any lie. The highway didn't bring anyone to our city. It brought them through and past. We had destroyed our downtown in the hopes of becoming the next Manhattan. But people didn't look at the facts under their noses. They believed President Nixon's lies about Vietnam and Cambodia and Laos—they believed him even when he was contradicted in *The New York Times*.

Howard Kramer, the former president of Carthage Savings and Loan, took his place at the front of the line. His large head blocked the view of the dais for most of the audience. The committee members could see the severe white part in his hair, but we only saw his slicked back hair. "Herbert Wilson wasn't just a good colleague and a visionary for our city. He was friend to many of us here. He never let me pay for a round of golf. He called me his mentor, when in truth I learned so much from him. I would like to go on record to note his personal generosity. And I would like to offer a plot of land for the statue and park. It's on the edge of town, near the cemetery, and at no cost to the city, I will hand over the deed for the property. We could use a park out there. As Mayor Sulliman says, let's move forward with this."

His cheering section of widows gasped and clapped for his generosity.

I muttered under my breath. The land he was offering was a plot of land designated for a section of the highway that had never been used. Families had been kicked out of public housing there, and the buildings had been razed, only to let the land lay vacant for fourteen years. Kramer was offering it because he couldn't sell it. I wanted to yell over the applause that Kramer was a crook as well, that they were all in cahoots with one another.

Another man got up to speak, my father's neighbor from Hiawatha Heights. He told another story of my father's personal generosity, and then he pledged a thousand dollars toward the building of the statue. "How much does it cost to build this thing?" he asked. Then, he turned to the audience and said, "If we pass a hat right now, I bet we can get the bulk of it."

All the money in the room. They could buy and sell Carthage ten times over. Every single one of them was convinced my father was a good man because he had lined their pockets. I wanted to scream. They envisioned a world where the rich could do what they wanted without consequence. They envisioned their wealth as a badge of honor. I wanted to bring the bank down. But I couldn't. It would be damaging to Joseph and Ginny, and my father had insinuated the bank could close Miranda's deli with a single phone call. I had to bite my tongue.

I counted to ten and then backward to one. I imagined myself on the fire escape in Francie's apartment in *A Tree Grows in Brooklyn*. The branches and leaves fluttered in a small breeze, and the filtered sun warmed my face. No one could see me from the other apartments, and I could pretend that I lived in a tree.

Joseph walked toward the podium. The line of people stepped back and let him take the microphone.

"I want to thank everyone for their kind words. As you know, Herbert Wilson was my mentor and boss and father-in-law, but he was also the father I never had. My life without this man would have been different—less. He helped me become the man I am today."

I gritted my teeth. I could feel a growl forming in my chest, rivaling the growl in my stomach that was short-circuiting my brain. Every other thought I had was of food. I tried to keep myself in Francie's hideout—tree, leaves, branches, sun—but the room didn't lend itself to my escape.

"And I have an update from the wings," Joseph said. "Sarah

is too shy to come back up, but she wants to say that she loves hearing all these stories, and she's a hundred percent for the statue now."

The crowd applauded and Sarah waved from her seat.

I felt like I was going to explode. My chest tightened, and my throat felt like an overstuffed duffel bag, about to burst its seams.

"I can't. I can't," I yelled from where I stood. "I held this back out of respect, but I can't let you make this vote without the full picture." I was now a star witness in *Mr. Smith Goes to Washington* apparently. I could hear the notes of drama in my voice.

"You'll have to get in line like everyone else, Miss Wilson," the chairman said into his microphone.

"I can't." I knew this wasn't going to help. I knew the crowd would turn on me. I knew Joseph might take revenge. None of that could hold back my words.

"If you people would take ten seconds to look away from your bank statements and investments, you'd see that Herbert Wilson was a crook. Just because he lined your pockets doesn't make him someone we should hold up to the next generation as a hero. He is not a hero. And Joseph Tower is not a hero either. I can paint a picture of corruption and venality that would make the hairs on the back of your neck stand up. I have memos that Joseph Tower personally profited from the razing of houses in the Old Ward Thirteen, even before he married my sister. I have memos that he controlled the press and the police. Do you want your newspapers and public servants working for Joseph Tower or for the community? Because right now, they're working for Joseph."

Joseph spun around from the microphone and stared at me.

Ginny stood up on the dais and looked like she might scream.

"Enough. Out of order. This will not be recorded in the minutes," the chairman yelled. "Out of order."

I saw police officers in the vestibule. One nod from the chairman and I'd be gone. I saw Miranda folding up our coats and struggling into the aisle. I was wrong to come; I was wrong to have her come with me.

"Think before you vote," I yelled at the dais. "You should know more about who you're voting for—more than just what they've done for you lately."

"Order," the chairman said again into his microphone. We heard him cough even as we left the room. The vestibule had stereo speakers broadcasting the meeting throughout the third floor. We could hear him no matter where we went.

We walked past the officers. I wondered if they would detain us, but I felt no hands upon me, no gun at my back. We didn't wait for the vote. We hurried down the stairs. Miranda handed me my coat and scarf. I looked at her. She struggled to button her coat. Her face was pale, and there was sweat on her forehead. She needed an ice pack for her shoulder and a long night of rest. When we got outside, I checked the money in my coin purse and put my hand up to hail a cab.

*   *   *

"Corner of Sycamore and 22nd," I said to the cab driver. He grunted his assent and arranged his heavyset body for the drive. I looked at Miranda. She was more than pale. I thought she was in pain. *Get her home, give her some aspirin, put this night behind us.*

"I'll pay for the taxi, don't worry." I put my hand on her knee.

She pushed my hand away and hissed, "Don't worry? You have no idea." I realized she was furious. We'd had so few arguments that I'd missed the signs. I thought she wasn't talking because she was overheated. I thought she pushed ahead on the stairs because she needed fresh air.

The vinyl seat was torn on my side, fitted back together with tape. Credence Clearwater Revival's "Who'll Stop the Rain" played on the cab's radio, mixing up memories of rain and anguish, both coming down by the bucketful.

The cab driver caught my eye in the rearview mirror. His double chin bounced as he drove over a pothole. He pulled at the brim of his hat and stepped on the gas.

"At least it's over," I whispered to her.

"It's over for you, not me," she said in a full voice.

I looked at the driver in the mirror again, but his eyes were fixed on the road.

"I'm sorry," I said. I regretted my outburst, but I was still shaking with anger at the way Joseph and Ginny had played me—how they had used Sarah against me. Everything in my body had resisted that vote, the push to hold my father up as a hero. It was wrong, what they were doing. And like a freight train, there was no way to stop it. I felt like my integrity demanded I take a stand, even if it meant getting bowled over.

"They'll come after me. You play it like a game." She turned her shoulder away from me and looked out the window. The streetlamps were lit, reflected in the puddles of melted snow on the street. "But it's my life," she said.

I felt my chest constrict and my eyes burn with tears. I didn't know how to fight with her. "It's our life," I said.

"Your brother-in-law is going to shut us down."

I could fix this. I would talk to Joseph and Ginny. I would apologize.

The cab driver turned a corner quickly, and I slid into Miranda, losing my center of balance.

"Stop." She pushed my shoulder, sending me back to the other side of the seat. The seat ripped open where the tape had held it. I felt the cushion pop out of its casing and the sharp vinyl edges.

"I've given up everything," she said. "I ran this business with my father, and I run it now for my father. It's all I have left of him. My father's soul is in the house. I can't lose it."

"We're not going to lose our house."

"It's not your house. It's my father's. He would be furious about the code violations. Furious with me. He never violated a code in his life. I haven't kept up. We needed new equipment, and I could never afford it. All the warnings are sitting in a file somewhere, and now your family is going to blow it up."

"I'm sorry." I didn't know she was hiding citations. This must have added to her stress—thinking her father wouldn't approve. I wondered what he would've thought about our relationship. He undoubtedly would have preferred Miranda to be with David. Maybe that's why Miranda let David hang around. None of us had been outed. They could still change their minds.

"I'll be evicted," she said. "I can't pay the mortgage without the store."

"We'll get other jobs," I said. "I'll apply for a librarian position."

"You haven't finished your degree," she said.

"I can finish it."

"You never had to finish it. That's why you haven't. It's not life and death to you."

That wasn't true. I hadn't finished it because I had been helping with the deli and trying to make money on the side. I never thought to take the time to finish my degree. It would have felt selfish in the face of the deli's enormous challenges. But I never said anything to Miranda because I felt guilty that my father had torn down her deli.

I tried to take her hand. She refused it.

I stared down at my hands. My cheeks burned, and while I should have just repeated my apology, I tried again to defend myself.

"I couldn't not say something," I said.

"But that's the thing," she said, further exasperated with me. "You protected your reputation, your sense of yourself, but you didn't think about the consequences for other people. You were caught up in your own story, with you as the heroine. What if you weren't the center of the story? How would you have acted then?"

I was shocked. I always saw myself as the supporting actress. I never saw myself as the heroine.

"I don't understand," I said.

"There was a girl at Fort Ontario. She lived in Oswego, and I went to school with her. She was white, Christian. We were friends. One day, she came back to the camp after school. We snuck into the commissary and took some Nilla wafers—still had the crumbs on our faces when we got caught."

I nodded, glad she was speaking to me but sure I wasn't going to be portrayed well as the stand-in for this young girl.

"She admitted everything. The director praised her for her honesty and sent her on her way. I was the one left with the consequences—no leaving the barracks for two weeks. It's not that I thought the punishment was unfair, but that girl went home to a cupboard full of cookies, and no one in her home ever knew of her offense."

Miranda pulled her knees into her chest and lay her head on them. I thought about the fire in my chest that evening, burning to set the record straight. I'd not thought enough about who else might get burned.

The solution was clear. I didn't know why I hadn't seen it before. Henrik wasn't telling me to make amends with my family. He was telling me to protect the relationships that meant the most to me. And Miranda meant the most. When he said family, he meant Miranda. I had misunderstood.

I remembered the vacation Miranda and I had taken together. The summer of '71, we traveled around New York: Oswego, Lake Placid, Rochester, Seneca Falls, Manhattan. In the cab that night, I vowed to put my head down and earn enough money to update our equipment and take her on another vacation. We'd go to Montreal and try their bagels. I wasn't going to let her down again.

*   *   *

The morning paper revealed, unsurprisingly, that the Historical Society had voted unanimously to approve the park and statue and that they would secure a location as soon as possible. The Wilson family would provide the land. The city would buy it from them.

This news was another strike against my nerves. I made a mistake attacking Joseph. I felt like I'd been screaming at my father over a curfew or an unfair punishment. My head pounded, and my throat was dry. I picked up the phone even though it was only 6 a.m. I had my first appointment at 7 a.m., so it was now or never.

"Ginny, this is Lucretia—Lucy," I said.

"I recognize your voice." She didn't seem pleased with the recognition.

"Did I wake you?" I asked in my friendliest voice, ready to apologize if I'd called too early.

"No," she said.

"I was calling, actually, well, I mean, I wondered if I could talk to you, of course, but I also wanted to talk to Joseph."

"He's gone," she said.

"What do you mean, he's gone?"

"He had something to take care of." She sounded like she had a cold.

"But it's early," I said.

Ginny was not going to tell me Joseph's whereabouts, but my mind spun out a few scenarios, and none of them spoke well for my getting to him before he did something rash.

"I wanted to apologize," I said.

"It's too late for that," she said. "And too soon. It's not the right time. We have to absorb what happened."

"I understand," I said. "But let's not do anything until we get a chance to talk."

"I can't promise anything, Lucy—I have to go."

I held the phone until the dial tone turned to beeping.

I went upstairs and got dressed silently while Miranda slept. She was curled in a ball like a child with a stomachache.

I went back downstairs and called George. I asked him to come in on his day off. I wiped down the counters, put money in the cash register, and then sat down to meet with my first client, a young man with a military crew cut and an impossibly thick accent.

"Full name?" I asked.

"Abraham Stein."

I typed in his answer. "Address?"

"11 1/2 Bleaker Street."

"Phone number?"

"None."

"References?"

"None."

"I can be a reference." I typed in my name and phone number and noted Abraham's name in my book along with his job application details. Abraham was the nephew of one of our customers, just over from Eastern Europe.

My form-filling business had started as a way for people to apply for federal compensation after the highway relocation funds were given only to property owners, not the residents who rented in Ward Thirteen. The forms were complicated and required proof of occupancy sent in triplicate. I tried to even the playing field by helping them work through the tangled requirements of bureaucracy. I was everyone's reference, everyone's former employer, everyone's sponsor. Everyone got glowing recommendations.

The cats paced under my desk. They wanted to be fed. Our entire routine was discombobulated with Miranda still in bed. I excused myself and fetched a can of food from the kitchen. I put it in their bowl on the little back porch and changed their water. I watched them eat with their tails swaying happily. I wished I could stay with them, in the easy world where all anyone wanted from me was a little food and water.

Back at my desk, I tried to give Abraham my full attention, but my mind turned to problems. Where had Joseph gone? Would my sister ever forgive me? Why was Miranda still asleep? She had slept for ten hours and woke up saying her lung hurt. I'd never seen her take a sick day. Even if she didn't work in the kitchen because of a sniffle or cough, she always worked in the back, organizing supplies or keeping the books. If she didn't feel better by noon, we'd go back to the doctor.

I made a mistake bringing her the night before. When we got home, she had immediately taken a bath. I stayed downstairs and ate crackers and a $100,000 Bar from the shelves. Then, she came down and showed me the paperwork that spelled our demise—warning after warning, violation after violation. She'd organized them in a folder but never acted on them. She'd kept the folder to herself and never let me know the inspectors had been there several times over the years. She carried the weight of that knowledge by herself. I told her we could move the store or rent an apartment. I would've said anything to make her feel better, but whatever the solution, it was going to cost more than we could afford.

George grabbed the beaded curtain in his fist and caught my eye. "I got someone else to come help. I hope that's okay."

"Who'd you get?"

"Alma," he said and then lowered his eyes.

"I won't tell your mom, but it must be getting serious if you're asking her to help in the store."

Abraham turned around in his chair to look at George. Abraham didn't speak a lot of English, but he was curious and a fast learner.

"I'll tell my mom soon," George said. "I don't want to get her hopes up. Alma's a whole other class of woman, and my mom will put a ring on her finger before she's even been asked the question."

I laughed at his characterization of his mother. He wasn't far from the truth. His mother's expectations of him were heightened since he was her only child. Now that I knew the story of his brother, or the shadowy outlines of the story, I could see why he felt the pressure to be both brothers in one. I couldn't imagine what it felt like to have your brother gone for fifteen years.

"I'll put Alma at the cash register while I prep in the kitchen," he said. "Hopefully, we won't be too busy."

The bell on the front door rang. David came inside with his camera slung around his neck. He adjusted his tie and pretended to study the shelves of jarred goods.

"Is Miranda in?" he asked.

"She'll be down soon," I said. "Under the weather today."

He looked at me sharply, waiting for more information. But when I didn't offer any, he went back out the front door.

As David went out, a young woman came in with an embrace for George. It was Alma. She was thin with plump cheeks and light brown skin. She wore a wool coat over a blue tweed dress. George guided her into the back room, like she was a treasure to be delivered with care.

"I'm sorry to interrupt again, but I want you to meet Alma Washington. She's in bookkeeping classes," George said, obviously proud. "Her father is a professor at the university."

He held the beaded curtain back for her to come into the back of the house. I stood up to shake her hand. "It's an honor to meet you again," I said. "I'll never let George's mother know I met you first. Don't ever tell her. We appreciate your coming to help."

"It's my pleasure." Alma spoke confidently. "I'm excited to learn about your business." She reminded me of the girls in librarian school, eager to be out in the world, taking on responsibilities, and showing how competent they were. She had the same neat appearance and spark in her eye.

"Miranda's upstairs. She's the owner," George explained to Alma. "She'll be down soon. I wouldn't be surprised if she's making bagels by midmorning." He walked Alma back into the front room with a gentle hand on the small of her back, and I could hear him explaining the systems and strategies of the morning rush.

My phone rang, and I took down another appointment. I finished Abraham's application and sent him to deliver it. I corralled my folders and put them in a box on the floor.

Lida Rosenthal came in the front door. "Miranda," she yelled. She wore a jumpsuit and a bright blue coat.

"Good morning, Mrs. Rosenthal," I said, coming into the front room. "Miranda is upstairs. George is in the kitchen."

"He's keeping kosher?"

"He is," I said. "He always does."

She nodded and went to the counter, where Alma was standing in front of our cash register, staring at its elaborate keys. We didn't have room for it, but it was gifted to Miranda's father, and it was a good conversation piece. It looked like something out of the Vatican—elaborate and expensive.

"Who have we here?" Lida yelled when she noticed Alma. There wasn't going to be a young lady in the store without Lida figuring out her marital status and finding a suitable mate—even if the color of her skin suggested she couldn't keep kosher.

"What can I help you with?" Alma asked, a smile on her face.

"I need some extra bagels," Lida said. "And while I wait, you can tell me all about yourself." If George wasn't already dating Alma, Lida would've had them fixed up by the end of the hour.

Miranda was going to be impressed when she came down. I couldn't wait for her to meet Alma. I went into the kitchen to make Miranda a cup of tea. I took a tea bag from our pantry and a mug of hot water from the urn on the counter. One of our code violations was from mixing personal and commercial storage. If we had personal milk in the same refrigerator as the customer's milk, that was a violation. We'd need an entirely separate kitchen with all new equipment to meet the codes.

A man rapped on the front door as if it wasn't a store he could enter at will. "Hello?" he yelled.

Alma answered the door.

"Miranda Fein?" he asked.

"She's upstairs," Alma said.

Lida Rosenthal stood behind her, watching.

"Please see that she gets this," the man said. Before I could get back into the front room, he took a piece of paper, a hammer, and a small nail, and he secured the paper to the outside of our front door.

Alma and Lida stepped aside so I could see it. The paper had a red stamp across its text. "Notice to Vacate. 30-day notice to quit the premises of 15 Sycamore Street."

My heart dropped. It's what Miranda feared would happen. Joseph had taken his revenge. They had condemned the building, taken it over "in the interests of the state." Joseph was evicting us for personal reasons, but he was hiding behind a law.

I heard her on the stairs before I saw her.

"Who was that?" she asked.

I thought for a second about hiding the paper and never

showing it to her, but I couldn't. We'd been through this before, and we had figured out a solution. The last time, however, we'd been much younger—in our twenties. That day of the first eviction could've been one of the worst of our lives, but it ended up being the gateway to everything I loved about our life.

*   *   *

Fourteen years ago, I had nowhere to run, but I ran. The backs of my shoes dug into my Achilles tendons and tore my stockings. My dress was stained with sweat.

On that day, in 1958, I ran past a poultry shop and a fish store, both closed for the Sycamore Street March that day. I ran past an appliance repair store with a man leaning in its doorframe. I ran past wooden houses with lopsided front porches and brick apartments with wastebaskets propping open the windows. An older man sat on a stoop—his wife yelled to him through an open window. They stared at me as I ran—a white woman running in Ward Thirteen was not something they saw every day.

I turned the corner away from Erie Boulevard and slowed to a walk, my chest heaving in the humid air. There were painted red X's on almost all the doorframes. At the corner of the next block, Sycamore Street I saw a low brick-faced building—Fein Foods. Its windows were covered in advertisements, faded in the sun: Kosher Meats, Barrel Pickles 15 cents, Dry Goods—Inquire inside—Fein Foods.

Miranda's last name was Fein. This must be her grocery store, her delicatessen. I'd met her at librarian school at North Carthage University. She was a year ahead of me then, and we were paired together for a project on the Dewey Decimal System. I loved how smart she was, and I sought her out in other classes. We had lunch together a few times, but once she graduated, I didn't run into her again until that morning when she'd witnessed the most humiliating moment of my life.

The red X's stopped at the beginning of the block, and I

exhaled. Miranda's store was safe. The shade was pulled down on the store's front door, and a sign said "Closed." I sat down on the stoop and buried my face in my hands. I let my breath slow. I could feel sweat tingling on my scalp.

A patrol car passed by slowly, its fenders taking up more than half the road. It was one of the cars that had arrived with my father at the Sycamore Street March. I recognized the uniformed men inside. They would probably report to my father that I was just fine—a little shaken up—exactly what he'd want to hear.

"Lucy, are you all right?" Miranda yelled from across the street. She waved her hand and hurried to my side. She had her long red hair in a bun, but it was escaping onto her shoulders. Her thin shoulders set bony angles under her cotton dress.

"I never thought I'd find you here." She sat down on the stoop and put her arm around my shoulders. She wiped a line of sweat off her forehead and looked me in the eye. We were both shaken.

I nodded.

"I saw what the police did. They questioned you. What happened?"

"I don't know—honestly." I shook my head back and forth, back and forth. My ears buzzed with my father's angry words—flashes of the violent encounter burned behind my eyelids. Black-and-white patrol cars. Batons. The sound of cracking bones.

"Are you all right?" she asked.

"That was my father." I grimaced as if that was enough of an explanation.

"What was he doing?"

"He wanted to know who gave me the flyer." I started crying. I had led my father to her neighborhood. He wouldn't have come if I hadn't stupidly left the flyer out that night. Ginny and I had been so cavalier about it. I told him I was going to the protest. I didn't think I needed to hide the flyer.

"It's not illegal to have a flyer," Miranda said, shaking her head.

"I know." I wiped away my tears.

"Why was he so mad?"

"I don't know. We got the flyer at the Fremont last week. I was laughing with my sister when we got home. He must have heard us say it was from a man w—" My head collapsed back onto my own arms, and I groaned. "Oh my God, what have I done?"

"A man who what?"

"I didn't think my father could hear us," I said. "I didn't even know he was up. I said it was from a man who couldn't keep his eyes off my sister."

She drew in her breath and took her arm off my shoulders. "At the Fremont?"

I raised my head. "But they didn't take the right man. It was Ray Washington who flirted with my sister. He was playing that night and came to our table. He kissed her. That's what my father must have heard us talking about. That's who he came here for."

Miranda shook her head. "We'll go to the police and explain."

"I can't. There's nothing I can say that they'll believe, and if they do, they'll go after Ray." I stared at her, trying to see if she understood.

"But they have the wrong man." Miranda stood up and wiped her hands on the sides of her dress. She was decided.

"But once they realize he didn't do anything, won't they let him go?" I asked.

Miranda looked at me long and hard. I knew I sounded naive, but I couldn't pinpoint what part of my vision was wrong. I didn't understand then that justice didn't happen for everyone, that a person could take the full brunt of a punishment even though they hadn't done anything wrong. I mean, I knew this could happen. I'd seen Alfred Hitchcock's *The Wrong Man,* but I didn't think it could happen in Carthage.

"If I go, it'll make it worse," I said. She didn't understand how well connected my father was.

"We have to go," she said.

"What happened to your friend?" I asked, still not standing.

"They smashed his camera and took his film. I thought they were going to kill him. I ran after you because I wanted to help, but David ran the other way. Everyone scattered. It was chaos."

I shivered even though it was the hottest day of the year.

An old pick-up truck pulled up to the curb. A white man with overalls and a painter's cap stepped around the back of his truck and pulled out a small can of paint. He looked at us on the stoop for a moment—Miranda standing and me sitting—and then busied himself with opening the can. He took a paintbrush already coated with red paint, checked a piece of paper in his pocket, looked at the address on the store, and stepped around us to paint a red "X" on Fein's doorframe. The paint dripped down the frame onto the top of the door. He put the can back in his truck and got in the driver's seat.

We watched him until he turned the corner onto 22nd Street.

Miranda got up and put her finger in the paint—bright red. Her face was set, her mouth in a tight line. "I thought this might happen." She looked over her shoulder like something else might be lurking behind the fire hydrant or one of the parked cars. "When I lost my mother, my father took care of me, but when I lost my father, I knew the full brunt of the world would come for me." She didn't look sad—only determined, like she'd been preparing for this all her life.

I hardly knew anything about her—I didn't know her parents were dead. She'd shown up for library training every day, like everyone else—dress, stockings, hair pulled back in a bun, fingernails clean. They checked our hands for cleanliness every day before we were allowed to work in the library. I had only been wiping dust from my hands, possibly some remnants of jam.

Miranda had been wiping off a whole other job—cash register grease, pickle juice, maybe blood, sweat, and tears for all I knew.

"That's what the protest was for—to avoid this," Miranda said.

"I know," I said. "But I think this was personal."

"We'll deal with this at City Hall," she said, "but right now, we have to get to the station. Gainer was the one organizing the whole event. They'll be looking to teach him a lesson."

"Gainer?"

"He was the man in the Army uniform. I've never seen him before today, but I heard people calling him Gainer."

I looked back at the red "X." Did she not see the gravity of the situation? Didn't she know the demolitions were set to continue next month, and she was now on the list? I looked at her, puzzled.

"One thing at a time," she said. "First, let's take the number 8 downtown before they book him."

It sounded like she was speaking a foreign language—what was the number 8? And what exactly did it mean to book someone? Librarian school hadn't taught me anything about the real world.

"How can you be so calm?" I asked.

"My father always said, 'It's not the adversity you face—it's how you face the adversity.'"

But this was more than adversity. They had Marine tanks lined up to aid the demolitions. The crews had already spent five days tearing down the AME Church, which workers said was one of the best-built buildings they had ever razed.

"I don't think I should go," I said. "What if my father's there?"

"You have to tell them what happened. You're a key witness. And you're not from the neighborhood, so they'll believe you."

My head reeled. How could I tell them my father had ordered that man to be arrested, that he had pushed him to the ground, attacked him?

"Let's wash up," she said.

It was twenty degrees cooler inside. The lights were off, and refrigerated cases glowed with tubs of cream cheese and other staples—stacked, labeled, and ready to go. I could see over the short shelving units to the deli case and the cash register—a baroque beast—Miranda could practically fit inside it if she were able to bend herself into a cash register shape. I couldn't believe she was the proprietor of this entire place.

She took me to a small back bathroom, pulled a string to turn on the lightbulb. The mirror was silvered and mottled with age. I splashed water on my face and smoothed my hair. I held my wrists under the cold water to bring my temperature down. It had to be ninety degrees outside and ninety percent humidity.

Miranda washed her hands, peeling the dried paint off her finger.

After walking a few blocks, we caught the number 8. I was drenched in sweat again. The air was stultifying. The neighborhood looked like it was melting—porches sagged, thin curtains drooped in open windows, men sat on stoops with their arms draped over their knees, like they were being smelted back into the earth.

I put my face near the bus window for a light breeze and watched the landscape change. Buildings went from wood to brick, then brick to stone. The street widened, and large patches of grass appeared. Tall oak trees lined the street—a complete transformation from one end of the city to the other. We went past my father's bank, which I knew was cool inside—marble floors and ceiling fans, wood paneled teller boxes.

The bus passed MacArthur Park. I peered up at the equestrian statue of Arthur MacArthur, Civil War general. I remembered reading about statues on tall pedestals. They were created in deformed proportions—the man much larger than the horse—so they'd look right for the people on the ground. If they brought it down, the horse would have the shortest legs and the man would have the largest head.

I'd seen that statue my entire life, but I'd never seen it from this angle.

Miranda leaned over me and pulled the string above the window. How did she know where to stop? It would have taken me an hour to find where the police station was and how to get there without asking my father for a ride.

Inside the station, people stood in clumps of two or three. Women held pocketbooks to their chests and men jingled change in their pockets. Their conversations created a low murmur in the room.

Miranda walked up to a man at a long table. He had a slew of binders held up with bookends, a telephone, and a stack of mimeographed papers.

"We're here to inquire after a man who was taken from the Sycamore Street March," she told the officer.

"Ward Thirteen, eh?" He looked at us with a question in his eyes. Ward Thirteen was predominantly Black and Jewish, but with Miranda's red hair and our white skin, we did not fit the bill. In fact, as I looked around the room, I saw we were the only white people besides a minister in the corner on a pay phone and the officer we were talking to.

"He was arrested at 10 this morning, brought here in a patrol car," Miranda said.

"Only the paddy wagon came in, sweetheart," he said. "Were you part of the protest?"

"There's no one being held?" she asked.

"We're processing a few disorderly folks, but—"

I had been at the protest. The only disorderly people were my father and the police.

"Could you just take a peek back there—maybe he hasn't been booked yet?" she asked.

"What's your interest?" he asked without moving.

Miranda took a notebook from her purse. "School project," she said with a smile. "They have us pretending to be journalists." She gave a minuscule roll of her eyes.

He laughed and nodded knowingly. He was charmed out of his government-issued socks by Miranda's ruse. He excused himself and went through the door to the precinct's inner sanctum.

I had been standing stiffly, hardly blinking my eyes, but when he closed the door, I risked a glance at Miranda, and we smiled like Cheshire cats. I felt such relief that the universe had brought me this dynamo of intelligence and energy right when I needed her. I felt like I had been living under a rock all these years, and I was finally blinking my way into the sun.

Our moment of suppressed glee was broken almost immediately.

"No one back there, young ladies. Can you describe the man?"

"He's a Negro, about twenty-five years old. He was in his Army uniform. He goes by the name Gainer," Miranda said.

"And what would you ladies be inquiring about a Negro for?" He cocked his head.

Miranda tapped her notebook. "School project."

He smiled and exhaled. "I wish I could help you, but he hasn't been here." He pointed to his mimeographed sheets. "I'd be the first to know." He adjusted his wide black belt and smiled at us again.

My heart sank. If they didn't bring him here, where did they bring him? I couldn't imagine what my father was doing—he was not one to operate outside the law—not to my knowledge at the time.

Miranda offered for me to spend the night at her house. We split a bottle of wine and she loosed her troubles into the air between us. She said she didn't own the land under the deli business. Her father had leased the building. She said her father would be crushed if she let the business go under.

We sat on her back stoop, the evening giving us a small breeze. We drank wine from juice glasses that we rested on the concrete stoop between sips. I felt exhausted and disheveled, but I leaned my back against her house's wall and felt a new energy buzzing through my body.

She told me the story of her house, a two-story clapboard with a wide front porch. The blue paint was peeling and the floorboards creaked as we walked across them. She said her father loved every doorframe of their house, every cabinet. He marveled at it every day and said prayers of thanksgiving every night. It's what he'd promised Miranda's mother—he would deliver Miranda to safety and give her a place to lay her head. The day he secured the mortgage, he had a neighborhood party on the front porch that spilled into the front room. They played klezmer music, and he danced with her, spinning her around.

"I'll show you," she said.

I shook my head, but she insisted.

I stood up and Miranda took my hand. She created the beat of the accordion with her mouth. "Da da da. Da da da." She tried to spin me under her arm, but she wasn't tall enough. Our arms got twisted, and we fell back on the stoop, laughing.

"We'll have to practice," she said. "It's not difficult." She held my eye as our laughter subsided.

Late that night, I asked her why she didn't want to move her deli to the South Side or up near the university. She said the only way she could afford to move the store was by selling the house. And she wasn't going to sell it. To her father, their house was the symbol of his American Dream.

In the morning, I heard her making coffee, and when I came downstairs, she had her grocery ledger, bank books, and a pad of legal paper. She sat at a wooden desk in the living room and chewed on her pen. She cradled a black phone with a long spiral cord under her chin.

"What permit do I need to sell sandwiches from a residential lot?" she asked into the phone.

"I need to move some heavy shelves and refrigerated cases out of a deli and into my home," she said on another phone call. "It's right across the street. I don't need a truck. How much would that cost?"

She wrote everything down, added up rows and subtracted columns.

Over the next month, the situation got more complicated. Employees relocated, and the deli manager took another job. No one wanted to work in a slapdash, fly-by-night operation. Longtime customers vowed to support her but begged her to sell the house.

I was impressed with her fortitude, but I was pessimistic from the start. The day she got permission to serve fresh food, she wanted to celebrate.

"They're going block your permit," I said. "They've probably already flagged your address. I'm so sorry."

"What are you sorry about?"

"This is all my fault," I said. "You never would have gotten a red 'X' if it wasn't for me sitting in front of your store."

"The only thing you have to apologize for is being such a spoilsport. I love a challenge, and this is a challenge like no other."

She patted me on the shoulder and waited until I caught her eye.

"My father never would let me quit," she added.

She gave my shoulder a gentle squeeze and headed to the kitchen. She pulled hand-formed bagels out of a drawer, opened the refrigerator for cream cheese and lox, and piled two bagels high with fixings. Then, she kindly asked me to shut up and eat.

*   *   *

Now, I stood in front of our second eviction notice—fourteen years after the first. Miranda walked into the front room, wearing her nightgown and a quilted housecoat, a faded floral print. She let the beads swing behind her and shuffled toward me in her slippers. She looked exhausted even after having slept for so long.

Emperor and Empress ran at full speed to wind themselves through her ankles.

"Who came to the door?" Miranda had a sixth sense for trouble. She could hear it sneaking up the sidewalk—she could read shadows and knew when to run.

I put her tea down on a shelf and stepped back to reveal the eviction notice. She stared like it was written in an ancient language.

When she lost the deli, she was determined to make the best of it, but when she saw this eviction notice for her home, her only home since coming to the United States as a child, she fell apart. She closed her eyes and slumped to the floor. Miranda was the strongest woman I knew, but she looked like she was fighting to even breathe.

I knelt to hold her. I thought she was crying, but she was holding her shoulder in pain.

"Call the hospital," I said to George. He and Alma were standing in the doorway to the kitchen.

"Dial 9-1-1," Alma said quietly to him.

"We have an emergency. We're coming to the hospital." He paused and listened. "15 Sycamore Street," he said into the phone. "Fein Foods. The owner of the deli has collapsed. It's a woman."

I lay her head in my lap. She rolled on her side into the fetal position. A truck drove past on Sycamore, its bed filled with wooden chairs. Above it, cars whizzed past on the elevated highway.

"Is it your shoulder?" I asked.

"My lung," she said. "My heart." The sides of her mouth pulled back in wincing pain.

"She's thirty-five, I think." George covered the phone with his hand as if he was going to ask, but then he said, "We're right by the front door."

I looked up at the door. The eviction notice was still there. The cold air swept inside, setting up camp around our bodies.

"They're sending an ambulance," George said as he hung up the phone.

I tried to run through everything we might need. I loosened her bun and removed her hair pins.

"Can you get her purse?" I asked George. "It's in the bedroom." I didn't want him to see that we shared a bedroom, but it wasn't the time to worry about decorum. I could already hear the siren in the distance.

From our spot on the floor, I looked around the store wondering if there was a drink or bite of food that might heal her. Tightly packed shelves, all the way to the ceiling—jars and bottles and cans and boxes—hundreds of products but not one cure. I had built this store with her, built this life of ours from scratch. We had given it every inch of our hearts and souls, and Joseph managed to snatch it away in a moment. How'd he even process the eviction notice so quickly? Unless he'd been planning it all along.

"We have to fight this," Miranda said, still holding her chest. Even in excruciating pain, her main concern was the deli.

"Don't worry," I said. "We'll find a solution. We'll move to the South Side or up near the university." I bent down and shooed the cats away from her.

"No." She gripped my wrist. "We have to stay here—my father." She didn't need to say anything else. Over the years, she had paused on the stairs enough times when she heard her father's voice in the wind or when she felt his presence in the kitchen.

I nodded. I felt the same way, but it wasn't her father's energy I felt. It was Miranda's. This house was where we had fallen in love. Upstairs had been our sanctuary for fourteen years. No one else ever went upstairs—we lived together in the big bedroom and had turned the small bedroom into a television room. After work and dinner and more work, we watched old movies, *The Mary Tyler Moore Show*, the nightly news. We had blankets and throw pillows and a window that opened to the minuscule backyard. How dare Joseph take this house from us.

"I'll get Joseph to pull it back," I said. "We have thirty days."

"Can we make the upgrades?" she asked through gritted teeth.

I thought about our weekly budget, already stretched as thin as it could go. Miranda knew our financial situation better than I did. She did the books. Buying new equipment was impossible. Getting a loan would be difficult with our sporadic income.

"I'll ask the bank," I said, but I knew I had burned my bridges with the town of Carthage.

"It's you, me, and George," she said. "That's who got us through the worst times. That's who should run the business. It belongs to the three of us. No one else."

I nodded.

Her eyes looked better, like the pain had passed, and I held her hand even as the ambulance arrived, looking too much like a hearse. Two young men jogged up the front steps, wearing blue jackets with insignias on their upper arms. I watched them carefully as they checked Miranda's heartbeat and looked into her eyes and mouth.

"We'll bring you in for a check-up, but your vitals look good," the driver said.

I helped her put on her shoes and took her purse into my lap.

They went back to get their stretcher, but Miranda struggled to her feet and took hold of my elbow as she made her way down the porch steps. She wasn't going to be carried if she didn't have to be. The air was cold, and the sky was filled with wet gray clouds. When she got to the sidewalk, she looked back.

"Meet me there," she said to me. And then she looked down our street—Sycamore Street, the only block she'd ever lived on, the one part of the neighborhood that had escaped demolition in 1958. Fluttering on the front of every building was a piece of paper nailed to the front door. Amos's Appliance Repair. The Salvation Army. Speedy's Used Cars. Eviction notices just like ours. The whole block was condemned—public safety.

I followed her eyes and realized what Joseph was doing. He was tearing down the whole block. This was going to be the site for their Herbert Wilson Park.

"No," she said. "No, they can't do this." She made a move to come back into the house. She would get on the phone, demand answers, challenge this in court. But she stopped, almost frozen on the path to our porch. She held her shoulder with one hand and then with the other. One hand on top of the other. She bent her knees and fell on the pavement.

My mind couldn't make sense of what was happening. I thought about her knees, if they were scraped. I thought about the canning, what we needed to prepare next weekend. I thought about the vacation we'd taken to Seneca Falls. We'd eaten lunch in a diner, had cider with our sandwiches. When we came outside, the rain was coming down relentlessly, and a long Pontiac sped up the narrow street with its windows down, its seats getting splattered with rain and its driver oblivious. He had Bob Dylan's "Highway 61Revisited" blaring on his radio. It was all too much: the irony of him being in a small town when he wished he was on the open road, the madcap decision to have his windows rolled down, his long hair and headband rocking to the tune. Miranda and I had clutched each other on the sidewalk, gasping for air, laughing so hard we had to go back inside to use the lady's room.

The ambulance drivers tried to revive her. They were trained to massage her heart. They were trained to tip her head back and clear a passage for air. But they were drivers more than doctors. I should have taken her to the hospital. I shouldn't have waited. I shouldn't have brought her to the meeting. I shouldn't have made her take on so much while I was chasing the phantom of my father.

I knelt next to her. The pavement was freezing and hard.

"Can't you do anything?" I cried.

They moved her body onto the stretcher and brought her to the back of the ambulance.

I saw George and Alma crying on the front porch.

She can't be gone, I thought. We were restocking. We were making corned beef. I was going to tell her about George's girlfriend. I was going to take her to Montreal. I was going to hold her face in my hands.

CHAPTER SIX

Her Private Face

As the ambulance took Miranda away, I crumpled to my knees on the sidewalk. Her battered purse was tucked against my thigh. I felt the cold air swirl over my lap, and my mind unraveled. The cracks in the sidewalk radiated out from the spot where she had lain, spreading like veins across the concrete. They branched tenuously, intersecting with roads, slipping beneath the highway, and creeping into thickly forested hills. The fissures stretched on, reaching the shores of the Great Lakes, tracing the path of the St. Lawrence River, and finally touching the vast expanse of the Atlantic Ocean. I stood motionless, acutely aware that even the slightest movement could disrupt this fragile network, sending ripples through an entire ecosystem.

Our neighbors came out with the noise of the siren. They had seen the ambulance and then heard the rustle of their eviction notices—too much to take in. They formed a semicircle, crying in each other's arms, shivering in the cold. Amos. Speedy. Lorraine.

George and Alma tried to help. I heard them as through a broken phone line.

"Do you want Speedy to drive us to the hospital?"

I nodded.

I don't remember the details of that trip—who drove, what car we took, the roads we traveled. But some things remain crystal clear: Alma's silhouette framed by the headrest in front of me, and George's warm hands steadying me in the back seat, holding me together when I felt I might fall apart.

The hospital walls were too white, the lighting too strong. I held my hand above my eyes and asked to see Miranda. A large white nurse came out and put her arms around my shoulders. She told me Miranda had died.

"Sit here," she said, pointing to a molded plastic chair.

George and Alma were there. They took the seats on either side of me.

"Do you have a funeral home?" the nurse asked me. "Religious affiliation?"

I didn't have answers. Miranda would know. I didn't know. I turned to George.

"Can you call the rabbi?" I asked him.

He nodded and went to the pay phone. Alma stayed near me, her fist at her mouth. Her eyes told me again that Miranda was dead. Miranda was my best half. She had helped me find the right path. I had chosen a life outside my father's home, outside marriage, outside my family, but it only made sense if she was in it. Nothing made sense without her.

"Ma'am," the nurse said. "Do you have a doctor? We can call one if you need one."

"I don't have one. She has one."

I wasn't making sense.

"Do you want to call him?"

I couldn't move. I shook my head.

"Do you want us to call him? He can come here."

I shook my head again.

"Give her a minute," Alma said to the nurse.

"And who are you?" she asked. Taking instructions from a Black woman seemed like uncharted territory for her.

"I'm a friend of the family," Alma said. She had never met

Miranda. Her first view of Miranda was in her death throes. But I appreciated Alma's voice. I needed someone to speak.

"Are you family?" the nurse asked me.

I shook my head.

"I'll take care of it," she said, as if she had been coddling the wrong person. Now that she knew she wasn't dealing with a sister or cousin, she could move forward, get back to her other patients, take a cigarette break.

The rabbi from Miranda's synagogue was suddenly in the waiting room with us. He bent down next to me and said a prayer in Hebrew. Standing up, he said a prayer in English:

> *We implore You, by the great power of Your right hand, release the captive.*
> *Accept the prayer of Your people; strengthen us, purify us.*
> *Blessed be the name of the glory of His kingdom forever and ever.*

"You did the right thing, staying with her," Rabbi Baum said to me.

"What do I do now?"

"We'll take it from here. Her body will be prepared for burial. We'll hold the service tomorrow."

I choked. Too fast. Miranda rose with the sun each morning, but she never rushed. She would call me outside to see any morning skies worthy of notice. Even with our neighborhood houses crammed in, one building next to the other, we could still see the sunrise over the highway when the sky was clear.

My teeth chattered.

Then, there was a doctor in a white coat.

"Release the body—" The doctor looked at Rabbi Baum.

"Temple Beth Israel," he said.

"You can release her to me," I said. The fog in my brain lifted enough for me to know she couldn't be taken away.

"What is your relationship?" the doctor asked.

"We'll take care of the body," Rabbi Baum said to me. "You're welcome to come to the service tomorrow."

"I'll take care of the body," I said, using their language to describe Miranda like she was an object. The key to form-filling is to mimic the language of the form provider.

"Her body must be washed," Rabbi Baum said.

"I'll wash it," I said.

"We have to say prayers."

"I'll say them." I didn't read Hebrew, but there must be a translation. I couldn't let them take her away, block me out.

"What is your relationship?" Rabbi Baum asked me.

I paused. I didn't know what they would say or do. I didn't want to jeopardize Miranda's burial next to her father.

"They're business partners," George said, stepping up next to me.

"They're very close," Alma added. "You can't take the body. Give her a chance to process."

The two white men looked at my two Black advocates.

"Just for tonight," I pleaded.

Rabbi Baum and the doctor consulted, and then Rabbi Baum told me that the body would go to the synagogue. He explained the importance of the time between death and burial, the sacredness of this interval. He told me that I was welcome to visit.

When the men left, my body deflated. I sank back further into the plastic chair. I felt the absence of Miranda's father who had deserved one last goodbye with his daughter. I felt the absence of Miranda's mother who would be heartbroken her daughter had died so young. I felt the absence of my mother who I would have turned to in this difficult time. I felt the absence of family. It wasn't death that separated me from my family. My sister wasn't here because of our differences. My brother-in-law and niece, the same. I didn't have family members to turn to, and in that moment, I felt the loss profoundly.

I looked up at the doorway to the rest of the hospital and saw a nurse with dark red hair. She had hairpins lining the sides of her white hat. She wasn't signaling me, but she was holding my eye. I stood up on my uneasy legs and went over to her, walking as if I were in a dream.

"Do you want to see her?" she asked me.

I nodded.

"Can you stay?" I asked George and Alma.

They nodded.

"They can come," the nurse said. Her tone made it clear that this was unorthodox, but she was offering us a consolation.

We walked toward Miranda through a labyrinth of corridors, passing rows of patients in beds, nurses methodically checking vitals, and doctors poring over charts. My mind, overwhelmed, soared upward until it breached the roof. From there, the hospital transformed into a vast dollhouse—each room a miniature stage I could distance myself from.

We stood around her body.

I wanted to tell George and Alma about my relationship with Miranda. I wanted them to understand. I wasn't just her business partner. We weren't platonic. We didn't have something that could be expressed in a contract. I wanted them to know Miranda was loved deeply, that I was her partner in life as well as business.

"I wish I could call my mother," George said. "But—" He opened his hand and gestured to Alma.

Alma took his hand.

I nodded and shook my head, not sure what I was trying to convey. George's mother was not going to appreciate being kept out of the loop of his romantic life. But I could understand their need to keep their relationship a secret. Just from the little I knew of Alma—that she lived near the university, she was taking college classes, her father was a professor, I could see why George wanted to be cautious. Alma had grown up in Manhattan. Her family wasn't from the South. He didn't want to scare her off with an overbearing mother.

George clasped his hands around Alma's, like he could draw strength from her skin. They understood the pains and pleasures of a secret romance. They knew the consequences of getting caught, that their relationship could be torn apart by its revelation, but they also knew the deep feeling of security that came from a relationship forged in the dark. Without prying eyes, they didn't have to conform to anyone's idea of what a relationship should be. I realized what a risk George had taken in bringing Alma to the store and now to the hospital.

I looked down at Miranda's face. She had a private face, its features close to one another, never giving much away. When others were around, even George, she looked at me without a hint of passion, but then after hours, she looked at me lovingly and spoke to me in intimate whispers. She sat close to me and held my hands, making up for all our play-acting during store hours. The first time Miranda and I kissed, we were upstairs, away from the glare of social expectations. We weren't even sure of each other. If we had misread the cues that afternoon, we could've ruined our friendship. It was a line we crossed, like jumping over a crevasse in a high mountain trek.

*   *   *

When I came back from losing my inheritance in 1959 so many years ago, I tried to sneak into Miranda's guest bedroom for a cry. She stood at the top of the stairs, saw the look on my face, and pulled me into her bedroom. Her window was open, trying to lure the tired breeze. We sat on the wooden bench at the end of her bed.

"What happened?" she asked. A short question with a long pause. I knew I could tell her the whole story.

"I'm sorry," I said.

"Enough apologies."

"I lost the money. I showed him our research, but he took my name off the papers. He took away everything—all the plans I had." Miranda and I had sat up the night before, weaving stories of what I could do with the money if my father put it in my name. I told her I wanted to use the money to create more opportunities in the neighborhood, more opportunities for myself.

"You still have plans," she said. "What are you talking about?" She took my face in her hands and pulled it toward her. "Your worth is not determined by your bank account."

I nodded. Her hands covered my ears and went up and down with my nodding head.

I smiled. I leaned forward until my glasses touched her glasses, our eyes too close to see each other's full faces. We laughed.

"Everything's a blur," she said, her voice dropped to a whisper.

My heart thumped a beat that drove to the far reaches of my fingers. My mouth went dry. I held her eye—I didn't want to misread her. I thought of the scenes in *An Affair to Remember* when the stars almost kissed but then didn't because of propriety—so many scenes. Throughout the movie, I had cried. I would never be as beautiful as Deborah Kerr. I had a stocky torso, small breasts, thick glasses. A man would never follow me to my stateroom on a cruise ship. A man wouldn't risk his engagement to an heiress in order to kiss me. I was beyond the borders of passion—I thought—beyond the reaches of desire. That was for other girls.

But here I was with Miranda, her hair as red as Deborah Kerr's. Her skin as smooth. Who did that make me? Cary Grant?

Our glasses bumped again, and I reached up to remove Miranda's. I didn't want to overstep. She kept her face close to mine as I pulled her glasses over her ears and lay them in my lap. It felt like a sacred ritual. She removed my glasses. Our faces stood naked. I could feel her breath on my cheek as we leaned toward each other. I don't remember who crossed the line. We let our lips touch. The softest touch. I felt like I had plugged into an energy source I hadn't known existed. It was like finding another room in my house that had been hidden in plain sight all along.

With one kiss from Miranda, I felt invincible. I wanted everything. I wanted to spend my life with her. I wanted to walk with her on my arm. I wanted to build a life together. I thought of Gertrude Stein and her partner Alice B. Toklas. I wanted to have salons and teas and conversations, all with Miranda at my side. I hadn't thought this was possible before our kiss.

We pulled away, let our hands nestle together in the space between us, our glasses tangled beneath our hands. I could not stop staring into her eyes. I wondered what she was thinking. Was she re-imagining the entire world like I was?

"We could go to jail for that," she said with a grimace.

My heart sank. She was right. Gertrude Stein might have gotten away with it, but she was famous, and she lived in Paris and California. In Upstate New York, women who kissed women did not have salons. They were ostracized and often went straight to jail.

"There are a lot of ways we could go to jail." I didn't mean to sound seductive.

She laughed and pulled at her mouth, puckering her lips with her fingers.

"We can't let anyone know," she said, holding my eye.

Her rule-making sounded like a green light. We could shut out the world and keep our affair a secret. We'd stay safe together. I hadn't known what the next steps would be. Would we kiss every day? Would we share a bed? I had no idea. We didn't need wedding bells, but there had to be something. I could see the weeks and months and years spinning out in front of us. I couldn't do it by myself, but with Miranda, anything seemed possible.

"How do you do it?" I asked. "How do you live here all by yourself?"

"I'm not alone. You're here," she said.

I smiled a goofy smile, ear to ear. "But before that," I said. I squeezed her hands, small compared to mine. "You did this all by yourself."

"The neighborhood watches out for me," she said, squeezing back.

"David certainly watches out for you," I said. He said he was taking pictures of the whole neighborhood, but his lens was almost always pointed at Miranda.

"I'm the only one who knows the neighborhood's recipes," she said. "They can't lose me!" She let her joke settle in the air and then turned serious. "That's why I want to keep going for everyone who's still here."

"And now we have no money." I turned my head away.

"Who has no money?" she said. "We just have to sell more sandwiches."

She laughed, but I shook my head.

"But no one has any money." I thought about all the people who came to the deli. Many of them were looking for work. Miranda was trying to find ways to hire more people. "We feed them for free more often than they pay full price," I said.

Miranda put her hands back on my ears. "Their worth is not determined by their bank accounts or the money under their mattresses or what's at the bottom of their pocket." She let her words sink in.

"Tell my father that," I said.

"You basically just did," she said. "You let him know that truth was more important to you than money." She looked at me with admiration—me! I was so busy admiring her I never thought she might be admiring me. This woman, this red-headed dynamo. Where did she come from? How was I so lucky to have found her?

After that first kiss, I knew I would take whatever risks I needed to preserve our relationship. I knew my family couldn't know about it; our neighbors couldn't know; her synagogue couldn't; our customers couldn't. And after all these years, we had even kept it a secret from George.

* * *

In the hospital, I lifted my eyes away from Miranda's body and looked at George. His smooth, young face carried its weight in his cheeks. He looked younger than his years, but his eyes looked older.

"I need you to know something." I couldn't let Miranda go to her grave without someone knowing our love for each other.

George nodded, his hand still holding Alma's.

"Miranda wasn't just my business partner." I didn't know if that was specific enough.

"I know." George wasn't a vociferous talker. That may have been all he needed to say on the matter.

I nodded.

"I've known for a long time," he said. "You are two of the kindest women I know, and you were happy. I didn't think anything more needed to be said."

I scrunched up my face, trying to hold my tears in. They burned behind my eyes, and I felt a tremor in my chest. I hadn't set out to have a relationship with a woman; I had assumed I wouldn't have any relationship at all. Looking back now, I realized that I was trying so hard to fit in as a straight woman that I had closed all other doors. I had been standing in a hallway of closed doors when Miranda opened one and came through like a burst of light.

"Your grief shows your love," Alma said tenderly.

"Do you want us to leave you alone?" George gestured to Miranda's body, still dressed in her nightgown.

I didn't want to be alone. We had grown our love in private, but that was only one part of our relationship. Miranda and I had missed out on double dates and anniversaries and scrapbooks of our life together. The private times had sustained us, but we had missed the glow of other people knowing we were together. I wanted to share a moment of that now.

I held Miranda's hand and imagined I was washing her body. I imagined that I had a bowl of warm water on the chair next to mine, a soft washcloth, and a sheet. I imagined that I pulled the curtains closed and turned off the lights. I imagined that Alma lit a candle and that George read a prayer. I dipped the washcloth into a bowl of warm water, squeezed it. I wiped her forehead, pushing her dark red hair back from her face. I washed her nose and chin, each ear, her throat.

I listened to the imagined prayers and my own breathing and the questions in my head. *Why would my heart keep beating and hers end at such a young age? Why did we think it was a shoulder muscle when it was her heart all along?* Miranda had worked so hard all her life. Now, she would never know the resting time of old age. We would never know the reflective time of our dotage together.

The imaginary candlelight flickered on Miranda's face, making it look like her eyelids were fluttering. I wanted to stay in that moment forever, not knowing if she was alive or dead, asleep or awake.

In my mind, I unbuttoned her nightgown. I slipped her arms out of her clothes and washed her hands, her forearms, her armpits. Her muscles were strong, ready to work. I washed her shoulder muscles and the space above her heart.

I touched a burn mark on the inside of her pale forearm. I

felt my brain rush in every direction. She must have gotten it from a frying pan or the edge of a boiling pot. She must have yelled out when it happened. *Szzzzz*, the skin reacting to the heat, pulling back from the pain. The mark had been pink and puckered when she was alive. Now, it was leeching color, gray and slack. *No*, my brain told me. *This is not allowed to happen. Do not accept the premise. Take your own skin and pinch it. Lose a finger to the meat slicer. Scratch your own face. But do not accept the premise of her death.*

I looked at George and Alma, my hand frozen on Miranda's arm. I looked again at Miranda's face and sighed. The clock ticked. I slid the washcloth down her sides, over her thighs and pubic hair. I let my tears fall on her belly and wiped them away. I washed her shins and calves. Her feet I held for a moment, thinking of the steps she had taken from Poland to Italy to New York with her father, the steps she took from her home to the deli and back again when she was a young woman, and up and down the stairs in the house with me.

I imagined that I slid a sheet under her back and wrapped it over her body, tucking it under her on the other side. Safe and secure. Clean and pure. I kissed her cheeks and held her head for one more moment and then another.

CHAPTER SEVEN

Contract

The synagogue took Miranda's body for burial. George, Alma, and I spent the afternoon cleaning the store, lethargically and frenetically in turns. George swept the floor and scrubbed the spot by the front door. I stacked and re-stacked the jars we had filled the day before. I thought of Miranda's meticulous cleaning of each jar and lid. I held the same jar of stewed cherries in my hand until the weight became too much.

The next morning, I wrote a eulogy for Miranda, something to read when they opened the service to remembrances. I went upstairs and dragged my black stockings out of the wastebasket. I pulled them on. I put on my black dress, the same one I had worn to my father's funeral.

I stared at the telephone on the bedside table, on her side of the bed. I sat down on our coverlet, the bed still not made from the morning. I dialed a number I knew by heart.

"Ginny, this is Lucy." I wanted to hear the voice of a loved one. I wanted someone else to carry this news. I wanted my sister to comfort me. It wouldn't fix our relationship, but she might send flowers or come to the funeral as a sign we were sisters before anything else.

"Lucy." She had a note of happiness in her voice, happy to hear from me.

"I have some terrible news. Miranda has died." It was the first time I had said the words aloud. They sounded false.

"She has? Of what?"

"They called it cardiac arrest. It was sudden. Yesterday morning. She had symptoms, but we didn't know what they were. Not even the doctor."

"I'm sorry," she said.

"The funeral is this afternoon," I said.

"So soon. How could anyone re-arrange their schedule to be there?"

"They'll drop what they're doing," I said.

"What about the store?"

I felt my body tense. What kind of question was that? How can a human being hear about the death of another human being and immediately ask about financial arrangements? Couldn't she even pretend to care about Miranda? Or me?

"You know very well what will happen to the store," I said. "You're the one who's tearing it down."

"Oh, Lucy," Ginny said, "let's not talk about that now. I'm sorry for the loss of your friend. I know she meant a lot to you."

I felt the condescension of her phrasing. Miranda wasn't just a friend, I thought. It's not only my loss.

Without saying another word, I hung up the phone. I sat on the bed. The mattress sagged beneath me, pitching me forward. I drove my feet into the floor and wondered how to fill the time before the funeral.

I went downstairs and looked at the eviction notice again. Miranda's death and the impending eviction swirled in my mind, confusing with their similarities. Final notice. Sudden eviction. No recourse.

I pulled the notice off the door and left it on the counter when we left for the funeral, but we didn't talk about it. Speaking of it aloud might give it more power. It had brought Miranda to her knees and then out of our lives forever. We weren't ready to process its other consequences in our lives.

We arrived early at the synagogue on the bus's schedule. Many congregants stood outside, dressed in black and navy, holding solemn expressions on their faces. The sky was gray over their heads, pressing down. The air felt as if snow were coming. The men smoked in small clusters, and the women wrung their hands. Many of them were customers from our store, and they came down the path to greet us.

"May God rest her soul, our sweet Miranda," Henrik said when he got to us. I couldn't imagine him not holding Miranda's head, pressing her hair in his hands. Every strand of hair on her head was precious to him. He had lost his friend Alexsander fifteen years ago, and he wiped away tears as he spoke about Miranda.

"Thank you, Henrik," I said. "I'm still not sure what happened. Her shoulder hurt. Her doctor said it was a strained muscle." The tears started up again, and Henrik pulled me in a hug. He was shorter than I was and thinner, but he gave me all the warmth he had.

Lida Rosenthal took up the hug where Henrik left off. She wore a flowered dress under her mustard yellow coat. "Anything you need," she said loudly in my ear. "Anything."

I nodded.

Lida gestured to the rest of the people heading up to the synagogue. "We're here for you," she said.

I wiped my tears and looked at the synagogue. The large stone temple was imposing, set back from the road on a hill. A path led over the frost-covered lawn and up to the double front doors. Three Stars of David marked the entrance.

Up the hill from the entrance, I saw a beat-up Dodge Dart pull to the curb. David got out of the passenger side. I almost didn't recognize him without his camera or bell bottoms. He was dressed in a black suit. Roger got out of the driver's side. David shook his head, and they had an argument. Roger slammed the door and drove off.

"I'm sorry I didn't call," I said to David when he was close enough to hear me. "I wasn't thinking. We're all in shock." I nodded to include George and Alma.

David shook his head. "How dare you? I found out from the office."

"I should have called you," George said, stepping in on my behalf. "You deserved to know."

"You told me she was under the weather," he said, still focused on me, his eyes raging, red around the edges. "I never would've let her die. How could you do this?"

"That's not fair," I said to him.

He leaned in close and said, "Never trust a lesbian."

I knew David was lashing out. He was grieving, angry. But my tears still came, hot on my cold face.

David stormed away, leaving me with George and Alma, perhaps the only three Christians at the service. I felt a chasm open between us and the synagogue. I didn't know if anyone had heard him. I didn't know if I'd been outed.

We walked the remainder of the path in a daze.

Rabbi Baum greeted us in the foyer. He wore a black suit with a patterned shawl around his shoulders, a yarmulke on the back of his head. "Friends, I'm glad you made it," he said. "Miranda would've wanted you here."

His words caught me off guard. I wasn't used to having someone speak for Miranda. I was still reeling from David's insult.

"May I speak to you for a moment?" the rabbi asked me. He looked both ways and then guided my elbow into a small alcove.

George stayed at the front table, getting a yarmulke for the service.

"I heard about the eviction notice at the store," Rabbi Baum said. "The entire block is going to be redesigned as a park. You must know the store's part of the Carthage Jewish community. Because of that, we'd like to move it up here near the university."

I stared at him, blinking but not comprehending.

"The store was given to the Fein family at the end of World War II," he said. "The recipes are part of our community."

"I know," I said.

"Now that Alexsander's daughter has passed, we'd like to continue the store even if we can't have it in that location."

I remembered Miranda's plea to keep the house. She wanted her father's spirit to remain there. The conflicting thoughts of grieving the past and planning the future hurt my brain. I couldn't do both.

"If there's any way to keep the store there—" I said. Maybe the synagogue had more pull with the city than I did. Maybe they could take care of it.

"Even without that location," he said, "we want to continue it in her memory, in the memories of many of our former congregants." He wasn't answering my question. "I have a man who's willing to take over the operations."

I couldn't believe how quickly the conversation had turned. I thought Rabbi Baum had been writing a eulogy for Miranda all day, but apparently, he had been creating a business model and hiring new staff for Miranda's store.

"We run the store," I said. "George runs it. He ran it with Miranda." I tried to get my verb tenses right. The store was there but may not be in the future. Miranda was not there now, but she had been in the past. I gestured to George and Alma to join us.

"This is George Pritchard. You know him from the store," I said.

"George, yes," Rabbi Baum said. They shook hands.

"This is Alma Washington," George said.

"Pleased to meet you," Alma said.

"Miranda has a contract with us," I said. "A binding contract."

The rabbi raised his eyebrows.

George raised his eyebrows as well.

"She gave us fifty percent of the business several years ago," I said. "The Jewish community started the deli with the original recipes, but the store has been a self-running entity for many years—unencumbered—Miranda had sole proprietorship upon her father's death." I tried to think of other legal words. There wasn't actually a contract, but I had all the forms to write one if I needed to produce it. She would not have wanted us cut out of the business.

"Is that so?" Rabbi Baum asked.

"Yes, and upon her death, it's a hundred percent." I was out of my league. I'd have to research estate law, but I wanted the rabbi to stop talking. Maybe George could run the store, and I could do the books, at least for a little while.

"George," Rabbi Baum said, "do you know the recipes?" He tilted his head as if to urge the young man to come clean.

"I do," he said. "Miranda taught me."

"And how to keep kosher?" the rabbi asked.

"Yes, sir," George said.

The store wasn't certified kosher, but George and Miranda were meticulous about ordering only kosher meats and keeping dairy and meat separate in the kitchen. They had carefully marked cutting boards, knives, and spatulas that were only used for their respective food type.

"Well," the rabbi said. "I'll have to discuss this with our community."

"It's best to have continuity," I said. "And we want to respect Miranda's wishes."

"We'll talk next week," the rabbi said. "And I want to see that contract."

"Yes, sir," George said.

Alma beamed by his side. This imaginary contract would make him the proprietor of a store, rather than just a worker. While she had fallen in love with him as an hourly wage earner, it would be easier to introduce him to her parents as a store owner.

*   *   *

The funeral was short. The congregation knew what to do and when. They sat and stood and sat again. They flipped pages in the prayer book as if they were answering questions on a quiz show.

George, Alma, and I sat in a pew by ourselves and tried to follow along.

Miranda's casket was at the front of the temple on a raised platform with the rabbi. I thought about her hair around her shoulders. I wondered if they had wrapped her in a white sheet like I had imagined. It would keep her warm.

"Grief is physical," Rabbi Baum said. "I tear this ribbon to show the grief for Miranda Fein's death. In memory of her family and because she was the last member of the Fein family, Henrik Neubauer will be the primary griever."

Henrik walked up the aisle and stepped onto the raised platform to have the torn ribbon affixed to his lapel.

"Baruch atah Adonai, Dayan Ha-Emet—Blessed are You, Adonai, Truthful Judge," Rabbi Baum recited.

I remembered the torn ribbon in Miranda's house, from her father's funeral. She had been the primary griever for him. I wasn't recognized as a griever at all. I felt a sting of resentment from my throat down to my stomach. I felt embarrassed to have shared the truth of my relationship with George and Alma only to be ignored at Miranda's funeral. And they had heard David's snarled insult. David was the one who should have been embarrassed by his behavior, but it was my face that shone with sweat and shame. I stared at the black ribbon on Henrik's lapel and wondered if it would be sacrilegious to tear my own ribbon at home.

"Adonai natan, Adonai lakach, yehi shem Adonai m'vorach— God has given, God has taken away, blessed be the name of God."

The rabbi gave a short eulogy. He talked about Miranda's father and the blessing of their arrival, escaping the Holocaust. He spoke of the shroud around her body, the *tachrichim*, representing the equality of all people, and I was relieved to picture her in this protective covering.

There weren't any personal remembrances. I folded my notes about Miranda back into my purse.

Six pallbearers lifted the casket. David was one of them. He had snuck himself into his congregation like a liquor bottle in plain brown wrapper. In my imagined funeral, George would have carried the casket with the others. Instead, we waited until we were told to rise, and we followed the congregation out to the graveyard. The land for the synagogue allowed for a substantial cemetery with pathways and trees, benches, and small stone grave markers.

Snow started to fall while we were standing around the gravesite—tiny crystals, hard like hail. A pitter patter on her casket, a sprinkling on our shoulders. I felt my stockings snag on my dress and knew I had ruined another pair. The cold air came through the run on the back of my calf.

After the burial prayers, the mourners took turns shoveling dirt onto the casket. An earthmover had dug the grave, and we returned the dirt to the hole it had made—shovelful by shovelful. The sound was horrendous, dirt falling on the casket. I felt claustrophobic for her. I had to shake my head to stop picturing her in the casket, terrified by the sounds.

When it was my turn, I took the smallest amount of dirt and put it by her feet. I stared at the coffin. I wanted to stop the burial, check one more time to see if she was alive. The line of mourners shuffled forward, and I handed the shovel to an elderly lady. I pulled my coat tighter around my body and walked on the frozen ground back to the path.

I looked for George and Alma. They were in line at the grave. I saw Henrik coming toward me. His black ribbon was hidden by his overcoat.

"I want to show you something." Henrik motioned with his gloved hand. I followed him to the front of the synagogue.

The snow had started to cover the pathway, and I wondered what the bus schedule was to get back home. I would be going home alone.

"Have you seen this?" Henrik wiped off a bronze plaque set on a stone pedestal near the road. Cars drove by with their windshield wipers on, their tires melting the snow underneath.

I looked at the plaque. *Temple Beth Israel, erected 1958. In honor of the survivors of the Holocaust and the members of this congregation who came to New York on the USS Henry Gibbins, this Jewish temple is deemed an essential part of Carthage history and can hereby never be destroyed or replaced without explicit agreement of the city of Carthage and its Historical Society.*

"A great security for you." I wished our neighborhood had a plaque like that.

"We fought for this," he said. His voice was well worn with age and grief, but his passion to be understood was clear. He wanted me to understand how they had earned it.

"How do you think we moved here in 1958?" he asked me.

"I can't imagine," I said. Most of the businesses and homes were razed without any plans for re-building. "Your temple was re-built almost immediately—the same year," I said, looking at the date on the plaque. "And in such a nice part of the city."

Across the street, women walked with blanket-covered baby carriages, and men crossed the street with newspapers tucked under their arms, heads bent against the wind. The window of Casual Corner was filled with winter fashions. The Kinney Shoe Store still had their Christmas decorations up.

"We fought for it," he said.

I hoped he didn't think the rest of us hadn't fought. We held marches, petitioned the city, went to the newspapers.

"We made the city see it was part of their self-interest to let us re-build here," he said.

"What do you mean?"

"We first rented a space in this part of town after the demolition of our synagogue in Ward Thirteen. Word got out that we were worshipping here. Someone burnt a cross on our lawn and left a Bible on our doorstep. We were confused by their choice of symbolism, but the message was clear."

"Why did you stay?"

"We knew we had to stay. We couldn't give into their threats. It was your father, I believe, who gave us the loan to get this land. We convinced him the empty lots near the university should be filled with historical and educational opportunities for the students. The Jewish students who came here and paid their tuition needed a place to worship, and our synagogue could create a partnership with the university. The way they saw it, our presence would bring in more tax dollars, and there would be more loans taken from his bank, and the interest rates would keep him in the black."

"My father?"

"Herbert Wilson," he said.

I shook my head. I didn't think my father ever made deals with the citizens of Old Ward Thirteen, and I didn't think anyone knew I was his daughter. Henrik had not spread that knowledge, and I stared at him. I had been sure that if one person had found out, then everyone would have known. But he hadn't told anyone. He had protected me.

"Then," Henrik said, "we secured our place in the city by making them see it was beneficial to them that we were protected."

"That was smart." I thought of the eviction notice back at home—one tragedy replacing another in my mind, like horses on a carousel. I tried to follow Henrik's logic.

"We didn't make them feel guilty. We made them feel generous. We made them look generous. We made them see that our history was their history."

I nodded. I didn't understand how it related to me.

"You have had two members of that same history in your house on Sycamore," he said.

"Oh no," I said. He couldn't be suggesting I try the same route. "I can't go back to the Historical Society. I'm not welcome there. And my sister is on the executive board. I'll never get a plaque like this."

"Find their self-interest." He took off his hat and smacked the snow off before putting it back on.

"What interest would they have in saving Miranda's house?"

"The city wouldn't want to make our congregation angry, for starters," he said. "We've created a deep heritage here, a strong community. They often point to us as a success story carved from the creation of the highway. That's not entirely right or wrong, but you have to let them see it that way. Give them what they want and they give you what you want."

"I wouldn't know where to start."

"What's your goal?" Henrik asked me.

"My goal?"

"What do you want to happen?"

"I want to save what's left of the neighborhood," I said. "And Miranda's house."

"And what about for yourself?"

"I don't know. I guess I'd like to have a spot in that neighborhood—a job—a place to live."

"And what would that job be?"

"I could keep running the deli with George."

"And if the deli moves?"

"Maybe I could still live in the house?"

"What do you offer to the deal? Your self-interest must co-incide with their self-interest. Like a Venn diagram. Where do your interests overlap?"

Henrik held onto my arm for balance and emphasis.

"I'm trained as a librarian. I have Miranda's papers—her father's papers." I pictured an archive of some sort. I could research all the families who had come over on the *USS Henry Gibbins* and transcribe their stories.

"I'll bring it forward," he said. "I'll ask them to call a special meeting. I know someone on the committee."

I nodded.

"And Mrs. Rosenthal knows someone in city planning who might be able to come down from Toronto to help us. She did a lot of good work for the neighborhoods in New York City."

"Jane Jacobs?" I asked. "How does Mrs. Rosenthal know her?"

"They grew up together in Pennsylvania. They're still close." Henrik paused and shook his head. "We have to fight for our city, even in grief."

"And you can make an argument for the archive?"

"We'll see what they have to say."

"Miranda has some documents from her father," I said.

"I have similar ones," he said, nodding grimly.

I thought about Henrik coming over on the *USS Henry Gibbins* with Miranda and her father. They had survived starvation and exile and terror for years before they got on that ship, and then once they'd arrived in New York, they had to learn English and new skills. They had to fight the prejudice that had been leveraged against them, and here was Henrik Neubauer standing before me with more power in Carthage than I had ever been able to claim. I wondered if his power was enough to save Miranda's house.

I looked back up the hill at the cemetery. George and Alma were waiting for me even though we would take different buses. The gravediggers were filling the rest of the hole.

CHAPTER EIGHT

Loss

The house was empty. The kitchen was quiet. The sealed jars were on the counter. The store was closed.

I made a cup of coffee, left it on the counter, and walked through the house.

In the back, my desk was covered in papers that no longer made sense to me.

I sat on the couch and cried. Emperor sat on my lap and purred. He didn't yet know that our world had changed forever. He sat curled in a circle, his tail wrapped around his body and his gray paws by his sweet, brown face.

I heard George let himself in the front door. He stood for a few minutes without moving, absorbing the loss.

He came into the back room and sat on the wooden chair at my desk, across the room from me.

I was in my nightgown and housecoat, my slippers. I stared at him and shook my head. He kept his eyes on the floor, his long body folded. He shook his head in the same pattern as I did. Back and forth, chin drooping downwards in exhaustion, and then some thought of Miranda would make it start again. Back and forth.

We hardly spoke. George came every day during his regular hours, but we didn't open the store. In the mornings, I mostly sat with the cats on the couch—they were my family. Customers and friends came by in the afternoons. Lida Rosenthal covered the mirrors, even upstairs, and Henrik sat silently in the kitchen each afternoon. Speedy and Lorraine brought a casserole that I never touched. Amos took off his hat and stood in the doorway, saying a silent prayer. David never came.

One morning, I can't remember which, I decided to make scrambled eggs for George and me. It was the only meal I knew how to make.

We dragged ourselves from our seats into the kitchen, which held the fault lines of Miranda's absence. Every corner held a reminder of her. Every countertop recalled her creations, her hard work, and ingenuity. I couldn't imagine working in here without her. I could never again knead dough or seal jars of boozy cherries. I could barely open the smaller fridge without crying, never mind the bigger fridge that she had organized so carefully, her handwriting on the containers of prepped food, marked with labels and dates.

Making breakfast reminded me of her. She made breakfast for me and George once a week, and we always sat at the tiny kitchen table, planning the next seven days. Now, George and I needed to plan the rest of our lives.

He took a loaf of bread out of the bread box and put two slices in the toaster. I pulled the cardboard box of eggs out of the smaller fridge. The bottom of the container was wet, and it sank toward the floor. The eggs followed in slow motion. *Splat. Splat.* I couldn't stop gravity. I could only regret I hadn't seen it coming. Half the eggs on the linoleum floor, the yolks decimated and smeared. I bent to wipe them up with a towel, but it was too much. I fell to my knees and cried.

He didn't say a word. He took the soggy container from my hand and put it on the counter, saving the last six eggs. He handed me the mop and dustpan from our utility closet. I didn't think I could get up, but he nodded at me. He was right—I could do it myself. I filled the dustpan and emptied it into the trash pail. He wiped up the remainder of the gooey mess with a towel, rinsing it in the sink.

I slunk back onto the kitchen floor. He sat down next to me, his knees and elbows a complex puzzle.

"I miss her, too." He closed his eyes.

"I know," I said. "She'd never drop eggs on the floor."

"I've seen her drop some eggs," George said with a smile. His eyes softened at the memory.

He was right. Miranda wasn't perfect. She constantly strove for perfection, but even that was a form of imperfection. I'd never heard her say, *I can't*. Only *I will* or *I can*. She had pushed herself every day until her life and the deli's had no separation. I realized that my life also had become melded with the deli's. Miranda was so motivated, so compelling, that it seemed natural to follow in her wake rather than make waves in any other direction. I didn't say any of that.

Instead, I said, "She wouldn't want to be remembered that way. She knew every inch of this kitchen. She knew how everything worked," I said.

"She was wonderful," he said.

I looked at the still-wet floor and the dustpan slick with egg residue and sighed.

"I don't think I can do the business with you." I hadn't known I was going to say that. My body had decided, and now my brain was catching up.

"What do you mean?"

"It's too hard." I knew I couldn't do it.

"Give yourself time," he said. "We don't know what's going to happen. It might be easier if we move to a new location."

"I don't think so." I didn't think I could ever eat another smoked meat sandwich or deli pickle or bite of coleslaw. I didn't think I could talk to another customer or balance another budget. I couldn't make an order or accept a delivery. Every time I walked through the kitchen, I felt like I was overriding some precious memory of Miranda. I didn't want to write over what was already written on my heart.

The toast popped up. We stayed on the floor.

"What else would you do?" he asked, his arms resting on his knees.

I shook my head. I had no idea. "I need to finish my library degree if I want a job."

He sat with that information.

"How long would it take?"

"I don't know. I have to take an exam and do a project." My voice petered out. It was too much to think about.

Emperor came in through the back door and went to George. George held his hand out, and Emperor rubbed his back against it, and his motor-like purr filled the room.

"I'll help around here," he said. "Packing up the store if it comes to that or re-opening the store here. My mom and I have to pack up our house as well."

"Have you found a place to move?"

"Not yet, but my mom's looking." George's house was slated for demolition, just like Miranda's. It was at the other end of what would soon become my father's park.

"Last time we moved," he said, "it was harder because my brother was angry about it. Then, when we finally moved, he was gone, and then our dad died, and I was grieving, I guess." He kept his eyes on his long fingers in front of him, like he was holding a book that held all the words.

"That's how I feel about my sister," I said. "I've lost Miranda and my sister in one fell swoop. It's exponential grief."

"And your father," he said.

I nodded. I hadn't even drawn him into the equation.

"I wrote to my brother so many times," he said, both of us thinking of our own troubles. "And he never wrote back. I don't know if he thinks of me as his brother anymore."

"I'm sure he does," I said. "Did you have the right address? Maybe he never got your letters."

"I don't know. I eventually stopped writing. I think he wrote some telegrams to my mom, but she won't talk about it. I don't know what happened. I thought he was going to stay." George's eyes filled with tears.

"He came for a visit?"

"This was when I was young. He was home on leave, and he told me all about Germany. Even when the Allied occupation ended, he was stationed in Berlin, part of the Cold War defense. Before the Berlin Wall went up."

"He liked being in Germany?" I couldn't imagine living there after the atrocities that had been committed. How could he like it when a belief in the superiority of the Aryan race had shaped their civic culture for so long?

"He said it was, in many ways, better than the United States." George caught my eye, unsure if I would believe him. "There wasn't any segregation, and everyone was trying to move past the racism that allowed the Holocaust to happen."

"But it couldn't have been better." I thought back to the movies about World War II. So much hatred and destruction. How could that be better?

"In Germany, my brother could go into any store and drink from any water fountain. His uniform made him an American first in their eyes. And the Germans loved that he gave them cigarettes and chewing gum. The white soldiers didn't love it, but segregation was illegal in the Armed Forces."

"It was?" I asked.

"They outlawed segregation in the Army before he even signed up. In the late 1940s. Ells showed me this one poem by Gwendolyn Brooks—'the white troops had their orders but the Negroes looked like men.'"

"I don't know it."

"It's from the 1940s. It's about white troops who are trained to discriminate against the Black troops, but when the Black men arrive, they look like men, of course, and the idea of discrimination seems ridiculous. 'Who really gives two figs?' was one of the lines. It's probably true. Given life or death, what difference did it make what color someone's skin was? That's what Ells wanted for us here."

"So he helped get rid of racial discrimination in Germany and worked in a desegregated Army, but he still faced racism at home?"

"He did."

"But he was still coming home to stay?"

"He was supposed to." George pet Emperor again, and then Empress put her paws on George's knee. He lowered his legs, putting them straight out on the floor, and she curled into his lap.

"Something happened," George said. "He left all of a sudden, and he told us to leave, too. He said he couldn't live in America anymore. He wanted us to move to Germany."

"Did you think about it?"

"I was too young, and my mother said she had moved enough. She thought Ells would come to his senses. He left me a letter." George unfolded himself to pull his wallet from his pocket, and from among his dollar bills, he pulled out a folded letter, soft with age. He read it to me.

Dear Georgy, I'm sorry that I have to leave. I know this is sudden, but I need you to listen

carefully. There's nothing but trouble and heart-
ache for us here. I want you to join me in Germany
as soon as you can. It's different there—not perfect, but better than what we've got. I need you to
convince Mama to let you come. I know it won't be
easy—you know how she is once she's made up her
mind. But you've got to try. Tell her she can run her
own business—there's a lot of missing buttons she
can sew on. Don't tell her I said that. And you can
do whatever you want. Stay strong, keep your head
up, and watch your back. Be smart about yourself,
whatever happens. Love, Ells

"But he never wrote again? He never came back?" My heart
broke for George. My troubles with my sister were heart-
wrenching, but at least I knew where she was.

"I never heard from him again," George said. "When our dad
died, Ells didn't even come to the funeral."

"For his own father?"

"He was our dad, not our biological father. We had different
dads, but still, Cyrus raised us for years. Gave us everything."

I thought about what he was saying, the rifts that he had en-
dured, losing his father and his stepfather, and his brother. The
worst part is that he didn't know what had happened. I sat with
his words and shook my head.

"Miranda had the best dad," I said. "I wish I had known him."

George nodded and pet both cats, one with each hand. The
cats loved George not just for the scraps he sometimes gave
them but because of his quiet presence, his calm nature.

"Miranda's dad taught her to dance," I said. "My dad never
taught me to dance."

"Cyrus taught me some moves," George said with a smile.

We sat in silence for a few minutes. It didn't feel
uncomfortable.

"My dad used to take me and Ells to work with him. He let us feel important, handing us a hammer or asking us to bring him a selection of nails. Some days, we got to hold his toolbelt or even carry two-by-fours from his truck. It was mostly Ells who got to do that." He sighed.

I exhaled through my nose, the closest I could get to a laugh.

That's the thing about grief; it overrides other concerns. It breaks down barriers. George and I were probably the only Black man and white woman sitting on the floor of a Jewish deli in the whole city of Carthage. Probably in all of New York. And if it wasn't happening anywhere in New York, I imagined it wasn't happening anywhere at all.

We talked about our families. We shared the burden of being children of overbearing parents. We had both kept our adult selves hidden from our parents. We had both hidden our true selves.

"My mom never wanted me to work here," he told me.

"No?"

"She wanted me to work with her as a tailor." He laughed.

"Not the same as being a carpenter with your dad?"

"No," he said. "Not the same as doing this." He gestured to the kitchen. "This is what I really want to do."

I asked him about Alma, and he shook his head.

"I'm going to tell my mom about her after we get the deli figured out."

I nodded. We sat together thinking about our uncertain futures.

"Thanks for cleaning up the eggs," I said. "I lost it for a moment back there."

"If it hadn't been you, it might've been me," he said.

George placed Empress to the side and got up. He made the scrambled eggs, and I watched the way he handled the frying pan, the oil, and the second frying pan as a lid. He had a flair for cooking. He buttered the toast and handed me a steaming plate of eggs, perfectly scrambled. I balanced it on my knees. Those eggs were the first bite of food that tasted good to me since Miranda had died. I had subsisted on crackers and coffee.

I had come into the kitchen to make him breakfast, and here I was sitting on the floor. I got up and set the table. I wasn't helpless. I didn't need to have people take care of me all the time. I had some agency—I just had to remember to use it.

"I think the business should be yours," I said as I took my seat.

"I would like that," he said, "if the rabbi agrees."

"I don't think we ask for permission," I said. "We just move forward as if it's inevitable."

"I don't know," he said.

The kitchen's empty chair couldn't be ignored. I got up and poured a cup of coffee for Miranda. It felt better to include her. I could picture her there. I wanted to give her everything, but I could only give her what I had. George and I grimaced and smiled and sighed and fell back into silence.

After breakfast, I washed the dishes, stalling. I didn't want to face the refrigerators.

But it had to be done. I opened the larger of the two refrigerators. Some of the produce was going bad. Miranda would have been horrified. I threw away the parsley and lettuce. I picked through the bag of spinach, taking out the slimy bits.

George took the cucumbers and made a batch of pickles. He took Miranda's big book of recipes and laid it on the counter. The handwriting started with Alexsander's and ended with Miranda's. It was a treasure trove of recipes and tips. Her story was contained in that book of recipes, but it wasn't enough.

No one would see that book but George.

I wanted to publish an obituary for her. I wiped my hands on my clothes without thinking and picked up *The Yellow Pages*. I found a number for *The New York Times*. After getting connected to the right department, I asked for the price. The price per line was more than we paid for butter each week, and I wanted more than one line. I couldn't fit Miranda into one line. It would cost hundreds of dollars I didn't have.

I hung up the phone, a bitter feeling in my gut. I hated not having money. I needed a job.

*   *   *

After seven days of sitting shiva as best we could and cleaning out the kitchen as best we ever had, I took the bus to the library. The sun shone too brightly through the windows. I shaded my eyes with my hand.

The library wasn't open yet. It made me want to cry. I didn't want to sit on the cold concrete steps, so I stood in a patch of sun and rubbed my gloved hands together. My breath came out like smoke.

"Dear child, I thought you were a homeless person. I was about to call city services." Mrs. Caravaggio found me in my patch of light and pulled me into her arms. "What is it?" she asked.

"Miranda died," I said.

"I'm sorry," she said. "She was so young."

I nodded, and my face crumbled. Mrs. Caravaggio took me in her arms, and I wept.

"I know how much she meant to you."

Mrs. Caravaggio did not, in fact, know how much Miranda meant to me. I hadn't shared the nature of our relationship with anyone. Only David and his friend Roger knew. Now, George and Alma. I could never bring myself to tell anyone else because I didn't know if they could be trusted. Mrs. Caravaggio was a nice woman, an important mentor and friend to me, but she was religious, and I didn't know how my life would fit into her ideas about the world—better to keep quiet.

"Let's get you inside." Mrs. Caravaggio unlocked the front door, turned on the lights, and motioned for me to sit in one of the chairs in the lobby. When she came back from the bathroom with a wet paper towel, she washed my face and handed me a brush from her purse.

I blushed. I had left the house without grooming myself. It wasn't the first time. I wondered if she had a toothbrush in that big purse of hers. She probably had a Dopp kit filled with accouterments to keep her face fresh and her hair aloft. Her hair was a helmet of solid perfection, while mine was a scraggly mess. I couldn't even get the brush through the back of it.

"What can I do for you?" she asked, sitting in the chair next to mine.

"I want to read a book by Jane Jacobs."

"Well, you're in luck. We have her book. You know, I met her one day."

"In Carthage?"

"No, I met her in New York City."

"Greenwich Village?" I said, still struggling with a snarl in my hair—the brush and I were trying our best. I had heard about Jacobs's long love affair with Greenwich Village, her ingenious plans to protect it from Robert Moses and his invasive highways.

"Yes, I went down there to see what all the fuss was about. I had seen all the destruction our own highway caused."

"Were you at the protest?"

"The Sycamore Street March? No, I wasn't, but I wish I had been. I think anyone who went to that was well informed and forward-thinking."

"I wish we had had a Jane Jacobs in our corner back then."

"Indeed. But it still can help to read her book. I'll bring it down."

We sat in silence for a couple of minutes.

"What else?" she asked.

"Well, I want to finish my degree," I said. "I need to finish it."

"I've been waiting for over a decade for you to say this," she said with a big smile. "You are already a librarian in the ways that matter. You have the skills. You've taken the classes."

"I need the degree," I said, nodding but not responding to her compliments. I had a hard time taking a compliment—they never had a class on that in school.

"I'll teach you anything you need for the exam, and I think we already know what your final project will be on."

I tilted my head to the side.

"Come with me." She took the brush from me and tucked it in her purse.

First, she brought me upstairs to get Jane Jacob's book *The Death and Life of Great American Cities*. Then, she brought me into the basement archives, where they kept property records and local history. Gray boxes were labeled and stored on metal racks. Mrs. Caravaggio checked the card catalog and then disappeared into the stacks.

She came back with two hard-sided boxes. One had letters stacked neatly from end to end. The other had cassette tapes. I looked at the labels. *O'Shea family, December 13, 1958. Ryan family, January 4, 1959. Walsh family, January 13, 1959.* There were at least ten cassettes.

"Do you know what these are?" she asked.

"Irish families from the local farms?"

"Yes, some of them related to the people buried in your great-grandfather's backyard."

I raised my eyebrows.

"The letters were gathered after the bodies were found. The families had kept them from the turn of the century. I haven't read them all, but the families donated them to the public record.

I've read the one from your great-grandfather to the family of the girl."

"One of the bodies was just a girl?"

"Well, she was nineteen or so. I think of her as a girl."

"And I can borrow these?"

"You have to read them here, but you can come as often as you'd like. I bet you'll have a final project in a month or two. Start with the letters. Then, transcribe the tapes."

I nodded. I hadn't expected to start right away, but nothing was waiting for me back at the deli until we knew if the building was going to be razed, and I was curious about what my great-grandfather had said to the families—and what the families had said to each other.

* * *

Every morning for the next week, George and I met in the kitchen for coffee, and then I headed to the library while he organized the deli. He organized the recipes, checked local sources for better prices, updated the menus, and cleaned the nooks and crannies of the kitchen. He pulled out the appliances and cleaned behind the stoves. I was glad not to be part of washing Miranda away, but I knew it had to be done whether we opened the deli here or not.

George sat at the small table. He had already made scrambled eggs for the two of us and poured three cups of coffee.

"What's on the agenda today?" I asked him.

"I'm meeting with the rabbi again. He wants to go over the kosher rules one more time. You know, he never asked about the contract, so I think he's okay with us taking over the deli."

"With you taking over the deli," I reminded him. "We'll still write up the contract in case you need it someday."

The phone rang. George answered it.

"Uh huh… We don't know… I'll tell her."

He sat down and looked at me. "That was Mr. Neubauer," he said.
I nodded.

"He says there's a special meeting of the Historical Society to-night at 6."

I shook my head—back and forth.

* * *

I didn't plan to go to the meeting. But I took the bus, and my feet took me to the ornate Victorian front porch and toward the open doors like an automaton. The crowd was markedly different from last time—not as many fur coats. The people were jocular. The men grabbed each other by the shoulders. The women at the top of the stairs yelled to their friends at the bottom. The noise was jarring.

Two men in the doorway talked about the day's news. "Watergate's the gift that keeps on giving." One of them laughed. A special committee was appointed to investigate the Watergate break-in. They were pleased the trial wasn't over. I thought the new committee would be as useless as the old. They weren't going to find anything unless they wanted to.

On the stairs, I saw the stooped, thin body of Henrik Neubauer. He wore a coarse wool coat and held onto the hand-rail like a life raft. I tapped him on the shoulder.

"Mr. Neubauer."

"Call me Henrik," he said. "I'm glad you're here." He craned his neck and then held me in an awkward hug. As we pulled apart, he held both my hands in one of his.

We let the crowd eddy around us.

His posture looked painful. I could almost feel the twinging of his joints and muscles.

"So many people," I said.

"Better turnout than at our Shabbat services," Henrik said with a small smile.

Rabbi Baum came up behind us. He nodded to me—I'm not sure he remembered my name. He put his hand on Henrik's back.

"You organized all this?" he asked. "It will be hard to vote against this crowd."

Henrik smiled. "We have the home-field advantage." His dry cough served as punctuation.

"I've got the first part ready to go," Rabbi Baum said. He and Henrik sounded confident—like they had the power to persuade the Historical Society. But I knew better. There was no logical argument that would convince Ginny to save Miranda's house and what was left of Old Ward Thirteen. She hadn't chosen that location for logical reasons; it was personal. Ginny and Joseph were punishing me for speaking out against them publicly, and if I knew my sister at all, I knew she could dig in her heels in stubbornness.

Henrik nodded and turned his attention to climbing the stairs. One step at a time. At the top, he and the rabbi got swept up in the crowd. I took off my coat and waited in line at the coat check. There wasn't anyone to hold my coat or save me a seat or tell me there was pot pie waiting at home. I held my mouth in a tight line and willed my tears to stay inside.

I stepped out of line and looked into the ballroom. Joseph sat near the dais with his chin held high, his sideburns shaved away. Sarah sat next to him and played with the lace on her dress's bodice. They had been outfitted as part of the performance.

I felt a tap on my shoulder. I turned to see Ginny. Her blue eyes were darkened by the spare lighting outside the ballroom.

"Lucy," she said.

"Ginny," I said.

A sisterly stand-off has no rival. We both could have held our ground without blinking—if we weren't afraid of making a scene.

"Why are you here?" she asked.

"I don't know," I said honestly.

She stared at me. She didn't smile, but her face was still soft and beautiful. Men and women deferred to her because of her face. It suggested innocence and purity. How could you argue with that beautiful face? Right now, her expression might tell others she was deep in thought, focused on the meeting ahead, but to me, her face said she pitied me. She thought I was here only for a moral stance. She thought I was trapped by my ideas of right and wrong. She judged me because I couldn't just take my father's money and keep my mouth shut—I couldn't go along with family lore. I couldn't let them milk the city's funds without exposing them. *Release yourself from your self-inflicted constraints*, she might say to me, *and the world becomes a bigger place*. Like releasing a shark from a cage and suddenly the whole ocean is its playground. Ginny and Joseph had been swimming in that water all their lives.

"You look a mess," she said, shaking her head. "You need to take better care of yourself."

Chairman Doyle hit his gavel and gave a rote call to order. We could hear him over the speakers in the vestibule.

Ginny walked up the aisle toward her place on the dais.

I looked down at my outfit. I wore a man's cardigan sweater over a white button-down shirt. Coffee stains down the front of both. The buttons and buttonholes on the sweater didn't line up. I hadn't thought about what I was wearing.

I slipped into the lady's room and stared in the mirror. I rebuttoned the cardigan to make the sides even. I put my scarf over the stains and ran my fingers through my hair as a comb.

A stereo speaker in the bathroom ceiling crackled. I heard Chairman Doyle getting started. No jokes about Gallagher's—no fawning over the audience.

I realized that I could listen to the whole meeting from the bathroom and not have to face anyone.

There was silence and then the rabbi's voice. "Our Jewish brethren have suffered enough," he said into the microphone. "The people you see sitting in this room are survivors, and we carry the memories of those we have lost." The rabbi went on to give the statistics of the Holocaust, pausing to let the numbers sink in.

"I propose, therefore, that the deli in Old Ward Thirteen, which started with the help of this congregation and was carried on by Alexsander Fein after his heroic escape from the Third Reich's grasp, be saved."

I stood at the sink and nodded. It was a good argument.

"Saved as a museum," he added.

I wondered if the committee was surprised by this, or if this was the plan. Did Henrik feed them this idea? I had suggested it, but I wasn't sure if I wanted it anymore.

"The deli can move into the commercial strip near the university," the rabbi said. "We have secured a location. And the current deli, which was the home of Alexsander Fein for the entirety of his time in Carthage, can be transformed into a museum, helping future generations understand the plight of refugees."

I could see the brilliance of the plan. The committee wasn't going to vote to keep a deli open and a place for me to live above it, but they might save the Fein house for historical purposes.

"Would this museum sit on the same land as the approved park for Herbert Wilson?" the chairman asked the rabbi.

Of course not, I thought. They would have to move the park elsewhere in the city.

"Yes," the rabbi said.

Yes? I let out a grunt of frustration. How could a museum to honor Alexsander Fein be set in a park to honor my father? My father had kept the members of what was called "Jewtown" in a veritable slum for decades and then delivered the final blow when he tore down the original Fein Foods deli. He had torn down Miranda's livelihood and her father's legacy, and now they wanted his park to contain a memorial to that same history? I pictured a statue of Miranda's father at the opposite end of the park as my father's—glaring at each other in perpetuity.

I held onto the sink and tried to breathe. In a dream I had the night before, I was sitting in a classroom in the women's college with rows of wooden desks and metal chairs. Miranda was in front of me, her red hair flowing down her back, more hair than she had in real life. She turned, but her hair blocked her face. No matter how hard I tried to see her, I could only see her hair. Then I saw a small, folded note on my desk. I knew it was from her. I opened it but couldn't read it. And then she was gone. I couldn't shake the feeling that if I had tried a little harder, I could have seen her.

Ginny's voice came through the speaker. "I oppose that decision," she said. "Having both attractions would water down the purpose of the park. The museum can be recreated elsewhere in the city."

"I concur," Chairman Doyle said.

The rabbi continued, "The house itself is part of the legacy. Our congregants have long-standing memories of the original deli and of the house across the street, which Mr. Fein's daughter continued as a deli in his memory."

"The house could be moved," Ginny said.

The bathroom door started to open—someone was coming inside. I rushed into one of the two stalls and sat on the toilet, my coat folded over my knees, my heart pounding.

"This particular house cannot be moved," the rabbi said. "The space itself is part of the legacy."

I remembered Miranda's plea to me to keep the house for her father. She didn't want the clapboard dismantled, the floorboards ripped out. She didn't want the home to be moved. Her father's spirit was housed there.

"I plead with you," the rabbi said, "in the name of history and in honor of the Jewish contributions to this city, to consider our proposal to leave the house where it is as a museum of the Jewish refugee experience."

The woman used the toilet in the adjacent stall and left without washing her hands.

I had missed the end of the rabbi's speech and didn't know what the long pause was for.

Then, I heard Henrik's voice. "I offer you a Talmudic saying: 'He who saves a single life—it is as if he had saved the world.' Let that phrase be understood in three ways," he said. "First, Alexsander Fein saved the life of his daughter when he made it to the *USS Henry Gibbins*. I was on that ship with Alexsander and his daughter Miranda." He coughed.

"The second understanding of the phrase is how we see the shelter New York offered us. The *USS Henry Gibbins* was the only ship of refugees in the entirety of the Holocaust to make it to the shores of the United States and not have its passengers turned away. The first ship came to Florida in 1939, and the passengers were sent back, many of them taken to death camps. The second ship came to New York in 1944, and you let us in. We are forever grateful to the state of New York, to the city of Oswego, where we were housed, and ultimately to the city of Carthage, where many of us were welcomed and allowed to thrive. You saved our lives. This museum would be a testament to your generosity."

I could see Henrik's plan of highlighting self-interest. If the committee helped him, they'd be helping themselves. People weren't motivated by shame and guilt. They were motivated by hope and if not hope, then fear, the two sides of self-interest. I wondered why I hadn't learned this technique earlier. What if, so many years ago, I had come into my father's bank meeting with this strategy? What if I hadn't attacked them? What if I had appealed to their self-interest to make them use the money for charity? I could have told them about tax breaks, accolades, and the sound sleep of the philanthropist. I would still have that money today. I could have updated Miranda's business years ago. I would have my choice of places to live today. I'd still be close with Ginny—Miranda might even be alive.

"This phrase," Henry continued, "does not refer only to Alexsander or the state of New York, but it is appropriate for Freya Hoffman, as well."

My coat slithered to the floor. I wasn't expecting Freya to be a part of the story. I pulled my cigarettes out of my purse and lit one, shoving my matches back into my purse's interior pocket.

"Freya Hoffman," Henrik said, "embodies the third understanding of this Talmudic phrase. She saved my life, and this should be remembered." He paused. "This is the woman who gave me the papers and money to escape from Germany to Italy. Without her, I wouldn't have been on the *USS Henry Gibbins*. I would never have escaped the Third Reich."

I held my breath. I couldn't imagine what she was feeling.

"Miss Hoffman may not remember me because we never met, but the papers came from her bank in Berlin, and I have it on good information she was the one who created them. I don't know how her other applicants fared, but she saved a single life and for this she has saved the world."

Freya had never spoken of this, not to me. She had never asked for any recognition. I remembered going with Freya to the movies, twice even seeing movies about the Holocaust with her. Nowhere in my memory did I connect her with this terrible history. I never pegged her as a hero.

I was ten or eleven when Freya and I went to our first Holocaust movie—*The Search* with Montgomery Clift came to Carthage, and Freya checked with my father to make sure the movie was appropriate. I already had my jacket, and we stood in our house's front foyer. Ginny sat on the stairs, still in her night-gown. Early on, my sister had been left out of my movie excursions with Freya because she was too young. Then, she didn't want to go with us. She made our father take her to the musicals instead of the dark films Freya picked for me.

Freya told my father it might be upsetting for me because the boy loses his mother in the film. My father had some practical response, something like, "Lucy knows she lost her mother, and she won't be surprised to learn other children have lost theirs as well."

"But then, the boy finds her," Freya said.

My father let that sink in and looked at me. I could imagine what they were thinking: that I would want to find my mother again if the boy was able to find his mother in the movie. But I didn't have any trouble distinguishing fiction from fact. Truth be told, Freya wouldn't be taking me to the movies if there'd been a chance of my mother coming back.

"It's okay," I said. "I want to see it—Miss Hoffman told me it's about the war." The war was over, but I knew about it from school. Freya told me she'd lived in Germany and worked in a bank there. She told me that many of the German bankers were bad men doing bad things and she'd left to start a new life in New York, but I'd never connected it to the Holocaust. To me, the soldiers were the bad men, not the bankers.

That afternoon, we sat in the theater with our popcorn and sodas. The lights dimmed, and the MGM lion roared. Of the movie, I remembered only doe-eyed children speaking foreign languages and tall men and women in uniforms. The protagonist was a Czech boy, and I remembered him running. Throughout the film, he ran. Through rubble, past bomb-torn buildings, into rivers, across fields, always running away from anyone in uniform because of his traumas in the death camps. He ran along a river and threw himself in to avoid being caught. His companion was swept away by the current and died.

Before that movie, to my young mind, the war was only for adults, for people drafted into the army. This movie brought home the vast difference between sending troops to fight in a war and having it fought in your own country. The Jewish people in Europe, when their native countries turned against them, had nowhere to turn. It's one thing to raise an army to fight against a foreign invader, but what happens when your own government is trying to eliminate you? Nowhere is safe at that point.

I admired Henrik for standing up and speaking. He possessed a broad perspective of the world, filled with hope and optimism surpassing my own. Growing up in Carthage had confined my outlook. Despite my extensive reading and my family's few trips to hotels in Europe, my view remained limited. In this narrow scope, my father's significance had magnified, and my sense of isolation had intensified. Until now, I hadn't considered the multitude of people around the world who might offer support.

In the bathroom stall, I pulled my coat back into my lap, folding its arms into a neat pile. I pulled out the metal ashtray from the wall and tapped my cigarette against the small edges. I couldn't stop thinking about Freya on the dais. If she had helped Jewish Germans escape from their country during the Holocaust, she had risked her own life. She could've been sent to the concentration camps or executed. "Nacht und Nebel" was the order from the Third Reich to make sure that citizens didn't help the Jewish population. It threatened them not only with punishment but with the promise they'd disappear into the *nacht* and *nebel*, the German words for "night" and "fog." Their families would never learn what happened to them. In the face of that, I returned to the same question I had from reading *The Diary of a Young Girl* by Anne Frank. Would we help a family in need if it meant sacrificing our own safety? What kind of heroes does the world need to make even the slightest difference? Henrik was right, philosophically, that he who saved one life had saved the world, but on the grand scale of a government trying to eliminate a population, how many heroes would you need? How much bravery is needed to stand up in the face of "Nacht und Nebel"?

Henrik finished his speech and then introduced Jane Jacobs.

I wanted to see her. This woman had stood up to giants and won. I had read her book and learned all the wrong moves Carthage had made during the creation of the highway. They hadn't consulted the people who lived in Ward Thirteen. Of course they hadn't. The residents were actively protesting the highway. They hadn't valued the diversity of the neighborhood. Ward Thirteen had been a bustling mix of Jewish and Black businesses—the highway tore all that down. And they hadn't listened to Jacob's theory that a car-centric city would rip the heart out of the community. We had done it all wrong. What could she possibly say to us now?

"Public land," she started and then stopped to let the word sink in. "You can't make public land decisions with the private land ownership parts of your brains. Public land is for everyone, but if you don't plan it correctly, it will turn into public trouble."

I heard some of the audience members grumbling. I came out of the bathroom stall and stood staring at the stereo speaker in the corner of the ceiling.

"A park without any destination within it will become a meeting place for drug deals and prostitution," Jacobs said.

The crowd roared in disapproval.

"Do you think you don't have drug deals and prostitution in your city? Go to your public parks after dark, and you will be illuminated."

She waited for the room to settle down.

"I have been asked to come here today to speak about the need to keep the Jewish deli in the park, to open it as a part of a museum or an archive. I agree with that need, but I also think the rest of the businesses should be kept on the edge of the park.

And the personal residences. The more variety of uses you can have for that space, the safer it will be. Don't knock down more buildings. Don't think that open space will fill itself with desirable activities. Be smart about it."

I noticed that Jacobs was appealing to their self-interest in a roundabout way, thinking about the success of the park, but she was also berating them, putting them in their place. How did she get to be so confident, I wondered? The answer was clear: her meticulous research and unwavering commitment to truth and integrity. These qualities were the foundation of her steadfast assurance. I wished I could bottle it and bring it home with me.

She finished her allotted time with some statistics and stories from Greenwich Village, trying to inspire Carthage to follow her example.

When she was finished, Chairman Doyle opened the microphone to public comment. There was hardly anything more to say, but some of the audience members added their own memories.

"My family sponsored one of the families from Oswego," a female voice said. She spoke more loudly than she needed to—as if it was her first time using a microphone. "It was the defining moment of my childhood. Those families from Oswego taught us what was important in life. We gave them shelter and food, and in exchange, they gave us a chance to understand life from a new perspective. Carthage needs a place to house this history." She left the microphone before she could finish her last word, but it was understood.

An older male voice took over: "When we decided to start Mr. Fein in a deli," he said, "we raised money quickly, and we compiled the recipes even more quickly. Out of tiny journals and handwritten papers written down from memory or passed from generation to generation, these recipes were our prized possessions. They spoke to the continuity of our families and traditions.

They spoke to the amalgamation of refugees. In Europe, we had nothing in common but our religion, but here, we banded together, eating each other's most prized family foods. Alexsander Fein is the man who brought these recipes to life for us."

I thought about all the food she and I had prepared over the years. Jars of boozy cherries and pickled fish parts. Some of the recipes didn't sell as well as the others, but she always reminded me that the original recipes weren't stocked for profit. They were stocked for community memories.

Another man with a salesman's voice started to talk: "I hate to be crass," he said, "but this proposal will help the city with tax dollars." He reminded the committee where most of the tax dollars came from. He argued that they could get people from the surrounding communities to come into the city to visit the museum and then send them to the deli. Maybe they would visit our shopping district or stay for dinner.

I felt nauseated. A line of sweat sprung along my hairline. Miranda's house was being bartered and sold like a piece of meat in a butcher shop. None of these people had ever lived there. None of these people loved her like I did. I felt divorced from the people in the ballroom—like they were floating away from me—like they were gathering forces to lock me out.

I tried to take a full breath and talk myself into breathing normally. *In through my nose. Out through my mouth.* I couldn't get the air to go into my lungs, not far enough to feel it at the back of my throat. My petty sibling voice rang in my head. Ginny would benefit from this deal. Her park would have an attraction to draw the public to its grounds; she would get city funds to maintain the park. She'd still be able to evict me from the house. I'd already lost my family home, and now they were conspiring to remove me from Miranda's home. I would lose the roof over my head, my refrigerator, and my bed. I had no skills to offer beyond filling out forms.

My brain spun out the possibilities of my demise. I counted to ten and then backward to one. I tried to access Scout's front porch or Francie's fire escape, but I couldn't concentrate. I held onto the toilet paper dispenser and imagined Miranda's voice. Smooth and calm. *Your body knows how to breathe. Let it do its job. You don't need a big breath. Small breaths for now. Each one counts.*

When I saw Ginny in the vestibule before the meeting began, her face told me she was sorry that I had chosen to lose my inheritance; she was sorry that I had chosen to stay single; she was sorry that I resented her easy path through life. It's the same look she gave me after I went to the Sycamore Street March while she sealed the deal of her marriage to Joseph. She stayed home even though she was the reason we were invited. I'd never forget how Ginny looked at me that day.

* * *

I'd spent the night at Miranda's house after the Sycamore Street March in 1958—no one in my family knew where I was.

I took a bus back to Hiawatha Heights. It was not a triumphant return. My seersucker dress was creased and stained—it smelled like I'd worked a double shift in a factory. The backs of my stockings had torn, and my bare heels squeaked in my stiff shoes. I walked gingerly from the bus stop to my house. Each property seemed longer than it had ever looked from the back seat of my father's car. From our neighbors' windows, I must've looked like a fallen daughter back from a night of revelry.

I had timed my visit to arrive after my father left for work. I wanted to get some clothes, books, and maybe the big electric fan out of the garage. That would get me through the week. I could help Miranda move the deli and then study for my final library certificate. I might be able to apply for librarian jobs by Thanksgiving.

I let myself in with the key that I kept in a zippered pouch in my purse. The front foyer was quiet, and the inner foyer was dark.

I tried not to look at the family portraits, but they beckoned me. My mother and father in separate frames, quarter turned poses toward each other, their eyes straight forward. My father's torso was wide, making his head look small. His pale face was lined with a short mustache. His face looked serene and intellectual: a thinker, not a fighter.

"Is that you, Lucy?" Ginny yelled from the kitchen. She came through the dining room wiping her hands on an apron—it must have belonged to our old housekeeper. I'd never seen Ginny wear an apron—I'd never worn one myself.

"Give me a hug," she said. "I thought you'd never come home." She sounded brisk and businesslike. This was not the Ginny I knew. Her mornings were usually filled with long cups of coffee and languid decisions about what to wear to the club that night. She was seventeen and vain and had an allowance from Daddy. What else was she going to do with her summer?

"Oh, Lucy," she admonished me, "you need a bath." She said it like it was a precondition for our conversation. "Why are you always such a mess? Did you brush your hair?"

I burst into tears. Wasn't she even going to ask what had happened? Where I'd been? For all she knew, I'd spent the night in the hoosegow.

"Why didn't you come with me yesterday?" I asked her.

"I'm glad I didn't," she said, holding my eye to see if I was joking. "I heard it got violent."

"It was Daddy who was violent."

"What are you talking about? He told me what happened."

"He told you about the man?"

"Daddy was trying to protect me. He didn't do anything to that man."

"You knew about it? Why didn't you come find me?"

"I knew you could take care of yourself." She patted my head, like I was the younger sister suddenly. She had her hair curled at the bottom and sprayed. She had rouge on. It was 10 a.m. and she was dressed like she was going to the club for dinner.

"I bet it's in the paper," I said. "I'll show you." They were taking photographs when the man in the Army uniform was taken away. I pushed past Ginny into the dining room and folded *The Carthage Register* back to its front page. Without thinking, I sank into the chair at the head of the table, where my father had taught me to read the paper beyond the headlines.

The good news was that there wasn't a photo of me. Thank God. The bad news was that there was hardly any coverage at all—nothing to show Ginny how brutal our father had been. There was a minor headline: "The Highway Marches On."

> Yesterday, at 10 a.m., Ward Thirteen residents protested the proposed highway project. They claimed they were not informed of the proposed route and were not adequately compensated for their evictions. Several dozen people showed up, but their efforts fizzled once the police chief asked to see a permit. Officers urged people to move along and arrested those who refused to comply. Mayor Sulliman claims that the residents were part of the decision-making process and they will benefit from the Empire Stateway as much as other residents.

The New York Times didn't cover the protest, not that I thought they would. And *The Wall Street Journal* didn't even recognize a possible downside to construction. "Build, build, build" was their mantra.

Ginny had walked away as soon as I opened the paper.

"He put a red 'X' on Miranda's deli," I yelled into the kitchen.

"Who's Miranda?" she yelled back.

"She's my friend from the library program," I said, pushing open the swinging door between the kitchen and dining room. "They saw me sitting outside her deli, and the next thing I knew, they were marking it for demolition. I swear, it was less than an hour later."

"Lucy, you sitting there didn't make them decide to demolish a building. They're knocking down that whole area."

"They put the 'X' there while I was sitting there. All the other buildings have been marked for months. It's not even in the right block. It's near 22nd."

"It's a coincidence. You're tired. Sit, sit, sit." Ginny pointed to the chairs where we sat when we were children. "I'll make you a snack."

I wiped my nose. "They're knocking down the Fremont."

"They'll build another one."

I was not accustomed to Ginny having answers. That was my job. From the time our mother died when Ginny was two years old, I'd been the secondary answer-giver. Our father gave answers about where we went to school and what we were having for dinner, but I was the appointed answer-giver for everything to do with the house, backyard, books in our playroom, and eventually about the mysteries and vagaries of human society. I helped her write her school papers, and I showed her around the women's college when she got accepted. She was supposed to start in the fall—until she decided to marry Joseph Tower. She had turned her whole life upside down in less than a week.

Ginny handed me a plate with crackers and a dollop of raspberry jam, our favorite childhood snack. We used to compete to see who could evenly parse out their jam, giving the same amount to every cracker. Of course, despite the rules of the game, we could always go back for more jam if we had miscalculated. And then, we could go back for more crackers if we had overcompensated on the jam.

One time when we were little, our housekeeper Mary was putting a roast in the oven, muttering about gravy recipes and types of potatoes. Ginny and I sat at the kitchen table with our plates of crackers. Mary wanted us to be quiet so she could concentrate. Our father was due home in an hour. He was bringing a dinner guest, someone from the city council or maybe from the bank. Ginny opened her mouth to show me her partially chewed crackers. Normally, I would have corrected Ginny's behavior, but there was something about her brazenness—I wanted to see how it felt. I chewed up a cracker, mixing in as much saliva as I could—I caught Ginny's eye—she was watching me. I positioned the clump of goo on my tongue, pulling the bits out of my teeth to congeal it in the middle. Ginny hummed a little tune as she waited for me and looked over at Mary who was setting a timer, her body bent over the oven like she was bowing for the queen. I had the crackers ready for their debut. I knew Ginny was going to get a kick out of it, but right as I went to open my mouth, a wave of hysterical laughter rose from my torso. The thought of it was so funny that I couldn't get it out without spitting the crackers. A big lump landed on my plate and a spray of crumbs flew across the table. Ginny screamed. Mary scolded, cleaned up our crackers without a word and sent us upstairs without our snack.

But now, Ginny and I were older, and we didn't seem to be on the same side.

"There's so much going on that we don't know about," I said, my mouth full of crackers and jam. "You wouldn't have believed it. Daddy showed up with two patrol cars."

"Can't we talk about something else? Daddy wants you to stay for dinner."

"Did he say that?"

"He says he'll forgive you."

"Forgive me? What did I do? Did he tell you what he did to that man?"

"He didn't raise a hand."

"He did," I yelled. I pushed the crackers to the middle of the table. "And then the uniforms jumped into action."

"They let him go. They were giving a show of power."

"You make it sound like a good thing. You should have seen Daddy's face. It was twisted—like he was a different person than he is at home."

"Well, that's impossible," she said. "He's the same person no matter where he goes."

I couldn't even swallow the mouthful I had taken. Where was Ginny getting this confidence, this surety? She sounded like she'd completed finishing school and was demonstrating her conversational skills. It was like talking to a radio host.

"You're not safe here," I said.

"Now, you're off your rocker. There's no safer place than home. Daddy told me to get dinner ready. Mr. Tower is coming. I've started to call him Joe."

"No, Ginny, are you kidding?" I could barely sputter out the words. She was only seventeen. I had been through the whole Mr. Tower, call-me-Joe rigamarole, and it was unbearable. Two years earlier, Daddy had brought Joseph Tower for drinks and asked me to meet them in the parlor. He told me to wear a dress and my mother's pearls. When I got there, Joseph jumped to his feet and took my hand. We had what I thought was a polite conversation about the origins of my name. I sparred good-naturedly with my dad about what it meant to obey the law and what civil disobedience had done for our country. I may have mentioned something about Eleanor Roosevelt being a better statesman than her husband. I held my own admirably. Afterward, Daddy told me that if I married Joseph, I would get the whole estate: the house, the checkbook, everything.

"I'm marrying him," Ginny said.

"You know Daddy offered him to me first?"

"But Joe didn't like the way you talked to Daddy."

"What?"

"He said you were too smart for your own good—an impertinent child."

"I was a child. And you are, too. Seventeen! I'll talk to Daddy for you."

"I want to do this. Joe's a sweet man. I love this house, and I want to be the lady of the manor."

Suddenly, the apron made sense, the confident speaking voice, the assurance she had all the answers. Ginny was joining forces with Daddy and Joseph.

"He's practically Daddy's age."

"He's not," she shook her head. "He's almost ten years younger."

I knew I'd been outgunned. I couldn't compete with a marriage proposal, a paid-off mansion, and the promise of a place in Carthage society. Ginny was putting aside everything I had taught her: the books we'd read together, our priorities. We'd promised that we were both going to finish college because we didn't want to be society ladies. We didn't want to look at roses all day and then sneak gin into our teacups at the clubhouse.

I decided I needed to pack a lot more for Miranda's house. I looked around the kitchen—as if a list of items would materialize. I needed clothes and a pillow. I thought about my mother's pearls.

I went into the inner foyer and picked up the phone while flipping through *The White Pages*. Fein, Fein, Fein—a whole column of Feins. I didn't know Miranda's father's first name, but right after Melvin came Miranda. I stared at the entry. Miranda had her own entry in *The White Pages*. I dialed the number and burst out my request.

"Miranda, can you get a car? Can I stay longer than a week? I'll work for my keep, I promise."

* * *

I shook my head in the bathroom stall. I had tears in my eyes and sweat down my back. But I was breathing. I realized I had missed some of the public comments. Joseph's voice was now being broadcast.

"If this plan for a museum goes forward," he said, "and I'm not sure it should, but either way, all the papers of Mr. Fein and the papers Lucy Wilson has regarding Mr. Wilson, her father, must be turned over for inspection. Their veracity must be determined."

"This is beyond our scope," the chairman said.

"It's not," Joseph said. "You can approve the project with the caveat that the research be verified. If Mr. Fein and Mr. Wilson are going to occupy the same space in our city park, this so-called research must be verified."

I got off the toilet and raced through the vestibule to the ballroom. I entered the room and slipped behind the mass of smoking men at the back. I looked around to see if anyone recognized me.

I thought about the Historical Society pawing through the papers, a shredder nearby. Joseph seemed especially keen. I still hadn't gone through everything Freya had given me. There was a stack of papers left in the folder. And he didn't even know what I'd found in the library archives.

I saw Joseph's back, his well-fitted suit. He turned to smile at the audience members closest to him.

I looked at Freya on the dais. She caught my eye. She gave the smallest shake to her head, back and forth. Almost imperceptible. She was as subtle as a spy in one of the war movies we'd seen together.

Joseph was still speaking, demanding to see the papers—using a conciliatory voice to show how reasonable he was.

I saw my sister nodding along with Joseph's words. She hadn't noticed me at the back of the room. I was baffled that she and

I had been raised in the same household, seen the same world around us, read the same news stories, and met the same people, but somehow, we'd reached such different conclusions about the world. In 1964, six years after our rift at the bank, she invited me to the World's Fair in Flushing. Daddy had given her and Joseph VIP tickets, and she wanted me to go with them. Everything I had read about the fair suggested shady dealings behind the scenes and unfair labor practices. I had read about a park-in where concerned citizens were stopping their cars on the expressway to display their opposition to the fair's discrimination in hiring. Ginny didn't care about any of that. The next day, she could only talk about the kitchens she'd seen and the display of modern cars.

I looked at Sarah sitting near the dais, her eyeglasses left at home so she wouldn't be tempted to wear them. Her understanding of the world was being formed. The more acrimonious this became with Joseph and Ginny, the more I feared they'd stop letting me see Sarah. I wanted to take Sarah back to my house and show her the evidence. I would explain things in words she could understand, let her make her own decisions. In that mansion in Hiawatha Heights, she was never going to get a true picture of the world. I felt like my education didn't begin until the day I left my father's house.

I scanned the audience and finally saw the back of Jane Jacobs's head. She was sitting with Lida Rosenthal and Henrik Neubauer. She was as tiny as Henrik. I was impressed that her strong voice had come from such a small frame. She had her gray hair cut short, and she wore a smart black pant suit.

The chairman summed up the proceedings: "The proposal on the floor is to allow the Sycamore house to stand as a museum to—" He paused. "Alexsander Fein and the Jewish refugees who the city of Carthage welcomed even when most of the world refused them. The proposal specifies the tax benefits and profit sharing from the museum with funds for construction coming from private enterprise. The rest of the buildings on the block will be razed."

I watched Jane Jacobs shake her head and exchange a glance with Mrs. Rosenthal.

I didn't have a copy of the proposal, but I was sure it was beneficial to the city. They'd contribute little, but they would reap the rewards of the museum visitors and the new deli. But without the residential houses and the small businesses, their park would remain vulnerable to troubling uses after dark.

"All those in favor," the chairman bellowed, "say aye."

The majority of the council said aye.

"All those opposed, say nay."

Ginny said nay.

"The proposal carries," the chairman said.

The house would be saved. Miranda's house would be saved. Even if the committee voted out of pure self-interest, there would still be a museum honoring Alexsander Fein. Even though we had won, I felt unmoored. I didn't have a place to live. The council looked generous for saving the house and creating the museum, but they hadn't done anything to save the rest of the neighborhood or move my father's statue. And once again, they had acted in their own interest instead of the city's interest. I didn't know what to feel.

Joseph didn't get his amendment to see the research, and I wondered what had prompted his public request. I wondered what was in that research that made him afraid, made him feel like he and Ginny wouldn't have the whole ocean at their disposal, like the cage was coming down on them.

I needed to see what was in the rest of those papers.

CHAPTER NINE

Protest

I woke before dawn and came downstairs in my housecoat. I saw a faint tinge of light through our back windows. I lit a cigarette, found an ashtray, and cleared my desk. The job application from Abraham and a host of unfinished projects sat frozen in time. My pen was uncapped—my chair askew.

I turned on my lamp and pulled out the overflowing file from Freya. I thought I was done with it, but Freya had shaken her head during the meeting. She held my eye. There was something I needed to find—something she didn't want Joseph to find before me.

Freya was a form-filler like me. She had forged papers for Henrik Neubauer and others. I knew it was cliché, but I pictured her smoking in a cafe. *I'll be the woman with the blue hat. You'll find an envelope on the chair next to mine. Do not speak to me or make eye contact.* It was like finding out your mother was a private investigator or that she had discovered uranium when you were a baby.

Empress jumped in my lap, pushing her head against my hand. She tried to twirl around and give me her tail, but I was too fidgety, and she dropped to the floor and looked at me with disdain. I took out the items I'd clipped together by date and dug into the rest of the unruly papers.

Receipts for lunches at Gallagher's. Memos for changes to bank policies. Country club referral letters. Donations to the sheriff's campaign.

Then, I pulled out a receipt for a telegram. It was sent from Germany but paid for in Carthage. I wondered if this was for Freya's family. They still lived in Germany. Why was she showing me this?

Then, I found post office receipts for air mail packages sent overseas to someone named Ellsworth Gaines. The name sounded vaguely familiar. George's brother was named Ells, but that wasn't the same. George's last name was Pritchard.

Finally, I found a voided receipt for one thousand dollars, with a carbon copy of a check made out to the same Ellsworth Gaines but never cashed.

I put those on the top of the pile, while I puzzled over their significance. Mr. Gaines—Ellsworth Gaines—I didn't know who that was.

I heard George's key in the lock. The bell above the front door jingled. He was early. I buttoned my housecoat but stayed at my desk.

"Lucy?" he said.

"Miss Wilson?" George's mother said.

I raised my eyebrows and bit my lip. I rested my cigarette in the crook of the ashtray and went to the front room. Ida Mae took off her long, heavy coat and handed it to me. I hung it on our coat rack. I wasn't dressed. I hadn't brushed my teeth.

"We don't want to take up too much of your time, but we're here about those papers," Ida Mae said. She was taller than George mostly because of her posture. She elongated her neck and stood erect. George hung his head and slumped his shoulders. He looked like a man who had suffered blows as a child.

"Which papers?" I felt my whole life was one piece of paper after another.

"You mentioned some papers Miranda had signed?" he said. "A contract?"

"Oh," I said. "Now." I paused. "There wasn't actually a contract—" I held his eye. He must have known this.

"I knew it." Ida Mae's eyes blazed at my admission. I felt the weight of her disappointment. Ida Mae was never thrilled George had hitched his wagon to ours. She couldn't see a future in the deli to benefit her son. She believed that we, the white owners, would keep the profits and opportunities for ourselves.

"But we can make a contract," I said, holding out my hands. "Mrs. Pritchard, I've no intention of letting this store go to strangers. Keeping it with me and George was Miranda's wish."

"People can wish things—doesn't mean they come true." Ida Mae's face was stern without her smile.

"We'll make it true. Come back to my desk. We'll do it right now." My mind was full of my father's papers, but the Pritchards had arrived at daybreak to get this contract. I'd promised it to them.

"George is twenty-seven," Ida Mae said. "He needs to have this official, not just one person's word against another's. Especially a white person's word against a colored person's." She looked straight at me. She wasn't holding punches.

I held her eye. I had never heard anyone talk about race so openly—not in front of me. I swallowed and nodded. I thought I might start to feel short of breath, as I often did in tense situations, but my breathing stayed stable. I knew what I was doing was right.

We went back to my desk. I saw the cats dart under the sofa, flattening themselves to nothing. I pulled out a standard contract form and slid it into my typewriter. I rolled the paper to the correct line and put "Fein Foods" and "15 Sycamore Street" in the proper boxes.

"George Pritchard and Lucy Wilson, sole proprietors upon the death of Miranda Fein," I read aloud. There was so much pain around that phrase and so much possibility. A final ending and a new beginning, all tied up in a legal contract. Someone might pull this out of a lawyer's file cabinet in fifty years and have no idea of the emotion behind every word.

But it wasn't right. I pulled it out of the typewriter and slid in a new, blank contract.

"George Pritchard, sole proprietor upon the death of Miranda Fein." I knew it was the right decision. My work in the library was almost done. I didn't want to stay with the deli.

I clicked the typewriter keys, filling in each box carefully with as much official language as I could muster.

"What's this?" George asked. He held up one of the post office receipts from my desk.

"I'm going through my father's papers," I said honestly. I'd rather have said I was doing research for a client or writing a book or making a collage.

"This is my brother," he said.

My fingers stayed on the typewriter, frozen on the home row keys, like I'd been taught in typing class. How could George's brother be in my father's papers? Was his house demolished by my father? Was he one of the people my father had bribed to keep the construction costs down? I thought of how bad this looked, and my cheeks reddened. Anything my father had done with George's brother was not above board. And my dream of keeping my lineage a secret was dissolving before my eyes.

"What do you mean?" I asked.

"What is it you have there?" Ida Mae's Southern accent came out more strongly in times of stress.

"Ellsworth Gaines," George said—like he was trying to process the syllables in a difficult word.

"That was your brother?" I asked. "Not a Pritchard?" Maybe he was wrong. Maybe it was a different person.

I stared at him. He looked injured. My cigarette burned in the ashtray. I could hear the clock tick on the wall.

"He's a Gaines," Ida Mae said.

I looked at her, wanting this to be a misunderstanding. I'd finish the contract, and we'd move past this terrible coincidence.

"He has a different father, different name," she said. "Show me that paper."

I handed her one of the post office receipts. It was for an overseas package, listing both sender and recipient. It had a description of the contents as clothing and personal items.

Ida Mae held it at arm's length, focusing her far-sighted eyes on the small print. "Why was your father sending a package to my Ells in 1958?" She sounded like she was throwing down a gauntlet—like we might come to blows over this.

I wanted to scoop the other receipts into my lap or rip them up. I wanted to know what my father had done with the city's money; I wanted to show my sister, but I didn't want anyone else to know—not like this.

I swallowed my fear and said, "There were three packages." I held up the other receipts. "And a returned check. One thousand dollars."

"Why was your father giving my Ells a thousand dollars?" Ida Mae put one hand on her hip, and I could see the woman who George had told stories about. She wouldn't broker concealment. She'd get her answer through force if necessary. But she used her eyes to threaten me without lifting a hand.

"Ellsworth didn't take it," I said. "He never cashed it." I handed the receipt to her.

"Why was your father paying him?" she asked.

"I don't know," I said. "There must've been a reason."

"1958. Ells was home then," George said. "And then he left. He got into some trouble. He didn't even pack his things." George used his other hand to support the hand with the receipt in it—like it was too heavy to lift.

"What kind of trouble?"

"Trouble with the police," he said.

"He went to jail?"

"A lot of people went to jail with him that day," he said. "He got bailed out, I think."

"We didn't bail him out," Ida Mae said. "Don't put my name on that. I didn't bail him out. I told him not to go to that protest. I told him not to call me from jail."

I knew, after she mentioned the protest, exactly who Ellsworth was. I knew exactly what my father had done to him. But I couldn't let my brain know I knew. The knowledge got stuck somewhere in the back of my mind, and I could only let the conversation wash over me.

"That was part of the problem, Mama," George said, not looking up. "Ells didn't want to come home. You told him he wasn't to set foot in our house."

"We still lost our house, whether he set foot in it or not." Ida Mae had a way of shutting down an argument. It wasn't through logic—it was through weariness. She and George had been cast out of their rented house without so much as a cushion. They got a notice on their door like Miranda did, but they didn't have a house across the street bought and owned. They were thrown out. Shortly after that, Ida Mae lost her husband Cyrus. She had to deal with grief and the hardship of living on one income. Her experiences gave her a gravitas in any argument.

"Mama, it was a bad time," he added carefully. "Ells was doing what he thought was right."

"Against what his Mama said." Ida Mae's voice went up in volume. Her neck strained with her words.

"And we lost him," George said almost in a whisper.

I knew what had happened. All these years, I had kept this secret, and now it was coming out.

"A man came and packed up Ellsworth's clothes." Ida Mae told us about a man, who looked like a lawyer. He came to their house and offered to pack up Ellsworth's things—said Ellsworth had been called back up to the Army and didn't have time to pack. Another man waited in the car.

"My father was the one who did it," I said, looking at the receipts.

"Well, he wasn't paying Ells for being at that march," Ida Mae said.

"The Sycamore Street March," I said. No reason to hide anymore.

"Exactly," George said. "He was handing out flyers."

My jaw went slack, and I had to compose myself. But there was no stopping now. I had to know for sure. "Did he print the flyers?"

"He organized it. After being stationed in Germany, he wanted to change the rules around here. He was fired up. But that night, he never came home. And the next day, he was gone."

"I was there that day," I said. "I saw him." I couldn't believe the man in the Army uniform had been George's brother.

"Everyone called him Gainer," I said.

George nodded.

George's brother was the one the police took away. He was the one my father had attacked—and it was all my fault.

*   *   *

I still lived at home in 1958, but unbeknownst to me on July 12th, I had just slept my last night in my childhood bed. I tried to wake Ginny, but she flung my hand from her shoulder and pulled up her covers.

"Aren't you coming? Ray invited both of us."

"I'm not coming," Ginny said. She rolled onto her side, her eyelet comforter gripped in her fist. "Don't talk to me about Ray."

Typical, I thought. Ginny had the forethought to set her hair in curlers the night before but not to tell me she was skipping the march.

I ran downstairs. I had never been to a protest before and didn't want to be late. In the dining room, Daddy didn't look up from his newspaper. I saw his bent head, brown summer suit, and black tie. His hat was on the table next to his coffee cup. I paused in the foyer, where I could watch him through the squared doorway. I wanted to have a conversation with him and let him know I wasn't going into this lightly. I wasn't going against his bank and the city's plans without careful thought. I'd heard about it. The proposed highway didn't need to go through Ward Thirteen. There was no reason to knock down that neighborhood.

Ginny and I had been to the jazz club, the Fremont, the week before. We didn't tell our father we were going. If he'd thought we might hear even a single strain of improvisation, we would never have gotten out the door. His worst nightmare was that we would mingle with the Black folks of Ward Thirteen. We had told him there was a dance at the university—a bunch of co-eds. He had called us a cab and waited with us in the front foyer.

"You look nice in your dresses. Your mother would be proud," he said. And to me, he said, "Watch out for your sister."

When we got in the cab, I told the cabbie we weren't going to the university. "Take us to the Fremont on Chestnut."

"No," he said. "No can do." He tapped his ash out his open window.

I'd heard about a popular jazz trio from a college friend, a fellow library student. I knew nothing about jazz except the fact that my father would disapprove. I'd been testing my father—choosing the opposite of what he believed just for the thrill of it. I took his assent as a signal for my dissent. Jazz. President. Senator. Protest. Vietnam. His stance was a sign for me to explore the opposite. Funny how we get locked into roles.

"It's okay," I told the cabbie. "We're meeting some friends."

We didn't have any friends there, but the jazz trio included Ray Washington, a big name up from the city.

Ginny and I smoked cigarettes and drank two martinis apiece even though we'd never had a real cocktail before.

Ray Washington cradled his saxophone like a woman and never took his eyes off Ginny. She had a few eyes for him as well.

My eyes were all over the place, watching the smoke float in front of the stage lights, the waitresses in short dresses, the men and women on the dance floor. And the noise! It didn't seem like the building could contain the decibels of sound the place produced.

Before we knew it, the set was over, and canned music had come over the speakers. We looked up to see Ray Washington himself standing at our table. He pulled up a wooden chair and sat with us, lounging back in it like a chaise.

Ray was the one who told us about the protest. "Four eyes," he said, snapping his fingers at a young man with glasses and a button-down shirt. "Give these ladies a flyer." That was Ellsworth Gaines—he hadn't been wearing his Army uniform that night, but he was drumming up marchers for his protest. He was going to save his family home and show his mother that change could happen.

Don't Destroy Ward Thirteen
March for Our Homes
10 a.m.
July 12, 1958

I asked Ray as many questions as I could think of, but I had known from the start I was going to attend. I'd already thought the highway was a bad idea. This march was my chance to turn my talk into action, just like my father had taught me. Even though he and I were on separate sides of this particular issue, we were both on the side of truth and informed citizenry and standing up for what we believed in. Or so I thought.

When we got home that night, Daddy was awake, but we didn't know it at first. He was in his study with the door closed. He must've heard us talking.

"He couldn't take his eyes off you," I said, teasing Ginny. "Maybe he'll be at the march."

"Don't be silly," she said. "I'm sure he kisses lots of ladies."

"Who kisses lots of ladies?" our father asked from the doorway to his study. He came forward like a bullet out of a pistol. "Have you been drinking?"

I hadn't thought to eat a mint.

"And smoking?" He looked at Ginny who had the flyer in her hand.

"What's this?" he asked, taking it.

"They were handing them out," I told him.

"At the college?"

I didn't want to lie, so I didn't answer. I turned the conversation. "I'm going. Ginny is, too. You always said I should stand up for what I believe in." I said, checking his face. But he was still looking at the flyer, and his shoulders were squared like he was protecting his lair.

I ignored the change in his posture, but I shouldn't have.

"This didn't come from the college. Ginny, where were you tonight?"

"Oh Daddy, I'm sorry. We went to a club." Ginny couldn't lie to save her life.

"A club? What kind of club lets a seventeen-year-old in their doors?"

"On Chestnut."

"In Blacktown? And that's where you kissed a man?" he asked.

He smoothed the flyer out on the foyer's table.

"It wasn't anything," I said for her.

He held his lips in the tips of his fingers, a tight bunch. He stared at Ginny until she cried.

"I shouldn't have," she said. "I'm sorry, Daddy."

I rolled my eyes. She didn't have to apologize for kissing someone, but she and our father seemed to accept this as the correct response. I could give Ginny all the ideas in the world, but if she didn't have the wherewithal to embrace them, there was nothing I could do.

"Off to bed, you two," he said. He must have started his plan right then—a good plan because I never saw it coming.

The next day, I left Daddy with his coffee and figured out the bus line. I caught the bus into Ward Thirteen. I sat behind a Black couple, both dressed in what looked like their Sunday best. I purposely sat behind them after all the trouble in the South about the buses. We went right down Erie. Daddy never went down Erie. He went downtown via the university, but it was faster this way. I saw the Fremont from the bus window, looking deflated without its neon lights and line of well-heeled patrons. I saw people walking on the sidewalks and crossing in front of the bus. Some of them carried signs.

Save Our Neighborhood.
Move the Road!
This is Our Home!

I smiled so hard it hurt. I was doing this. I might get arrested. I might get my picture in the paper. I couldn't wait to tell Ginny about the vinyl seats on the bus and the rickety windows that came down only halfway. I scanned the sidewalks. I would tell her if I saw Ray, but he was probably back in Manhattan sleeping off his latest set.

What a different world this was—the same city with a different set of rules. Where I grew up, just blocks away in Hiawatha Heights, the city shut down at 9 p.m. and the only dancing was at the country club with a measured distance between the dancers. Last week, I had seen bodies swaying together so languidly it was hard to tell where one dancer ended and the other began. It was a place worth saving, and Ginny would be proud of me for helping. Where were we going to drink martinis if they tore down Ward Thirteen?

The man in front of me pulled the string to signal a stop, and I realized it was my stop, too. As soon as I stepped off the bus, I saw Miranda, my old classmate. A good omen. She was three years ahead of me in school, my mentor the first year in the library program. She didn't become a librarian when she graduated—I didn't know if they had any Jewish librarians.

"Miranda!" I yelled.

"Lucy? What are you doing here?"

I smiled broadly. "I'm here for the march."

"That's capital! You know I live here?"

"In Ward Thirteen?" I thought all the college girls lived near the college.

"My dad left me his deli—I live across the street from it."

"Is it—"

"It's not set for demolition. It's right on the edge. But my customers, they're losing their homes. That's why we're here."

My mind was officially blown. Miranda ran a deli? She had customers? She wasn't much older than I was and she ran a business and trained to be a librarian? She held a small notebook, and a man behind her held a camera with a detached flashbulb.

"This is David," she said. He was a short, compact, young man with eyes only for Miranda. "We're covering the march today." David gave a little wave above his camera.

"Maybe I'll get my picture in the paper. Make sure you get my good side," I said, sticking my hip out in an awkward pose. Ginny would have been better at posing.

Miranda and David went down the street to talk to the organizers. I tried to look like I belonged. There were a few white men from the college and an older white couple, but Miranda and I appeared to be the only young white women. I had worn a fitted seersucker dress that was too tight under my arms. I could feel the sweat dripping down.

Out of nowhere, I saw my father's car approach the edge of the demonstration and park at an angry angle, ignoring the parking lines. Two police patrol cars pulled up behind him and another black car. Men poured from the flung open doors.

My father was at the breakfast table a few minutes ago. How did he materialize here so quickly? And where did he get this backup?

Police officers joined my father as they pressed their way through the crowd. Police Chief Arnold Manley, who had been to dinner at our house several times, stood by his cruiser in the background. He was tall and stocky, a former football player. He and my father had gone to high school together. His wide head supported an even wider hat—a shiny brim and a large insignia above his forehead.

Someone was speaking through a megaphone a block away, and people were starting to chant. The demonstrators pointed at the approaching men, but my father pointed at me. My chest tightened even as I told myself I'd done nothing wrong. I'd explained this to him—he knew why I was here.

I felt the demonstrators gather near me. I saw the man from the Fremont with his stacks of flyers. He was wearing an Army uniform, khaki pants and a khaki button-down shirt, double pockets on his chest. I saw Miranda with her photographer friend. I saw a colored woman with her hair in a perfect bouffant—she wore heels and pantyhose. Behind them, the crowd swelled, and the man with the megaphone shouted, "March for our homes. March for our lives."

"Where is he?" my father yelled at me. He stood three feet from me, creating a stand-off that drew more and more notice from the crowd. His eyes told me he would not back down.

My face burned. I stared at him, but my mouth didn't come close to opening.

"Where is he?" he repeated in a tone he only used when Ginny and I were in the worst sort of trouble.

I honestly had no idea who he was talking about. I'd come alone, of my own volition. I was standing by myself. No one had forced me to come.

My father scanned the demonstrators and then pointed at the man from the Fremont, a young Black man with glasses and a military spine holding a cardboard box filled with flyers.

"Is that him?" my father asked.

I couldn't grasp his question. Before I could answer, he gave a little flick of his fingers, and the police officers advanced. They grabbed the man's arms and wrenched them behind his back. His flyers fell to the sidewalk and spread like a straight-edged fan.

"You can't arrest him," one of the organizers said. "What has he done? This man has served in the U.S. military." The crowd echoed their endorsements.

"This is a peaceful demonstration," Ellsworth said, struggling to arrange his shoulders. "I am within my rights." He seemed to be saying it like a litany that would not get any results, words for the record in case anyone was keeping a record.

But my father wasn't interested. He lunged at Ellsworth, grabbing his throat. Ellsworth stepped back and stumbled, slipping on the flyers spread at his feet. The police still held his arms. The crowd receded and then pressed back toward them. Police officers held their batons across their bodies to push back the crowd.

My father put his leg between Ellsworth's legs and tripped him to the ground. He held his neck, pushing the back of Ellsworth's head into the concrete.

The two police officers holding Ellsworth pulled his elbows to make him stand up and handcuffed him. Their faces were drenched in sweat. They brought him over to stand in front of me.

I looked at Chief Manley, who was looking down at his shoes. His thick neck had turned red, but he did not stop my father.

"Is this him?" my father asked me for the last time.

I didn't understand. Was he the man who had given me a flyer? Yes, but I wasn't going to say yes. Not with those batons aloft. Tears sprang in my eyes. What did my father want me to say? I looked at the crowd of people, the demonstrators, and then back at my father. I opened my mouth, but no words came out. One of the great failures of my life.

"I've never seen this girl before in my life," Ellsworth said, his voice raising, his feet pushing against the pavement. The officers jostled him, and his glasses fell to the sidewalk.

"You're a liar," my father said, a hatred in his voice I had never heard before. He advanced at him from the side. Ellsworth turned toward him, and my father pushed Ellsworth's chest. Two police officers held Ellsworth from behind, stretching his Army uniform sleeves.

My father reached out and tore Ellsworth's dog tags from his neck. The silver chain snapped, and my father held the tags in his hand. He looked at the name and then shoved the tags into his pocket. He stole them.

"Did you see my other daughter?" my father asked him.

Ellsworth shook his head but held my father's eye.

"This will help you remember," my father said, and he punched him—drew back his arm and punched him on the side of his face. Ellsworth was handcuffed and held by two officers, and my father attacked him. I felt something tear inside of me. I had never seen violence up close beyond a few scuffles in my high school. Even then, I was never a part of the crowd pressing in to see the fights. I skirted the conflicts and walked toward the perimeter of the school, neatly avoiding involvement. But now this was my father, and Ellsworth was restrained. It was like seeing my father attack a child, someone defenseless. I felt nauseated.

But then, Ellsworth leaned back toward the police officers, gained some slack in their hold, and lunged at my father. He threw his forehead at my father's face and made contact. My father spun backward and held his face. Blood came from his nose. He staggered away from the crowd. The demonstrators stared at my father. They leaned from side to side to get a better look.

Chief Manley went up to my father to check his wounds, and then he signaled his officers to wrap it up. A paddy wagon arrived as if summoned from the chief's mind and they started making their arrests.

The officers dragged Ellsworth in the opposite direction from the paddy wagon—into one of the patrol cars. As soon as he sat down on the edge of the back seat, a short, young officer smashed Ellsworth's leg with a baton. I could hear it hit his bone, a noise I would never forget.

David snapped photographs, deftly replacing the flash after each shot. Then, he turned the camera toward me and I ran.

*   *   *

Sitting at my desk in my nightgown and housecoat, I shook my head. I could feel the adrenaline from so many years ago. I could feel the heat of the day, the sound of the baton, the sight of my father's image crumbling before me. I had always thought if Ginny had come with me that day, we would have been on the same page going forward. If she had seen what happened, she would have known our father the way I did.

I sat with my elbows on my desk, both hands holding my head, my forehead heavy on the heels of my hands.

George sifted through the other papers on my desk and pulled out a typed letter on letterhead from a law firm. It was addressed to my father and referenced a pending case.

George read it aloud. "Dear Mr. Wilson, in response to your inquiry about liability for a protestor's injuries, we are pleased to inform you that the police report does not implicate you. With an abundance of caution, however, we recommend that you offer an incentive to the plaintiff for his future cooperation. The bank has informed us that they would like to avoid any unnecessary publicity."

"That's the incentive. That explains the check," I said. "Did your brother open a lawsuit against my father?"

"I don't know," George said. "I don't think so."

"He was probably threatened," Ida Mae said. "I always thought that." Her face fell, and she seemed miles away from Carthage as she thought over this new information.

"He warns me in the letter to be careful and watch my step," George said.

"What letter?" Ida Mae asked.

"He left me a note in our room at home. He slipped it through the window frame," George said. "He said to watch my back."

"He left money in the mailbox," Ida Mae said. "But I never saw him. I don't even know if it was him."

"And you've talked to him since then?" I asked the Pritchards without moving my head.

"I haven't," George said, looking at his mother. "He blamed us for what happened. He felt like we didn't support him, that we were cowards when it came time to press charges. Instead, he was charged with assault and battery." George sat down in my extra chair. Then, he quickly stood up and offered the chair to his mother.

"Our neighbors and church members forfeited the bail they posted. Ells never showed up for his court date," Ida Mae said.

"No letters? No phone calls?" I asked. I thought of the powerful men involved in Chappaquiddick and how a story could get retold by the perpetrator instead of the victim.

"Ells didn't talk to us before he left. He didn't pack a thing. I don't even know if he dropped off the notes and the money or if he had someone do it for him." George paced from the front room back to my desk.

Ida Mae said, "He didn't listen to me."

I felt a chill run through me. "You haven't heard his voice in fourteen years?"

"We don't talk to him," George said. "He turned his back on us." He gripped the back of his mother's chair.

"What do you mean?" I asked.

"We argued. Well, Mama and he did." George waited for her to turn and look at him. He wanted permission to tell the story. Ida Mae nodded. "Mama didn't want him organizing that protest. She was furious. He left that morning after saying some awful things."

Ida Mae shook her head. "You don't know as much as you think you do," she said. "I've lived through more than you have. I've protected you."

George stopped talking.

I looked over the papers we had uncovered, trying to form my worries into words. "And you haven't seen his handwriting since those notes he left at your house?"

"What are you asking?" George said to me.

"What if that's not Ellsworth sending the telegrams?" I pushed my typewriter to the side. I stood up and pulled the receipts in front of me. The telegram paper was blue, the writing coming through a carbon sheet from the original. I opened the folder again, looking only for blue papers.

"What are you saying?" Ida Mae stood up and looked at the papers I was pulling out. We huddled over the desk.

"I have a suspicion," I said. "Look at this, another telegram receipt. 1960."

I handed it to Ida Mae who handed it back to George.

"It doesn't say the recipient," he said.

"It's from Germany," I said. "But paid for from here. He could've called it in."

"What do you think this means?" Ida Mae emphasized the word "you," like she was going to be judge and jury on the thoughts inside my head.

"I've always had a suspicion about that day," I said. "My father was so angry and if Ellsworth was just as angry—I don't know. I've always thought my father acted strangely in the days after the protest."

"Strange how?" he asked.

"There was a grave in our backyard."

"Lord, have mercy, child, what are you talking about?" Ida Mae said. She held onto the table and then sat down in the wooden chair like she had given up on ever making sense of my words.

"Years ago," I said, "they found two bodies in our backyard and had them removed by the police. They thought they were family members, but my father made a comment about it being a good time to bury something," I said, "if something needed to be buried. He was joking, I think, but he said it right after the protest. They were digging up the backyard for my sister's wedding. He was trying to tell me something. He was taunting me."

"What are we going to do with this?" Ida Mae asked, pointing to the telegram receipts and then spreading her arms to the whole problem before us.

"Can you send Ellsworth a telegram and see if he responds? Ask for his phone number. If you hear his voice, you'll know he's alive."

"Alive?" George asked. "Do you really think—" He couldn't finish his question.

"I have it on good faith that my son is alive and thriving in Germany. He's not the only one in the Army. We have people in our community who have sent back word that he is alive. They say he was writing for the squadron's newsletter. I have it at home."

"You haven't shown me that," George said.

"It's written under a different name, but I'm sure it's him."

"What name?" George asked.

"I don't remember, but it's Ellsworth who wrote it. The article is all about Germany and how it's great for Black people. That's my son. He wanted us all to move to Germany. I had never heard of such a plan in my life. With George still in elementary school, I couldn't think about it. I had already moved here. I wasn't going to move again."

"But in case it's not him, I still think we should look into this." I couldn't shake the idea that my father could have made Ellsworth disappear and then faked his correspondence.

"What are you going to do?" Ida Mae asked.

"Let me finish this contract. You'll have to leave before I sign it. I want you to have plausible deniability."

"You're forging it?" he asked.

"I'm signing for my partner," I said.

Ida Mae covered her eyes and let out the loudest sigh ever heard this side of the Mississippi.

"And then we're going to find out if anyone's been forging those telegrams or other correspondence from your brother," I said. "Don't you think it's strange you haven't heard his voice?"

"That doesn't mean that he's buried in your father's backyard." Ida Mae wasn't going to let me run away with my cockamamie theory.

My father could lose his temper and get violent. I'd buried most of those memories. Every summer, when we went to our beach house, our Uncle John and Aunt Rosemary would come with their kids for two weeks. It was the only time Uncle John got to stay at the house because my father had inherited it as the oldest son. John was younger and shorter than my father, but they shared a similar physique, a large chest with narrow shoulders.

It was an old house—had been in the family for generations. For the two-week visit every year, the house got an overhaul. The staff beat the rugs and brought out the silver. Cases of wine were delivered, and my father hired a cook.

I remembered one year; we were sitting at dinner with fresh lobsters and corn on the cob on platters in the middle. We had metal tools to crack the claws and small handles to stick into the ears of corn.

They were talking about how nice the house was. Uncle John said something like, "It must be nice to have been given all this so you didn't have to start from scratch."

My father grumbled, and his face turned red, but he didn't respond. My uncle started talking about the wine, swirling the yellow liquid in his glass and talking about a glass of wine he'd once had in the South of France.

My father pushed back from the table. I remember thinking it wasn't a good sign. I looked around the dinner table at the smiling, sun-burnt faces of my cousins. I couldn't understand why Uncle John kept talking. My father came back with a bar of soap tucked in his palm. He stood behind Uncle John and covered John's mouth with his hand, shoving the soap between his teeth. John dropped his wine glass and struggled to pull himself free. That's what our father did when he thought heresy had been spoken. I had tasted the soap more than once.

John grabbed the tablecloth, and the plates and platters smashed to the floor. The lobster shells scattered across the room. My father and his brother stumbled backward away from the table, and they knocked a bowl off the sideboard. Our nanny ran in and pulled me and Ginny into the kitchen. Our cousins ran behind us. A chocolate cake sat on the counter for our father's birthday, its icing melting in the heat. I could smell the bar of soap still lingering. I could almost taste it myself. We heard more crashes. Aunt Rosemary screamed and threatened to call the police. Ginny started to cry. I held her in my arms and tried to cover her ears. I didn't want anything bad to happen to her.

The next day, John and Rosemary and their children were gone. Ginny and I tiptoed down from our bedroom. He was reading the newspaper out on the deck.

"Good morning, you two," he said. "Today's a good day to take out the boat. We'll pack a picnic."

I stared at him in disbelief. Ginny cheered.

I didn't know if we ever went back to the old beach house after that. I did know that Uncle John and Aunt Rosemary never came back. I didn't think I ever saw them again, and Uncle John wasn't at my father's funeral. My father had been leaving wreckage behind himself all his life, and he was never held accountable. And he made it seem normal—we did go on the boat that day, and I remembered that outing more than I remembered any conversation about why we never saw Uncle John anymore.

"There's someone I have to talk to," I told them. There was only one person who wanted to hold my father accountable as much as I did.

I organized the papers on my desk and put the cover on my typewriter.

"I'll go with you," George said.

"Not a chance," Ida Mae said to her son. She stood up, which was the same as putting her foot down.

"Mama, I'll be safe," he said.

"That's what your brother said," Ida Mae said. "And no."

CHAPTER TEN

Hidden

I took the bus to Little Italy on the North Side of Carthage. I walked up a steep hill, small houses lining both sides of the street—chain-link fences and painted wooden doors—empty window boxes waiting for spring. I checked the address and knocked on the door.

Freya opened her door. "I thought you might come," she said.

Her house was compact and tidy. I could see a narrow hallway, a sitting room, and part of her kitchen from the front door. On her walls, she had small, framed landscapes with blurry forests and lakes. On the sitting room wall was a mirror and a faded sampler—stitched letters and numbers and *Freya Hoffman* embroidered across the top. She must have done it when she was a child in Germany.

Freya pointed me toward a fussy, velvet loveseat and offered me a cigarette. I could feel the heat coming through the air vents in the ceiling. I took off my coat and tucked my gloves in the pocket. I set the coat as far from me on the loveseat as I could. I didn't need another source of heat.

"Coffee?" she asked.

"No thanks." I held her eye for a moment.

She sat in a hard-backed chair across from me. Her sitting room was stiff and uncomfortable, not designed for entertaining. She had seemed so "with it" when she drove me to the movies—her outfits were bold with colorful jackets and high heels, even during the daytime. But her home was old-fashioned. A small crucifix hung on the wall behind her.

"I found the receipts," I said, "the ones for Ellsworth Gaines. He's the man from the protest, isn't he?"

"You're right," she said with a nod—like she was the gate-keeper for whom I had to answer three questions to receive the golden key.

"Did my father have him killed?" I looked at the floor. "I hate to even say that, but I don't think Ellsworth went back to Germany."

"I was worried what would happen to him. I set up a phone call with a lawyer. The lawyer suggested your father cut his losses and offer a payoff. As vice president, your father couldn't risk the scandal. He knew he was in the wrong."

"You set up the call?"

She nodded. "There were photographs. When I mentioned that to the lawyers, they jumped into action. The sheriff agreed to get Ellsworth safely to the train station and give him the check." She lit her cigarette.

"But Ellsworth didn't cash the check."

"I found that strange as well. I couldn't contact him, but I know some young lawyers went to his house and sent his clothes to Germany."

"But did he make it to the train station?"

"I don't know."

"You gave him a chance," I said. We both knew that giving him a chance didn't guarantee his survival.

She leaned back in her chair and nodded.

I noticed her posture, her phrasing, the look in her eye. She was closing the door on her involvement. She was happy to talk to me, but she wasn't going to confront Joseph and Ginny with me. She wasn't the woman sitting in the cafe with the blue hat, like I had pictured her. She was the one behind the scenes. She had saved those papers for me. My heart beat faster, and I looked around Freya's house as if I might find some other source of support. I wanted to go to the movies, sit in the dark, and watch other people take chances. It was much harder to do it myself.

"Why did you do it?" I asked.

"Do what?"

"Save all those papers."

"Well." She leaned her head from side to side as if weighing how to phrase her words. "I worked with your father and brother-in-law. I heard their private conversations. I wrote up their back-room deals. I knew they were planning to honor him with a statue. After thinking and praying, I knew your father should not have a statue and that I could do something about it."

I nodded. "I can't imagine it was easy."

"It wasn't." She smiled again.

"Joseph will be furious if he finds out."

"I'm retired," she said. "I'm safe. I may go home to Germany."

I thought it strange she thought of Germany as home after all she'd suffered there. I thought home was wherever you felt most comfortable and safe, but then again, I'd never lived anywhere but Carthage.

"Do you keep in touch with your family?" I asked.

"My brother and I see the world differently," she said carefully. "He served in the SS. I never understood how he could fight for them. He tells me he joined to keep our family safe. He regrets what he did."

"Are you close?"

"We aren't," Freya said. "But I'd like to meet his children."

I thought about what she'd risked during the war. Her brother joined the SS to keep their family safe, but she'd forged those papers to keep others safe. Family bonds weren't paramount to her. She knew the crimes of powerful men often go unpunished, and after time passes, no one remembers the details—unless someone saves the evidence.

"You did me a big favor," I said.

"Honestly, Lucretia, I was waiting for the day when the bankers would be prosecuted. A day when their crimes would be brought to light. I would've brought the information forward earlier if I'd thought anything would have been done about it. Americans are still not ready to see rich people as anything but heroes."

"We have a lot to learn," I said.

"America is not self-reflective," she said. "If your father gets a statue, he will be revered for generations to come. Americans don't question what is placed before them. They don't reckon with their history."

I nodded. I knew what she was saying. We were a distracted people, concerned with our own bottom lines. I felt again the limitations I had created for myself by living in the same town for my entire life.

"Germany has a horrific history," she continued. "My brother was brainwashed by the SS The whole country was, but we don't hide it. The Holocaust is taught in schools. And, we don't have Hitler statues in our town squares."

I agreed the world wasn't any more ready to hear about my father than it had been to hear about my great-grandfather. My library project had brought me deep into the memories of Carthage from the turn of the century. The cassette tapes in 1958 had the voices of families still grappling with their losses from 1918. Two families had lost children, and those children had lived in my great-grandparents' house. And they were buried there until we found them in 1958. I would have their voices inside my head for the rest of my life: *"My daughter." "Our son." "We needed the money." "There was no other work." "We didn't want them living there." "We had worked so hard to build a life here in America, and it was taken away in a moment."*

Freya and I were sharing an ashtray, pulling it back and forth along the coffee table as we needed it. It made me feel like an adult. I had grown up, always wanting to be like Freya, but I never had her panache. Freya always had smart outfits and co-ordinated accessories—I was always tearing my stockings and smearing my mascara, if I even wore any at all. I was always for-getting my purse somewhere, if I even remembered to carry one. I didn't act and dress like a lady. I was always told I was too loud, too rough, too much. As a kid, I never noticed if I had leaves in my hair or if my bathing suit was misaligned or if I had jam on my face. I tried to fit into their neat models of femininity, but I was messy.

And I was about to get messier. A person who was about to dig up a grave in a backyard couldn't worry about their nails breaking or stockings ripping. I kept my nails short, and I had worn my hard-toed kitchen shoes. They were perfect, and I real-ized I was the right person for the job.

"I'm going to confront them," I said to Freya. I needed to hear myself say it aloud.

"I knew you would, Lucretia. I'm proud of you. You're living up to your namesake."

"Lucretia Mott?"

"A great abolitionist, unafraid to stand up to the status quo. But also the Lucretia from Roman history. She was raped by the king's son. After naming the perpetrator, she took her own life to prove her dedication to her virtue—in front of some of the most powerful men in her empire."

"I don't think I'm brave enough for that," I said.

"Bravery can be defined in many ways. You're taking your life into your own hands, and that takes its own kind of bravery."

I nodded. I had let decisions be made for me about my own life. When I lost the battle against my father, I had thought I had to live quietly in defeat. I hadn't imagined, until now, that I could do something more.

Freya stood up and gave me a hug. I leaned over the coffee table and felt her love alongside the unnerving buoyancy of having nowhere else to turn. I either moved forward by myself, or this crime would go unpunished.

"Thank you, Freya," I said, wiping away a tear.

"You're welcome, dear one," she said, brushing my hair back from my face.

"I mean, for everything." I remembered Freya picking me up from school, picking me up from my house, picking me up over and over. She always dressed elegantly with a hat and a pair of gloves. She could have been in the movies, not just watching them. I remembered her ever-present smell of talcum powder and hairspray mingling with the theater smells of popcorn and butter. Those smells marked my path toward maturity. After each movie, Freya would ask my opinion. After a while, I learned to form my opinions even as the plots were unfolding. Not just opinions about the stories or cinematography but opinions about what the characters should have done, how they figured out who to trust, what the right move was in a difficult situation. Tough questions that shaped my view of the world. While Ginny was going to musicals, I was being brought to movies that helped me figure out the world. I owed Freya credit for almost all my good qualities as a thinking adult and blamed her for none of the bad ones.

"I know," she said. "You'll always be in my heart."

"And you'll be in mine." I stabbed out my cigarette and gave her one last hug.

*   *   *

Razed

On the bus, I sat in the back row and exhaled. My mind was two stops ahead of my body. I knew where to point my shovel, but I didn't know if I had the strength to dig into the winter earth. If I could get far enough along, the police would be called. They would want to see what was down there. They might have shrugged their shoulders at a pair of questionable deaths from 1918, but they weren't going to ignore one from 1958. It was a long shot, but I needed to know once and for all if my father was a murderer.

The bus chugged along—spit and shuddered, like a beast making its way through the morning traffic. I stared out the window at the commercial strips, narrow residential lots, and half-empty parking lots. A man took out his garbage cans, his jacket unbuttoned. The sun cast his shadow along the sidewalk.

Our father had duped Ginny. Maybe he sent her out for groceries while he had his men bury the body in the backyard. If this was the case, then Ellsworth Gaines had been at Ginny's wedding, buried beneath the rented chairs. None of us had any idea.

Except Joseph. I had a feeling he knew all along. The day of their wedding, he'd stood in his suit at the top of the aisle. He had taken Ginny's hand from my father's. Did they exchange a glance, knowing what was beneath their feet?

I thought of Mr. Brown in *The Big Combo,* the quiet gangster who could safely circulate in the light of day—a man so powerful he could get other men to risk their lives and reputations for him. He was cruel and unyielding in business and then expected a normal family life when he got home each night.

As close to Hiawatha Heights as the bus could go, I got off and walked toward Onondaga Way. I kept my head down, watching my hard-toed shoes appear and disappear from my line of sight. I didn't look at my neighbors' windows. A child's game—if I don't see them, they won't see me. I hoped Joseph had already left for work.

My father's house stood solid and stolid, its windows impassive. He hadn't built the house, but it embodied his characteristics. He had pedigree and ambition, tradition, and creativity. My father always said he was building on his family legacy as a steward of their wealth. He was born in 1900, too young for the first war, too old for the second. He had to make his mark through his career. He was trained as a lawyer but excelled in banking. He was competitive and always a bit smarter than his opponents. He was driven, as if the family gravestones spoke to him at night and kept tabs on his progress.

Through an otherwise blue sky, a cloud drifted behind one of the peaked roofs. I let myself in the side gate. They never locked it. In their backyard, I felt as if I were levitating above myself. Never had I trespassed before. Never had I stood in a place I wasn't allowed to stand. It felt freeing and terrifying. At the garden shed, I creaked open the door. It didn't sit right on its hinges. My father would never have let it sag like that. He would have had workers fixing it as soon as it showed signs of misalignment. But Joseph and Ginny had let it sag.

The shed was dark and dusty. Tools hung on the wall—my father's tools still in their regular places. I selected a sharp shovel and grabbed a pair of men's gloves from the potting table drawer.

In the yard, I looked under the oak tree where the bodies had been found fourteen years ago. I could picture the workers smoking their cigarettes as Ginny and I waited for the police. I remembered her crying in my arms, worried it was a bad omen for her wedding. She was always a bit shallow, missing the big picture when it didn't pertain to her. That was partly my fault. And my father's. When our mother died, we turned Ginny into a barometer of our family's health. If we could keep her happy, then her happiness reflected back on us. We worked to bypass any struggles for her, but in the end, she had turned out incapable of coping with even the smallest inconvenience.

Before I could touch the shovel to the ground, my sister found me.

"What are you doing?" Ginny yelled. "Is that you, Lucy?"

I didn't look up. The ground was too cold to gain purchase, but I thrust the shovel at a muddy section. I had to dig only enough to make them call the police.

The gardening gloves were big, and they slipped each time I moved the shovel. The sun tucked itself behind a darkening cloud.

"Lucy, answer me." I could hear from her voice she wasn't entirely sure it was me. She hadn't seen my face, but after all these years, we knew each other's movements and body structures, even under winter coats and sweaters.

I didn't answer. I felt like giggling. While I was primarily driven by a righteous search for the truth, a smaller part of me eagerly anticipated Ginny's fall, the moment when the truth finally hit her brain. A petty, sisterly moment of reckoning.

Ginny went back inside, and I heard only my shovel hitting the earth and my breath escaping my mouth. The shovel was heavy with melting mud, and the canvas gloves scraped against my palms.

I felt someone behind me. I stepped on the shovel to push it further down, pulled up another lug of sod. The oak tree shook its branches above me.

"What are you looking for?" a young voice asked. I turned around to see Sarah. She peered into the hole I had started, gathering her own intelligence.

"Something your grandfather put here many years ago." I wanted to say "someone" instead of "something," but I didn't want to terrorize her. Then I asked myself why we always try to protect girls from the truth. I decided not to commit the same mistake we had made with Ginny. I rested the shovel and turned toward Sarah to tell her why I was there.

Sarah wore boots but no jacket, and she held her arms around her middle. The snow was melting, but it was late January, and she was cold. I wanted to pull her into my coat. I wanted to be the best aunt to her, but my relationship with my father had made that difficult. I was on the outside, and I had no control over how they talked about me when I wasn't there. But Sarah and I still shared a special bond. I don't know if it was our love of books or our need for eyeglasses, but we always had identified with one another.

"Your grandfather—" I started.

"Are you crazy?" Ginny strode across the yard in full outdoor gear. She'd put on heeled boots and a belted wool jacket. Her hair was not yet coiffed for the day, but she wore slacks and a plaid wool scarf. She practically barreled into me as she came to a stop, inches from my shoes, stepping between me and Sarah. I looked at her face and saw wrinkles around her eyes. I hadn't seen her without makeup in years. Maybe since before she was married.

The ground was harder underneath the melted top. I was not going to be able to go six feet. The shovel bounced off the frozen ground, but I thrust into the closest edge.

"Lucy!" Ginny grabbed my shoulder.

My shovel flung back and hit her in the shin. Slush and mud splattered on her pant legs.

"Shit." She held her shin and let out a wail. Sarah went over and helped her balance.

I held in my apology. I wasn't sorry. A glove had flown off in the collision, and I bent to pick it up.

"What is going on here?" a man yelled. I didn't need to look up to know who it was. Ginny retreated, holding her shin, and Joseph came forward. He stood in front of me, next to the tree trunk.

"What are you doing?" Joseph was dressed for work: gray suit, shiny black shoes.

"You know what I'm going to find under here," I said.

"What are you talking about?" He looked perplexed.

I didn't answer him. I stamped on the shovel to push it back into the ground. I could hear Ginny crying behind me. She was going to have a bruise, and for a woman who didn't encounter bruises often, I could see how a shovel to her shin would make her cry.

"Call the police," Joseph said to Ginny.

"Good idea," I said. "They should be notified. I found some interesting items in my father's papers—items you might've forgotten about." I paused to catch my breath. "Ginny, you'll want to hear this. Then, please, do as your husband says and call the police." I felt as if I were reading lines from a screenplay.

Ginny walked closer but out of the range of my shovel. I thought about chasing her with it, anything to get her attention. I liked seeing her without her makeup. I liked seeing her age. I longed for a day when her pretty face would stop giving her favors in life.

"What could possibly be buried here?" Joseph asked. "Do you think you'll find a treasure?"

"I think it's a man's body. I think it's Ellsworth Gaines's body."

"What the hell?" Joseph yelled. "There isn't a body under here. Are you trying to prove, once and for all, that you've lost your mind?"

I paused, leaning on my shovel. "I'm trying to prove to Ginny that our father railroaded the people of Carthage." I turned to Ginny. "The day of the Sycamore Street March—I've been trying to tell you this for fourteen years, Daddy attacked someone. He had him taken away, separate from the other protestors. And in his papers, I have found that person's name is Ellsworth Gaines."

"I know that name," Joseph said.

"I'll bet you do," I said. "You've been part of this all along."

Joseph held his hands up, like he was surrendering to a woman's irrationality.

"Daddy, is this true?" Sarah asked over my words. She held onto her mother's elbow, but her eyes went from me to Joseph, back and forth.

"I was not part of attacking a man," he said. "I wasn't even there that day."

"You were part of the cover-up. I have the receipts from Western Union, the post office. What else were you sending to Germany? Why were you sending telegrams from Germany?"

"I didn't do any of that." He shook his head.

I didn't believe him. Joseph always did whatever my father asked of him. Nothing was too small or strange. He would run upstairs and get my father's slippers, like a dog. He surely didn't draw the line at sending telegrams from a dead man to his family.

"Daddy is dead, Lucy. You have to let this go." Ginny lowered her voice. She was trying to calm the situation. She stroked Sarah's hair and then rubbed her arms for warmth.

"It doesn't matter that he's dead. I'm trying to save you, not him," I said. "I want you to see what he did." Every family interaction for the past decade had been overlaid with my desire for Ginny to know the truth about our father. Every time our father talked about his bank's ruthless maneuvers or hinted at his own ambitions, I caught Ginny's eye and tried to make her hear him, what he was revealing about himself, but my one-track mind only made her less likely to believe me, more likely to think I was making a mountain out of a molehill.

"Just me? Is that why you went to the newspaper?" Ginny asked.

I shook my head. I regretted going to the papers after the day at the bank. "I went to the papers because Daddy wouldn't listen. You wouldn't listen." I bit my lip. How could I explain? "I want Sarah to see," I said.

Without my own children, my heart was set on Sarah. I would throw it all away to have Sarah on my side.

"What does Sarah have to do with this?" Ginny asked.

"What if we listened to you now?" Joseph said over Ginny. He reached out to take the shovel. I pulled it back.

"You're not listening," I said to him. I had come to their house, tried to reason with them. I had presented at the Historical Society. I had done everything in my power to show Ginny what she abjectly refused to see.

"But if we did," he said. "What if I showed you something that confirmed what you were saying about this Gaines man?"

"That he was killed and buried here?" I hit the shovel against the ground.

"He wasn't killed. But you're right, your father did orchestrate his removal."

"Removal? He wasn't a blighted store front. He was a human being."

"And he's still a human being. He's in Germany, living his life." Joseph held out his hand. His clean-shaven face looked younger. He looked like a man who wanted to make amends.

I wanted to believe him. I wanted to give that news to George and Ida Mae.

"How do you know?" I asked.

"I'll show you." Joseph beckoned for me to follow him into the house.

I put down the shovel and gloves and motioned for Ginny and Sarah to go ahead of me. If anyone needed to see this, it was them. I felt another wave of excitement bubbling up in my chest. I could only be happier if I could go home and tell Miranda all about it. I'd been waiting for this moment for over a decade.

"I'm going to show you this on one condition," Joseph said over his shoulder.

"That I don't go to the newspapers?"

"Well, that. But if you want to prove to Ginny that your father treated this man unfairly, then you have to leave the other evidence alone."

"Then, you're admitting to the other crimes?" I asked the back of his head.

"Not crimes. But some questionable financial moves," he said. "If that's not what you're interested in, I'll give you what I have about the man at the protest."

If I gave up the other evidence, about the buying and selling of property, the influencing of elected officials, the insider trading, then Joseph's fortune would be secure—Ginny's fortune. I hated that they made their decisions based on how it affected their bank accounts. They'd do anything to protect the bottom line, even give up their facade of morality.

I knew I'd be giving up a chance for redemption, but if I could tell George and Ida Mae what had happened that day, I would be satisfied.

"Fine," I said. "But I need to know what happened to Ellsworth."

I followed Joseph into the house, through the kitchen and dining room. We went through the foyer. My mother and father looked down on me from their quarter-turn portraits. I couldn't decide if my father would be proud of me for figuring it out or angry with me for pursuing it—probably a bit of both. We went down the hallway into my father's old office. The same pictures hung on the wall, the same family Bible stood on its wooden pedestal.

Ginny and Sarah stayed in the doorway. Joseph went into my father's filing cabinet and pulled out a file.

I stood there with sweat on my forehead and dirt on my face. I looked at the window seat with its velvet curtain and thought about disappearing behind it. It was a prime location for hide-and-seek when we were children.

Joseph took his time with the file, removing the papers and placing them on my father's desk. Taped to the inside of the folder was a metal necklace. He un-taped it and handed it to me.

Dog tags. I turned them over. Gaines, Ellsworth. His ID number and blood type.

"What is this, a trophy?" I asked. "They did kill him." The tags felt heavy in my hand, cold.

"No one killed anyone," he said. "You have to understand your father was only trying to protect Ginny. You told him a man—"

"A Black man," I said.

Sarah stared at her father without blinking.

"A Black man was hitting on Ginny," he said to me, "and your father wanted to send a message, but no one was killed." Joseph lifted his head to look at Ginny and Sarah.

"Then, why hasn't his family heard from him?" I asked.

"You'd have to ask them. But no one was killed. Your father said he was burying something in the backyard. It was after that night when you and Ginny went to that jazz club. He was teasing you." Joseph closed the filing cabinet but held onto the folder.

Teasing? What kind of father teases his daughter over something so important, stands back and lets her make a fool of herself? Only a man with impunity could play with the truth like that. What was I supposed to do? Believe him when he talked about the crimes in the newspaper, but not when he joked about his own crimes? Take note of the glint in his eye and the tilt of his head—believe him only when the stars aligned?

"Did you know he had the wrong man?" I asked Ginny. "Do you remember? The saxophonist was interested in you—not the man handing out flyers."

"Your father didn't know anything about that," Joseph answered. "He swore he had the right man. He wanted to send a message."

"Was there a police report?" I asked.

"Not one that mentioned your father." Joseph closed the folder and patted it, like the deal was done. "He tried to pay the Gaines man, but when he refused to take the money, your father made it more enticing for him to go back to Germany."

"What do you mean?"

"Your father had a bruised face, a cut above his eye. Mr. Gaines could have gone to prison for a long time. There were pictures." He opened the folder again and took out an envelope of photographs, small and blurry. I grabbed them. They showed Ellsworth hitting my father with his head. They showed my father's injuries. These were the photos that David had taken. The police had grabbed his camera and developed his film. These were the photos that told only one side of the story.

"Where are the rest of the photos," I asked. "These show only one side. He attacked this man," I said to Ginny. "Look at how Ellsworth's hands are held back. Look at his head. You can tell he was attacked. Our father did that." This was the moment I'd been waiting for. I stared at Ginny, waiting for her answer.

"Your father was scared about Ginny," Joseph interrupted again. "That's when he called me. That's when we got engaged." He looked at Ginny.

"There was more to it," Ginny said, still standing in the doorway with Sarah. My heart stopped. What was she going to tell me?

"They showed me some other pictures," she said. "A boy down south who was beaten to death for flirting with a white woman."

"Emmett Till?" I asked.

"I think so," she said. "The pictures were awful, and they told me a white girl was responsible for that. I didn't want anything to happen to Ray."

"But look what happened to Ellsworth. It happened anyway. There was nothing between the two of you. That was in Daddy's mind."

"It's what he knew at the time," she said, shaking her head. "What he thought he knew."

"But it wasn't information, it was a gut reaction," I said. "And Ellsworth lost fourteen years with his family." I held up the dog tags. "He was furious with his own family for not supporting him. He wanted to press charges against our father."

Ginny nodded and wiped a tear from her cheek.

"You think it's okay what our father did?" I held up the dog tags again.

"I think it's complicated," she said.

Sarah looked sharply at her mother. I couldn't imagine what she was thinking, but I was glad she was hearing this, even if it might undo her memories of her grandfather. He didn't deserve a burnished reputation. Even if she only looked back at this when she was older, after the shine of her parents had faded, the words would still be lodged in her brain.

"Are you kidding?" I asked Ginny. "Nothing is less complicated than this. Do you think it's okay our father physically harmed a man because he thought he might've made eyes at you? You were also making eyes if I remember correctly," I said.

"I already said I was wrong," she said.

Why had I been civil to them for the past fourteen years? I had sat at the dinner table with my father even though I had known he was a criminal. I gave a remembrance at his funeral and didn't mention his cruelty. If Ellsworth had gone back to Germany, furious with his family for not supporting him, then maybe he was right not to talk to them or answer their letters. I was the one hemmed in by my ideas of politeness.

"Let's put this behind us and get back to normal," Ginny said. This was all she ever wanted. As I looked at Ginny's pleading face, I knew she would accept me back into the fold. But at the same time, I realized I couldn't live in Carthage any longer. I couldn't make small talk with Ginny over Easter brunch. I'd been trapped in this standoff with my sister for over a decade. It had taken over my field of vision.

"Why did he save these?" I held up the dog tags.

"He wanted to make sure he could prove who had attacked him, if a lawsuit ever came through. The bank was adamant that he save any evidence."

"Did you know?" I asked Ginny. The most important question. "Did you know all along that Daddy attacked that man?" My voice rose in an ugly way. I wanted it to convey violence. I elongated my words until they cracked and distorted in the back of my throat. I wanted to shatter her with my voice.

"It doesn't matter what I knew. I knew Daddy had good motives," Ginny said. "He wanted to take care of his family." She pulled Sarah close to her side. To her, the conversation was over.

"To think only about your family and lining the pockets of your family's purse is not a good motive. You were in no danger." I looked around the room, raging. I wanted to pull the books off the shelves, smash the windows. I couldn't hear her justify his actions.

I always thought if I could prove what I'd seen, she would come over to my side, but I was wrong. I grabbed the family Bible on its pedestal, filled with its names of our ancestors, births and deaths. I threw it to the floor. It landed at an awkward angle, and the pedestal tipped and crashed.

"How dare you!" Ginny yelled. She came toward me and pushed my shoulder with both her hands. I stumbled and then pushed her in the chest. She fell to the floor.

"How did you not tell me this?" I screamed. "How did you not tell me you knew all along?"

"If I told you," Ginny said between her crying gasps, "I would have lost you."

I had spent all my energy trying to convince her that our father was culpable, and she had known all along. If that was true, then none of this needed to happen.

"Why did you agree to the statue then? If you knew, why did any of this have to happen?"

Ginny wiped her nose with her arm and looked at Joseph.

"It pays off a debt," she said quietly.

"What do you mean?"

"We told you," Joseph said.

"The city's paying for those lots," Ginny said. "They really wanted this, and they were willing to pay triple the market price. We needed to pay off Daddy's gambling debts." She pulled herself up by holding onto our father's desk.

"That's why you're tearing down my neighborhood?" My breathing was too heavy to hear myself think. It was like a railroad station in my brain—trains heading in every direction, and horns from every track.

"All right, all right," Joseph said, pulling me into the corner away from Ginny. "We've kept our end of the deal. You promised you'd let this go."

"I don't always keep my promises," I said, pulling my arm out of his grasp. "And I never promised to keep quiet about anything to do with the other bodies, the one our great grandfather buried."

Ginny stared at me.

"It wasn't influenza," I said. "You probably already know this, but the people from the farms, from Eastern Carthage, said there were signs of trauma on the skeletons. They were kids." My sentences didn't make sense, but I wanted them to know. I'd been waiting to tell them. "The two victims worked and lived in this house."

Ginny looked down at the Oriental rug. Could she have known this as well?

"She lived in the servants' quarters above the kitchen," I said to Ginny, "where we used to play. She was killed, and so was the boy. They were teenagers."

"How do you know this?" Ginny asked.

"Not from our father. He wrote a book of lies and got it published, so it seemed legitimate. He probably thought he was so clever. He didn't sign his name because he knew he was lying—Amos Pendleton. That's how he dealt with the knowledge that his grandfather, or someone in this house, was a murderer. He wrote a book in praise of him—just like you're doing with the statue."

"Daddy's not a murderer, and we don't know that our great-grandfather was either."

"We have found out a lot about them, and I'm still looking. And we don't know yet what we'll find out about Joseph."

"That's absurd," Joseph said. "I have nothing to do with this."

"You're doing the same thing as my father," I yelled. "You're destroying a neighborhood to pay off a debt. You have a negative balance, and you're putting it on the backs of my neighbors."

"I've never had anyone pay off my debts," Joseph said.

"My father. He paid your debts before you even owed them."

"I did all the work myself," he said, turning away from me.

"If I can't see my father convicted, I'd love to see you go to jail."

Joseph grasped my arm and held it to my side. I could see a store of anger brewing behind his eyes. Joseph, like my father, could be charming as long as he got his own way, but when threatened, he turned to violence. His pride wouldn't allow him to back down, certainly not to a woman.

He pushed me into the wall. A framed map fell to the ground. He held my arm and pushed my shoulder with his other hand. I swung my free arm wildly, but I couldn't hit him. I tried to get his hand off my shoulder, but his grip was too strong.

"Joe," Ginny said.

"No, Daddy," Sarah screamed.

Just as abruptly as he had grabbed me, he let go. Plato once said that a virtuous man, accused of a crime he has committed, will take his punishment with grace. But the same man, wrongly accused, will rage against his accuser until one of them lies dead. But here was Joseph, rightly accused, and he was raging. It either meant that he wasn't a virtuous man or that his entitlement deluded him into thinking that any accusation against him was unwarranted.

"You think everyone's so stupid," I said to both of them, "that they'll take your word. But not everyone's stupid. People are going to keep asking questions. Our great-grandfather is going to be unearthed as a murderer. Our father's true nature will come out someday." I realized the words I was speaking were filled with hope. I'd always thought these men were too powerful to be taken down, but my words suggested that somewhere in my body, I still hoped for redemption.

I straightened my sweater and wiped tears from my eyes. "I always knew you were capable of that," I said to Joseph.

"He didn't mean anything," Ginny said. "You're fine."

"I'm fine, but this is the tip of the iceberg. You and Joseph have caused so much damage, as much as Daddy."

"That's ridiculous," Ginny said.

"You killed Miranda," I yelled.

"You killed Miranda," Ginny yelled back at me. "What did you think would happen? Creating that ridiculous public drama. No one needed that. It's what you've always done, ever since you didn't get your way at the bank. You've embarrassed us, treated us like pariahs. I've wondered many times if you should be locked away. You never apologized to our father before he died. All those times at our house, eating our food, sitting there like you were doing us a favor." Ginny sputtered out her last words, spent by her outburst.

I heard the words, but shock prevented them from sinking

in. I thought more about them after I left Carthage—that she could turn this around and blame me, question my sanity. I also thought more about how her words might have been true.

I'd always been gentle with her, patient—holding her hand on steep staircases and letting her sound out words from our picture books. Daddy and I both softened the rules for her, set the bar lower. We thought she needed protecting, a kinder type of up-bringing because she would never know her mother. But she had come to expect these graces, and the world did not disappoint her.

"It's time for you to go." Ginny opened the door to the study and motioned for me to leave.

I stared at her. Her hair was a mess. She wiped saliva from her chin. I couldn't imagine this was the same human being I had grown up with. I thought back to the night at the Fremont, the week before the protest. How differently I thought it was going to turn out—how differently I thought Ginny would turn out.

*   *   *

The night we went out in 1958, Ginny had looked impossibly pretty. In the dim lights of the Fremont, candle lamps attached to each table, her seventeen-year-old face found every inch of light and reflected it. Her skin glowed, and her eyes looked mis-chievous around the corners. I wore our mother's pearls, a way to have our mother with us for another milestone she would miss.

Carthage hosted a steady stream of jazz greats. Singers. Saxophonists. Drummers. Trombone players. Close enough to New York City to make it easy for them, and their reception was always worth the trip. They didn't get a cool round of applause; they got rapturous and clamorous delight. Carthage hosted John Coltrane, Dizzy Gillespie, Count Basie, and that night, the Fremont had Ray Washington.

"What'll you have?" I asked Ginny once we caught the wait-ress's attention.

"What?" Ginny yelled over the trumpets and drums and piano and saxophone.

"What do you want to drink? A Tom Collins?" I could barely hear myself over the music.

"No, no." She arranged herself in the booth, sitting up taller, about to savor the moment. "I will have a martini," she said. "Shaken not stirred."

We laughed. It was not a lady's drink, but it fit the moment. We had seen *Casino Royale* with our father, and that line stuck with us as the pinnacle of panache.

"Make it two," I said.

That evening marked our first night out on the town together. We had been to dinners with our father and out with friends, but this was sister time. Just the two of us. And we were trailblazers. One white couple at a corner table and a few white co-eds at the bar, but the rest of the tables were filled with Black faces, every shade of skin color. The Fremont was a Black bar in a Black neighborhood.

I smiled. The world was charged with an electrified sense of possibility. Back then, power dynamics seemed to be changing. Neighborhoods were mixing, jobs were opening for women and Black people.

Our drinks came. We didn't even know how to lift the glasses to our lips without spilling them. *Martinis are served in ridiculous glasses*, I thought. How could you not spill after having one too many? We tasted them with the smallest of sips. I almost gagged, but Ginny held a smile on her face even though she must've been grimacing on the inside. She wouldn't back down once she had taken a chance on something. And like an actress, she could keep a smile on her face through any obstacle.

That night, I believed in her. She soaked in the atmosphere of the Fremont. She wasn't intimidated. Even though she'd had little contact with anyone of another race, she seemed at ease.

Ginny and I leaned in close to each other and talked in between songs.

"This is wonderful," she said.

"This is the direction we need to go," I said. The South had fought for civil rights through a dense wall of racism, but here in the North, we could take small steps and get to know one another, and it was going to turn out much better, I thought.

"Better than the country club," I said. I'd always hated the phony country clubbers, smiling at each other as they stabbed each other in the back, comparing the sizes of their cars and diamonds, the marriage prospects of their children.

"Absolutely." Her eyes sparkled. She smiled at me like she was seeing me for the first time. I felt in that moment we were going to forge a new type of life together, and our father couldn't object if we both took the same path. We'd offer each other cover.

I held onto my pearls and let them settle between my fingers. They represented family to me, stitched together and passed down, always linked.

My reveries ended when Ray Washington noticed Ginny. He was a big star visiting a small city, and he noticed my sister. The entire audience followed his gaze. Over the top of his saxophone, he held Ginny's eye, and at the band's break, he came to our table.

I didn't have the slightest idea how to react, what to say, where to look, but Ginny acted like this was an everyday occurrence.

"Pleasure to meet you, Mr. Washington, may we offer you a seat? What wonderful music. What do you think of our fine city?" Ginny had an endless stream of patter and polite filler, and I suppose Ray Washington was keeping up his end of the conversation but like the rest of the place, I couldn't take my eyes off Ginny.

The next thing I knew, Ray was snapping his fingers to bring someone to the table. This man handed me a flyer and I know

now he was Ellsworth Gaines. He was tall and fit. He wore glasses. Not the thick black rims all the academics wore at the college, but a pair of thin, brown rims that complemented the shape of his face. He wasn't interested in me or Ginny—he was interested in getting as many people to the protest as he could.

"Why do you think this will work?" Ray asked him.

"People will see the injustice," Ellsworth said. "The bus boycott worked down South. Times are changing. I've lived in Germany where it's not segregated, except for our Army."

"It's not segregated here," I said.

Both Ray and Ellsworth looked at me.

"I mean, not like the South."

They still didn't say anything. Ray handed me a flyer.

I wish I had talked to him more—Ida Mae's son and George's brother. I'd never gone to Ward Thirteen before, not even in my father's car. My father wouldn't approve of my being there, and his mother wouldn't have approved of him coming to my neighborhood. We thought we weren't segregated in the North, but we were. The Sycamore Street March shifted our lives forever—Ellsworth and me. Neither of our parents had wanted shifting. But shifting had happened.

Ray moved his chair and rested his hand on the banquette behind Ginny, and she stared into his eyes.

"I think your friends are calling you," Ray said to me.

"What friends?" I looked behind us at the bar.

"Those friends," he said, but he kept staring at Ginny.

And then they kissed.

I looked away.

I don't know why I made such a big deal about it, but I felt like Ginny had earned some high achievement. Ray Washington kissed her in a banquette at the Fremont. Wasn't that the greatest? But I went too far. I told Ginny they could get married and move to New York. My mind was always racing ahead of the present moment. I'd have us in our graves by suppertime.

"He has a glamorous life," I said to her. What did I know about his life? "He travels to Europe and South America. He plays in all the best clubs. He's famous worldwide."

Looking back, I can see it was more important to me than her. But it was poignant. Ginny and I had just discovered the Fremont, and suddenly it was all going to be torn down? I pictured Ginny and myself walking in the march and fighting for Ward Thirteen and meeting up with Ray Washington for lunch. That is not how it turned out.

*   *   *

I left my father's house with the dog tags of Ellsworth Gaines in my hand. I abandoned the shovel in the yard. I could still feel Joseph's grip on my shoulder and the spot where my back had hit the wall. I felt my ties to my sister, my childhood, and the house unraveling—a frayed edge, dragging on the ground. The only tie that still tickled at my back was Sarah. I didn't know if I'd ruined my chance to ever see her again.

On the bus, I sat in the back row, huddled near the window. I held the dog tags. The inscription was punched into the surface—the chain was strong. The tags were designed to survive a soldier's death. I didn't know for certain if Ellsworth was alive or dead. I had to tell Ida Mae and George what I had learned, but I stayed seated even as the bus passed our stop.

I couldn't stop thinking about Ginny. She was convinced our father had done everything with the best of intentions, and I couldn't change her mind. If the dog tags didn't shock her, then I couldn't think of anything that would.

I watched black tree trunks fly by and building facades change from wood to brick to stone, some close to the road, some set back. Moving in and out, forward and back. The bus lurched from red light to red light and took wide turns through the city, opening its doors at every stop. For one ticket, I could ride all day. I felt the rhythm of the bus driver's route as we started a second loop around the city.

I was tired in my chest; my legs felt limp. I closed my eyes and let the movement of the bus lull me. Only the chill of the dog tags in my hand kept me awake.

I got off when the bus reached the Old Ward Thirteen stop for the second time. It was afternoon, and the day had gone dark with storm clouds. I put my gloves on as I passed under the highway to the other side. The cars on the Empire Stateway turned on their lights. The highway was illuminated like a privileged path, while our neighborhood was cast in darkness. Even the streetlights were dark.

At George's block, I saw the low-slung apartment buildings built to the edges of their lots. They wouldn't come alive until the sewing machine factory blew its whistle. It wasn't quitting time yet. Only one house on the block was lit from stem to stern. I heard animated voices, the peal of a woman's laughter.

A red Volkswagen Beetle was parked on the street.

Through the windows, I saw yellow lamplight. George and Alma stood arm in arm. He must have told his mother about his relationship. I wondered if Ida Mae was mad about being kept in the dark for so long.

I stood for a moment, then turned away.

"Lucy." I heard George's voice. "Come have a toast with us."

George stood on his porch, holding a bottle of whiskey. I'd never seen him look so happy. He wore corduroy pants with a flare at the bottom.

I stood on the sidewalk and gave my excuses. I didn't want to disrupt his celebration. I could show him the tags tomorrow.

George ignored me. "Mama, could you bring another glass?" he yelled into the house. Alma came out on the porch. She was wearing a tweed dress and a cardigan with pearl buttons.

"I don't want to interrupt," I said to Alma.

She shook her head. "You're not interrupting."

"Come inside," George said—as if it was already decided. He seemed confident and lit from within.

The front room was warm and tight, crowded with boxes ready to be filled for their move. I took off my jacket and held it against my middle. George arranged small shot glasses on the coffee table.

Alma held out her hand, so I could see her ring. I hugged her and then George. I felt tears in the corners of my eyes. Ever since he and Alma had sat with me and Miranda's body, I felt a closeness to them. It was an experience none of us would ever forget, and I wondered if it had prompted him to propose.

"My parents are over the moon," Alma said. "I don't know why we were worried, keeping it a secret for so long."

I smiled for Ida Mae. This was all she ever wanted. And she couldn't have asked for a better daughter-in-law.

"My parents are coming for dinner tonight, so we're fixing a feast." Alma smiled like a girl on Christmas morning.

"Let's get you back to your cooking, then," I said.

"Stay." Alma came over and fussed with my hair, smoothing it down. She wiped something off my cheek.

Ida Mae came out with another glass but stopped when she saw me.

"Miss Wilson." She hadn't been expecting me. I hadn't been expecting myself. I wanted to tell her about the dog tags and talk about the contract from this morning. I wanted to ask about the telegram to Ellsworth and see if he had responded, but this wasn't the time.

She nodded and placed the extra glass on the coffee table.

"Introduce yourselves," Ida Mae said. She handed each of us a filled shot glass. "No hoity toity around here." She didn't look at me.

"Nice to meet you," I said to Alma, holding her eye. Some secrets were meant to be kept.

"To Ellsworth," George said, thrusting his glass into the air and holding it still.

My heart stopped. I didn't know if we were toasting his life or death.

"Amen," Ida Mae said, raising her glass into the same space as George's.

I clinked glasses with them and drank my shot of whiskey. It went down to my toes. I hadn't eaten all day.

I put my glass on the coffee table and looked around the room. I didn't understand the toasts.

"Ellsworth's coming to visit," Ida Mae said without elaboration.

"He got your telegram?"

"He did and he called," she said. "Cried like a baby and apologized to his mother." She wiped a line of sweat off her brow.

"It was him?" I asked.

"It was him," she said, looking at me like I was a fool to question a mother knowing her son's voice.

She was right. I'd be a fool to question her. My heart hadn't caught up with the logic in front of me.

Ida Mae smiled. "My Ellsworth had the spirit of God inside him from a young age. He used to stand on a chair in our house, he couldn't have been two years old. It was before he had words. But he had sounds. He would stand on that chair, raise his chubby hand, and squint his eyes, and pour out the most impassioned speech. He had dramatic pauses and facial expressions. He would raise his voice to its highest volume, and he'd hold you in his eyes. I thought he would become a preacher—he could have. But as his words came in, we found that he wasn't talking about God but, instead, about justice. I know that God gave him those words. He had a plan we couldn't see. God has always known that a mighty justice will come rolling down, and it's people like Ellsworth who sing of its coming."

Ida Mae had tears in her eyes as her vision of her son came into focus with the reality of his life, and she saw that they were the same.

I took out the dog tags. "These belong to him," I said. "My brother-in-law had them with my father's papers."

Ida Mae took them from my hand and tightened her mouth.

"If there was ever a thing that didn't belong to your father," Ida Mae said slowly, "a set of dog tags with my son's name on them would be at the top of the list."

"My brother-in-law said—"

"They threatened him," Ida Mae said. "And tore him from our home. All these years, I've been blaming Ellsworth, but I can finally see the truth of what happened." She didn't look at me. I felt the room change. I was complicit. And she had no idea how much.

"I was there that day," I said. "I never knew it was your son. But I was there. My father did attack Ellsworth. It's haunted me all these years."

"Not as much as it's haunted me," she said.

Nothing I could say could change the past, but I could stand and listen. I could face the fact that I didn't do enough at the time, that I had ignored the sinking feeling in my gut and focused on keeping a relationship with my sister rather than hunting down the truth when it mattered. I had waited until my father had died. So had Freya. We had both been too scared to do anything at the time.

"Ellsworth said he asked a public defender to press charges," George said. "The bank tried to strike a deal with him, but he refused. He went away to protect us more than anything. He told us there was no reason to rile the beast."

Ellsworth was right. That beast took many forms—the earth

movers in Ward Thirteen, my father causing bodily harm, the billy club to Ellsworth's leg, the police taking my father's side no matter how wrong he was.

Ida Mae tucked the dog tags behind a picture of Ellsworth on her side table. "I'll give them to him in person when he comes. And then we have to set about finding him a wife."

We laughed. George and I smiled at each other. All these years of his mother hounding him—and now she finally had another project.

"You were good to get these for us." He touched the dog tags. "You're a brave woman." I didn't know if it was his whiskey or his engagement, but he had a new swagger.

Ida Mae shrugged her shoulders. I'm sure she had some other words to describe me and my family. But I took George's words to heart. I'd been feeling cowardly without Miranda. She had mothered me to a certain degree, helping me to see the good inside of me, and I had mothered her, helping her to reach her dreams. Two motherless women trying to fill the missing pieces in each other's lives.

"I had a friend tell me I've gone about this all wrong. I should have created a Venn diagram to help Carthage see their interests were my interests. It's what we should've done with the protest to begin with."

Ida Mae let out a sound of disgust and raised her eyes to the ceiling. "Lord have mercy, their interests and our interests were never the same."

"But the highway project hurt Ward Thirteen and the whole city—if we could have made them see that." I had been thinking over all the moves I'd made and wished I'd followed Mr. Neubauer's advice from the beginning.

"That wasn't their goal." Ida Mae shook her head. "There is no diagram or piece of the pie that could convince a group of people who think they've got a God-given right to the whole pie."

I looked down at the floorboards. I didn't have the answers or the fortitude to make a change in the world. I only misunderstood circumstances, misread cues, and failed to see what was in front of me.

"No need to look backward," Alma said to me. "The construction's already begun on the new deli and—"

She was right. Moving forward, I would see the world more clearly.

"Did George tell you?" I asked. "I've got the contract changed. He will be the sole proprietor."

Alma nodded and smiled. "Lots of changes," she said.

"What are Amos and Speedy going to do with their businesses?"

"They used that form you gave them," he said. "I think they'll get enough money from the city to start over on the South Side. Lorraine says she'll be glad to be away from the highway."

"Where are you going to go?" Alma asked.

"I'm thinking. Maybe down South?" I'd never had that thought, but the lilt of Ida Mae's accent had put the idea in my head. I wondered if I had that kind of courage inside of me. Could I leave this place? Start again somewhere else? I knew I couldn't live in a city that would create a statue of my father after all he'd done.

"No," Ida Mae said. "You don't want to be with the white people down there. The colored folk are good folk, but they won't have you. The white people? That's a different story."

"Not all the white people," Alma said.

"I can tell you stories, Alma. And when we're family, I will," Ida Mae said. "But my parents were born into slavery, and their lives as free people were not dictated by their oppressors— burning down our churches, stealing our crops, killing our animals. We had to run twice as hard, and even then, we only got half as far. It's different if you've never lived it."

George hung his head.

"I used to believe in the promise," Ida Mae said, "if I kept my head down, there would be a just reward—there'd be a day when I crossed the line, and life would be easy. It's like I had my jaw clenched trying to get there. Ells and I butted heads over that. He said there wasn't any promised land unless you changed the land you were in. I thought I'd delivered him when he joined the Army. I wasn't worried about the bullets and the enemy—I felt he was safe with that uniform on."

Alma nodded. She would have to walk carefully with her soon-to-be mother-in-law. Their experiences of life were different.

"But we got here," George said. He stood up for Alma with his statement. He moved the conversation. I could see his relationship with his mother changing.

"And you brought your recipes," Alma said to Ida Mae.

"I did," Ida Mae said. "They were stitched to my heart." She paused and looked at me. "George can sell our Southern fare at the new deli when it opens. Your Miranda started the ball rolling on that."

"It's what she would've wanted." I preferred speaking for Miranda rather than hearing other people do it.

"We're collecting more recipes, and Alma is designing the labels," Ida Mae said. "A clever girl we have here."

Alma added, "We're going to call it 'Remember Where You Came From.' A section for the Jewish recipes and a section for the Southern recipes. All the people who came here but can't forget where they came from."

"Your barbecue sauce has to be there," I said to Ida Mae. I wondered about the trouble George might have with the rabbi and the kosher requirements, but if anyone could figure it out, it was him.

"It'll be the first thing you see when you walk in the door," she said. "It's a wonderful taste of the South, but I don't think it's worth going back down for. You've got other places to go."

"Maybe north then," I said.

"Can't get much further north," George said.

"Canada." I didn't know where these ideas were coming from. Miranda always stayed prepared for a sudden move. She'd kept her passport renewed even though we hardly had money to travel, and she kept all her important papers in an envelope she could grab with only a moment's notice. We had talked about going to Montreal.

"The North Star," Alma said.

"Whichever way I go, I need to get away. You've helped me see that. My family here still doesn't think my father did anything wrong."

"Karma will prevail," he said.

"Right," Alma said. "Bad actions eventually come to light, and people go to jail or pay a fine or folks stop doing business with them."

"None of that ever happened to my father," I said. "He died feeling like he'd gotten away with it all."

"History is longer than a man's life," Ida Mae said.

That gave me comfort. That's what refugees understood. They hurled themselves into the unknown not just for themselves but for their progeny. They needed to leave to continue to tell their story. I needed to leave to change my story.

"Will you stay for dinner?" George asked.

Ida Mae looked up sharply.

"No, I'll be getting back. It's been a long day."

I offered my congratulations again and turned to Ida Mae. She gave me her famous smile. We embraced—a long, heartfelt embrace, enough to make me realize we could outpace the circumstances of our families. I'd find my people. Maybe no one as perfect as Miranda, but the world was filled with every sort of person.

CHAPTER ELEVEN

Remembered

Late in February, workmen put a wooden sign in front of Miranda's house: "Home of a Jewish Refugee." The name appalled me. Why did they think there was only one refugee? Why did they reduce the Feins down to a generic category? But the sign was painted and mounted and shellacked. It would be there for a while.

The sign arrived at the house with the news that I had until the middle of March to gather my things and leave. It was now the middle of March.

The night before I left, I packed my books in a box to be delivered to my new home. The museum committee asked me to leave Miranda's books. I flipped through the book she'd been reading when she died, *The Men with the Pink Triangle*, about homosexual men who were prosecuted and killed by Hitler. I put it on the low bookshelf next to her copies of *The Tempest* and *The Adventures of Huckleberry Finn*. I wondered if the museum would leave it there. Probably not.

I looked around the living room. I ran my hand along the dining table scuffed with the hours I had worked there. How many times had she touched this table or tapped me on the shoulder as she went past?

I walked through the deli, already packed into crates. There was a handcart and a stack of cardboard boxes. The movers would leave the cash register and canned goods for the museum store, but everything else would go. All the onions and pickles and spatulas and potholders and spice jars. Tomorrow, they would go, and so would I.

"Knock, knock," a voice at the front door called.

I recognized David's voice and froze. I hadn't talked to him since Miranda's funeral.

"I come bearing gifts," he said quietly.

He let himself in. His slim blue corduroys clashed with his plaid jacket. The space between us sparked with remnants of our last encounter when he had dismissed me hatefully and then had been honored as one of Miranda's pallbearers.

"I'm sorry," he said. He put his camera on the counter and took out an envelope.

I took it from him. I could see photographs inside, but I couldn't look at them. I nodded and held them to my chest. Tears filled my eyes as my face tried to clench them back. I had already cried so many tears.

"I don't know what I was thinking. May I claim temporary insanity?" He grinned at me and wiped his palms on his pants. He looked like Miranda in a way, his facial features close together, a youthfulness around his eyes.

"I forgive you," I said. In the throes of surviving the slights of this world, it was a wonder we didn't all lash out at each other. "I really do."

Years ago, Miranda and I had seen the movie *Judgment at Nuremberg*. It had been heart-wrenching to hear about the crimes against Jewish people during the Nazi Regime. I thought about the scene when the defendant argued that if one of the judges was guilty, then everyone was guilty. All of humanity was guilty. And he was right. We were all guilty.

David smiled and looked around the deli. "Everything's going?"

"Pretty much." There wasn't anything else to say. It was late, and I told him I had to get up early. We laughed that some things never changed, but the laugh never reached our eyes.

After David left, I shut off the lights and climbed the stairs. I could almost hear Miranda puttering around in the kitchen. I sat down on our bed and took off my pants.

When I got in bed, I looked at her pillow and patted the mattress where she should have been. I could feel her there. I knew what she would say. *Don't worry. You're going to be fine. I believe in you.*

I felt calm and breathed deeply.

I hadn't succeeded in stopping the statue of my father or convincing my sister of our father's crimes. My sister's life had shaped her thoughts, and my life had shaped mine. I could still love her from a distance.

I had trapped myself in this conflict, feeling like I had to win. I had turned our relationship into a battleground. No evidence would ever convince her, but I had kept trying. I know now that the world didn't need her to be convinced. The world only needed love and understanding and gentleness.

The statue would go up. The rich people would go to Gallagher's. The poor neighborhoods would be vulnerable. But George and Alma were creating a new life near the university. Ellsworth was coming home to reconcile with his mother. Freya was heading back to Germany to see her brother. She may wish his life had gone differently, but if they could look over the sea of time since they'd last looked into each other's eyes, they'd see the sibling still there, the one they giggled with over ice cream, the one they sang made-up song lyrics with while riding bikes, the one they held hands with while going down rickety stairs. That person was there—the world tried to hide them, bury them; they put up defenses and protected themselves with justifications and theories. But if you peeled back the layers, they'd be there.

*   *   *

The next morning, I wandered through the house and thought through everything I had to do. I had already packed my clothes, given away my skirts and dresses to the Salvation Army, thrown away my tights, and bought some polyester pants in a range of colors. I'd lost weight since Miranda had died, no one urging me to eat, and my new clothes felt like a costume, as if the wardrobe department had commissioned a new script and changed my outfits to match the altered plot lines.

I found myself in front of Miranda's armoire. I bent down to the bottom drawer and pulled out the box of letters and papers from her father. I wanted to read the items she'd shown me over the years, committing each to memory. I held onto the black ribbon she had ripped at her father's funeral. I thought about the one Henrik had ripped and worn. That should've been my ribbon, my place at the front of the synagogue. I could feel her fingers on the grosgrain fabric, and I wanted to keep it, but I placed it back in the box. It would serve as part of the museum's exhibit.

Near the bottom was a leather billfold. Inside, a note and a thick fold of cash.

In case of emergency. For Miranda Fein and Lucretia Wilson. To escape. To live. "Awake, dear heart, awake. Thou hast slept well. Awake." And Miranda's signature.

Wrapped in the note were dollar bills: ones, fives, tens— money she must have set aside each month—almost five hundred dollars—a significant amount. All that time, Miranda had scrimped on her present to secure an uncertain future—a stash of money in case we had to leave in a hurry, in case someone found us out. This was the province of refugees, to imagine a scenario where the only option left was to run.

I left the empty billfold and took the note and money. I might be able to rent an apartment instead of staying in a boarding house. I could get a foothold in my new city. Money in hand, I sat down on the couch and sobbed, holding the bills until my hands loosened and the money fell in my lap. Emperor jumped onto the cushion next to me and purred. I pulled him into my lap and buried my face in his fur. I wanted to remember his smell and his soft fur and the way he looked at me when he was hungry. No one knew where Emperor or Empress had come from. They had claimed us with their hunger and need, and we had given them a place to live because we wanted to help them, and we had grown to love them. Perhaps George most of all. He had promised to take the cats to his new home, despite Ida Mae's protests. She knew he would be moving out with Alma soon enough, and she had a soft spot for the cats even if she would never admit it.

I wiped my eyes and sat for a moment. I wanted to remember the sag of the center cushion and the cat hair on the back of the sofa. I got up and put the money in my purse. Strange to have such an influx of money to lay against the $120 I had saved for the trip.

Out our side window, I could see the land for the new park stretching the length and width of the block. Where we had once seen the wooden siding of the house next door, there was now only open space. At the far edge, I could see some movement. There was my sister Ginny, standing on the road, framed like an Alfred Hitchcock still, arguing with two men. She held blueprints in one hand and gestured toward the elevated highway with the other. A crane idled in the foreground. Weeks ago, they'd installed a tiered pedestal, and it waited for my father's statue. The historical committee had voted to save the Fein house, but the rest of the block went down almost immediately. The Salvation Army. Amos's Appliance Repair. Lorraine's swept porch. Speedy's Used Cars. The earth movers razed each building, leaving a barren landscape of exposed earth. Not ideal, but this would have to serve as the backdrop for our goodbye.

I slipped on my boots and went out the back door. Ginny

could see me approaching, and I could see her see me. We didn't wave or yell. I moved toward her with the inevitability of a train pulling into a station. I thought of the westerns I had seen with Freya, the gunslingers pacing out their steps for their final confrontation.

I was glad to see Sarah sitting against the empty pedestal, reading a book. I had worried I wouldn't see her before I left. Her ponytail was askew, and her glasses sat higher on one side of her face than the other. She nibbled on a fingernail and held her book in one hand.

The two men walked to their parked trucks. Ginny stood alone, in a matching sweater set and our mother's pearls.

"Trouble in paradise?" I asked when I got close enough to talk. It wasn't a great opening—I regretted it as soon as I said it.

"Not that you'd care." Her hands were clenched around her purse straps and a tube of blueprints. Her heels dug into the over-watered ground. It had been six weeks since Joseph had shown us the dog tags—six weeks since he had thrown me against the wall. And as with everything else, Ginny and I had drawn different conclusions. To me, these actions were the absolute, concrete proof that our father and her husband were corrupted by and sick with their own power, but to her, they were a sign of their love for her and how far they would go to protect her.

"I'm sure you'll figure it out." I gestured to the statue's pedestal and the rest of the park. I wanted to let her know I was leaving, but she had missed so many of the initial steps that she was going to be shocked. For weeks, since the day I had delivered the dog tags to George and Ida Mae, I'd worked on a plan to move to Canada. I wanted to cross a border, go someplace where the laws were different, where justice hadn't been misshapen into a bank account, where men couldn't cover up their wrongdoings with a donation to a sheriff's re-election campaign. I wanted to join the draft dodgers who opposed the Vietnam War, the men and women who crossed borders to get married without miscegenation laws to stop them. I wanted to join the history of men and women who had escaped the Fugitive Slave Act and the Jim Crow laws—the Jewish men and women who had escaped the Nuremberg Race Laws. Sometimes, you had to put a border between yourself and the absurdity of what lawmakers could put down with pen and paper.

I had finished my librarian credential by sitting for the final exam and turning in my final project—a study of rural servants from Eastern Carthage. I had listened to the cassettes from the gray library box, and I had read my father's book. I found discrepancies in both. My thesis was titled "Incomplete and Imperfect Sources: A Study of Rural Servants from the Archives of the Carthage Public Library." I fact-checked my father's book and scrutinized the oral histories of the families who had lost their children. They knew at the time it wasn't influenza, but because the bodies were buried so quickly, there wasn't any chance to prove it. A lot of people had died in the area, and the public cemeteries were closed during that time. But in 1958, when the bodies were exhumed and turned over to the police, the families had asserted that the bodies had signs of trauma. The victims were teenagers who had worked in my great-grandfather's home, one as a house servant and the other as a stable boy. Listening to their voices hour after hour, I could hear the pain of their experience but also the threads of their community. They all called the girl by her name, Esme, and they never called her a servant. They called her a "helper." And the boy was Patrick, and they called him a "groomsman." I heard the Irish lilt to their voices in the cadences of their sentences.

Their theory across the board was that Esme and Patrick had become romantically involved. They might've been caught together in the stable. No one knew if my great-grandfather had killed them or if it was a family employee, or a jilted lover.

They had successfully covered it up. By putting their words on tape and securing them in the archive, the families must have held some hope that my family's narrative might be challenged someday. They all talked about damage to Esme's and Patrick's skulls and the indignity of the bodies lying in storage for so long. They talked about bringing their bodies home and how their mothers were singing in heaven. They talked about the protest they had held when my father's book had come out. They may not have gotten immediate results, but they became a part of the public record. Mrs. Caravaggio's library archive had preserved these voices, and it gave me hope that there were projects like this in libraries across the country.

In contrast, my great-grandfather's letter also stood as part of the public record.

> Dear Mr. and Mrs. O'Sullivan, It is with a heavy heart that I write to inform you of the passing of your daughter Esme. She served faithfully in our household for several years, and her presence will be sorely missed. With her gentle demeanor and diligent work ethic, Esme made our home a place of warmth and comfort. Following local burial restrictions, I have arranged for her burial on our property, under the shade of the old oak tree that she loved so much. Please accept our deepest condolences during this difficult time. You will be able to re-bury her once the restrictions have been lifted. You are welcome to visit at any time. Esme was a cherished member of our household, and her memory will forever remain in our hearts. Yours sincerely, Chester A. Wilson

There was a similar letter written to Patrick's parents. My great-grandfather hadn't even made up a cover story. He simply said that they had died. The families had demanded the bodies, but the city had protected the Wilson family by enforcing an influenza burial restriction until both sets of parents had died. I kept the letters as part of the archive and donated what I had of my father's papers to the library. Maybe someday, someone will find them and write a book.

Once I finished the project, I sent my resume far and wide and heard back from only one location—the San Francisco Public Library system came back with an offer. San Francisco didn't have many different laws or circumstances than New York, but it had enough. It certainly had better circumstances than Carthage. By bus, I would cross the borders of New York, Pennsylvania, Ohio, Indiana, Illinois, Missouri, Kansas, Colorado, Utah, and Nevada, and finally arrive in California. I wasn't a refugee, but I felt like I was running.

The San Francisco of my imagination had Victorian houses and steep streets and progressive ideas—home to Alice B. Toklas and the Daughters of Bilitis. Women who loved each other had joined together and given themselves a name. That couldn't happen in Carthage, a place where Miranda and I had worried about being condemned or ostracized for a kiss or even a passionate glance.

"It's an engineering problem," Ginny said, jolting me back to the present. "I want it tall enough to see from the highway but short enough that people can see it from the ground."

I couldn't believe that we were going to talk about sight lines and viewer perspectives when we had so much else to discuss. But maybe we had to cover the banal before we could get to the crucial.

"It looks strange," I said, looking around. "A whole neighborhood used to be here." I could see the elevated highway in front of me and a block of houses to my right, now edging the side of the park. Maybe they'd change the street name to Park Place and charge an arm and a leg for rent.

"I can't even see straight," Ginny said. "What this project has cost me. If I'd known, I'd never have done this. The die is cast." Her sentences weren't coherent, but I understood we were having separate conversations. Listening wasn't her strong suit, nor mine.

Ginny went to the pedestal where Sarah was sitting and laid down her blueprints and purse. She straightened up, as if renewed, and put her hands on her hips. She pointed to a large tarp-covered lump on the ground. Stones held the corners in place, and sharp edges pushed the tarp up like elbows or knees beneath the cover. "This was all meant to honor our father," Ginny said. "It's not too much to ask. The city deserves this."

I looked at Ginny. I wasn't going to fight her on the topic of what the city deserved. I'd fought that narrative as far as it could go, and it had only pushed Ginny further into her corner, and it had driven Joseph to push me up against a wall. No one had shown their best side during our confrontation, but Joseph had crossed another line. I didn't think I'd ever reconcile with him. But that didn't mean I couldn't try to salvage my relationship with my sister. I wanted to tell her about San Francisco, but my stubborn side wouldn't give up the information until she asked. If she didn't care enough to ask where I was going after I was evicted from my home, then I didn't care enough to tell her. Childish, I knew, but that's what you get with siblings.

Ginny's eyes were creased at the corners, and her makeup couldn't hide the dark circles underneath. I remembered one night when she was two, fresh out of the bath. She didn't understand why Daddy and I were sad. She pulled off her towel and danced naked in front of us, her wet hair clasped to her tiny head and droplets flinging off her arms as she spun around the bedroom. Daddy covered his eyes and laughed, his first laugh since our mother died. And then he cried. I remembered it clearly, an anomaly of emotion from our childhood.

How did Ginny go from that light-filled child to this woman before me? How did she go from the young woman ordering a martini to this steely-eyed matron ordering the demolition of houses? We were all born naked babies—where had we gone wrong?

Ginny undid Sarah's ponytail and retied it without Sarah looking up from her book. Then, she raised a finger to me even though I wasn't talking and went back to talk to the workmen by their trucks.

I put my face up to the sun and took a deep breath. The air was getting warmer even though the groundhog had predicted a lion-like March. I'd be gone before the prediction could be confirmed. I hoisted myself onto the pedestal's first tier, happy all over again that I had traded my skirts and dresses for pants.

"Have you seen it?" Sarah asked me. She put her book into her B. Dalton bag and laid it on the pedestal.

"That?" I asked, gesturing to the large tarp.

She nodded and slid off the pedestal.

I jumped down, and we each lifted a stone and pulled back the tarp.

"Oh, Sarah." I didn't know what to say. I took a walk around the statue.

"His hat is so big," she said. "His legs are too short."

My father's statue was hideous. His stiff arms pushed him into an unnatural pose on the ground—his legs diagonally uplifted, though they'd be straight once they raised the statue onto the pedestal. One hand grasped his hat, waving it over his head, but his face was in the ground.

"It looks grotesque." I couldn't turn away.

"Not how he looked in real life," she said.

"No, indeed."

"My mom says it's more like a symbol."

"A symbol of what?"

"I don't know," she admitted. We shared a smile.

I didn't want to put Sarah in an awkward position, but I needed to know. "Did your mother ever say why it had to go right here?" I asked her.

"Because you had a fight." She held my eye. "My mom and dad were pretty mad."

"I guess your mom and I have been fighting about our father for over a decade."

"That's a long time," she said.

"Your mom finally won, though." I pointed back to the pedestal.

She grimaced and shook her head. "I don't think anyone's won."

She was right. I'd been fighting for justice, I suppose, but mostly I had been fighting to have my sister see our father the same way I saw him. And Ginny had been fighting for our father to have an untarnished reputation. Neither of us had reached our goal.

"I've stopped doing research on our ancestors in the graveyard," Sarah said. "I'm afraid what else might turn up about our family."

"It's always better to know," I said, nodding because I knew exactly how she felt.

Sarah and I shook the tarp together and tried to cover the statue back up. My father's hat peeked out from one of the corners. The tarp wasn't large enough to cover his whole being. I pushed my glasses up on my nose at the same time Sarah did. I smiled to myself. We'd inherited the Wilson look. I was sad I wouldn't see her grow up and wondered if she'd ever visit me.

"I don't know what they'll do about the perspective," I said. "If it looks right from the ground, it will look wrong from the highway. It's like the MacArthur statue, but the MacArthur one can only be seen from ground level." Statues weren't meant to be seen from two perspectives.

"What's that?"

"The General MacArthur statue in MacArthur Park?"

"I don't know it."

"Don't you play field hockey there?"

"I do, but I've never seen a statue," she said.

She hadn't seen it? The statue had been a civic project on the largest scale. Carthage had done everything in its power to make General MacArthur a household name, and their efforts hadn't made an impression on the latest generation. The long arc of history was nothing if not unpredictable. I looked again at the tarp-covered statue. My father might've been able to fool the people of his generation and half of the next generation, but Sarah's generation wouldn't be so easily fooled. Herbert Wilson might go from adoring crowds of well-wishers to a squawking population of pigeons. By the time I died, maybe his influence would have died as well.

Sarah pulled her book back out and hoisted herself back onto the empty pedestal, leaning back against the second tier.

"What are you reading?" I asked her. I picked up her B. Dalton bag and saw *The Autobiography of Miss Jane Pittman*, a book of short stories by Alice Walker, and a new novel by Judy Blume.

"Did your mom see these?" I thought Sarah was a follower, but she wasn't. She was a reader. I had worried that her only influence was coming from her parents, but she had already discovered a host of other voices.

"Nope. My mom doesn't look at them. Just pays for them." Sarah shot her eyes up to the sky.

I had been disheartened by the world's uncanny ability to absorb the protests and marches and disruptions and milestones and simply continue with its status quo. Nixon had put the sixties behind us, and Joseph had grown sideburns, briefly. But maybe some of the changes were yet to come. Maybe my relationship with Miranda would eventually have become acceptable, even in Carthage. There had been the Stonewall Riots and the San Francisco March. Maybe change would radiate out from the cities. I felt again I had made the right choice in my destination. I looked forward to being seen with kinder eyes.

"She lets you read what you want. That's admirable," I said.

"My mom says that's how you became so smart." Sarah looked at me to see my reaction.

I was surprised to hear Ginny had anything good to say about me. She thought I was smart. I couldn't hide my smile.

I looked at Ginny, finishing her conversation with the two men. She and I had been trapped by our circumstances. Neither of us had committed our father's crimes, but in the re-telling of them, we had parted ways. There'd been too high a cost all around. Ellsworth had lost years with his family. Miranda had died from the stress of the conflict. Ginny had lost her older sister and had her daughter's faith in the family shaken. She'd also seen Joseph attack me, and she had to live with that knowledge—she was living with a man who would put his hands on her sister. I noticed Ginny was less combative toward me when I was less combative toward her.

Ginny walked back to us. I didn't need to make her suffer. That wasn't my goal. I wanted to leave her with the door open so she might come around someday.

"Can you come in for a coffee?" I asked.

"We don't have time," Ginny said.

I swallowed my habitual response here. *Too busy? Fine, go do your stupid errands. Your loss.* I didn't say any of that.

I said instead, "I want to show you something." I didn't know exactly what I wanted to show them, but I wanted them to see the inside of the house before it became a museum. "It will only take a minute."

"Mom, I'd like to see it," Sarah said.

"Okay, no coffee though, a quick visit," Ginny said.

We walked down the flattened walkway that had been marked through the park. A path from my father's statue to Miranda's father's house. With all the time they were going to spend together, I thought Alexsander Fein might enlighten my father. They were both readers. Maybe my father could open his mind to understand where he had gone off the tracks. Or maybe he'd be too busy waving his hat at the passing traffic.

"This is your house?" Sarah asked when we went inside. "You have a store in the front?" She loved the cash register and the books.

"You're packed?" Ginny asked. "Where are you going?" She put her hand on the box of books, looking for an address.

"I thought you'd never ask," I said. "I'm going to San Francisco." I loved watching her face as she absorbed the news.

"California? That must be a thousand miles from here." She couldn't take her eyes off my face.

"Almost three thousand miles," I said.

"Why are you going so far?" Sarah asked.

"I could say it's where I got a job—"

"You got a job?" Ginny asked.

"I've had a job all these years. I just didn't have a job title. But yes, I got a job." I couldn't help feeling the excitement of sharing this. I hadn't been able to tell anyone about it. "Look at this, they sent me a brochure." I rummaged in my purse and pulled out a well-worn brochure from the San Francisco Library. "It's a Beaux-Arts design. I don't know how to pronounce it, but look at how beautiful it is. And on the next page, you can see the murals by a Swiss artist who studied in Paris. San Francisco invests in its libraries. I can't wait to see it in person." I realized I'd just spoken more words to my sister in one fell swoop than I had in months.

I didn't feel like I'd gotten my point across. I opened my

suitcase and pulled out David's envelope of pictures. Miranda and I didn't have a lot of pictures together, but he had printed every one of them for me. I dealt them out onto my desk. Miranda and me standing in the doorway of the deli with our aprons on. Miranda and me sitting on the front porch, our legs touching, and both of us laughing—a picture of Miranda looking at me, her eyes soft and gentle.

Ginny understood what I was showing her. She looked at me for a long time.

I felt some tightness in my chest release.

"Do you want to see upstairs?" I asked.

"No," Ginny said. "We ought to be going." Upstairs was too much for her. I could hear the door closing in her mind. There was only so far I could go with my sister—like a typewriter carriage hitting the end of a line.

But it didn't hurt me like it might have a year ago. I was glad to see the doors she had, so I could see the shape of her house. She couldn't quite hear what I was saying about Miranda, but sometimes we heard things in our ears and only later did we hear them in our hearts.

I reached into my box of books, not yet sealed, and gave Sarah some of my books—Elie Wiesel. Viktor Frankl. Anne Frank. Frederick Douglass. Harriet Beecher Stowe.

"They all wrote about escaping, surviving. This one, Anne Frank, there's not a day I don't think about this book."

"You talked about it at the funeral," Sarah said.

I was surprised she remembered.

"Well, then, I have the same question for you I asked your grandfather. 'Would you take a family in?' How would you decide?"

Sarah thought about it for a moment. "I'd only ask one question. 'Do I have room?'"

I smiled at Sarah. She was melting my heart. I looked at Ginny, and she softened her eyes as well. She wanted her daughter to grow up with a heart and a conscience.

"I love that question, Sarah," I said. "I'm going to think about it on my trip. 'Do I have room?' I think it's a question we could apply to a lot of situations."

Sarah nodded and looked around my house.

"What are these?" She picked up my stack of composition notebooks.

"I'm going to write down everything I remember from the last few months. A few pages every day. I want to have a record of it. Maybe I'll turn it into a book someday."

"Will I be in it?" my sister asked.

"Of course," I said, though I didn't know if she'd like what I had to say.

"Make me skinny," she said. We both laughed.

"Will I be in it?" Sarah asked.

"Of course," I said. "You're the reason I'm writing it."

"I'll miss you," she said.

I gave her the biggest hug I could manage. I wanted to say so much more to her. I loved her beyond all reason and wanted to be part of her life, but I also had to leave, and I felt that in leaving, I might be able to give her a better version of myself once we saw each other again.

"I'll miss you, too," Ginny said.

I nodded. I wouldn't cut Ginny out. There was no good to come of that.

"Sarah," I added, "let me know what you think of the books, and I can send more from California."

"Okay." She balanced the stack of books and then put them in her bag.

I hugged her and hoped we'd come together again. I knew I'd

be sending a lot of letters, and I hoped she wouldn't forget me.

I turned to Ginny. I couldn't help but add one more thing. "I hate that statue—I just want you to know."

"I hate it, too," Ginny said.

I guffawed. She had taken me so much by surprise that my laugh turned into a cry. I had pushed so hard for fourteen years, and the moment I stopped pushing, Ginny gave in.

Ginny was crying as well. We wiped our eyes with the backs of our hands at the same time. I hugged her. I could feel the little girl and the young woman and even the woman she had become. There was so much we could never heal over, but we could start here.

As I pulled away, wiping my eyes, my sleeve caught on her pearls. I always thought Ginny wore the pearls to needle me or because she was trying to fill the shoes of our mother and take her place in society, but as we untangled ourselves, I thought maybe she just liked the feel of them against her skin, a warmth from the mother she'd never known.

I didn't long for our mother's pearls anymore. I might buy myself some pearls of my own someday. They'd remind me of my mother, that someone had once loved me as a naked baby. I remembered so little about my mother, but I did remember her putting me to bed. She climbed into my bed with me and pulled the covers over both of us. My father would stand in the doorway, somewhat aghast at her playfulness. I remembered snuggling against her, feeling cared for.

I wondered what Sarah would cherish most about her mother. I had no access to their private relationship. I had only judged them as I watched Ginny fixing Sarah's bangs and straightening her hems. I imagined a sign outside her house, "Home of a Superficial Society Woman," a sign I had created and maintained over the years. Just as generic as the refugee sign. But in private, Ginny and Sarah must be silly together, dip their heads together over a book and exchange a glance over their breakfast cereal. My sister was the silliest little girl I had ever met. Funny noises. Funny faces. A born entertainer.

I hugged Ginny close one more time.

After they left, I sat at my desk. The house was creaking with silence. I could hear every breath from my chest. I had wanted to show Ginny my house so she could see Miranda. I wanted her to know. My relationship with Miranda was the best thing I had ever done, and I didn't think Ginny would know me if she didn't know that.

I would leave the house this afternoon, but there was nothing to show I'd been here. I wanted to carve something on the desk to leave my mark. *Lucretia + Miranda.* Put a heart around it. I wanted to leave a trail of breadcrumbs so people could learn about us later.

I took my typewriter out of its case. One last document.

I wrote from my heart:

> Miranda Fein, daughter of Alexsander Fein and proprietor of Fein Foods, died on January 12, 1973. She shared her house with Lucretia Wilson, her companion and partner, in Ward Thirteen in Carthage. Ms. Fein was an integral part of the Jewish and colored communities in Carthage, having served them for decades at her family deli. Ms. Fein arrived in the United States on the *USS Henry Gibbins*, and after a long detainment in Oswego, New York, she and her father settled in Carthage. She will be remembered for her dedication to preserving the recipes of refugees from around the world.

I made three copies and sent them to *The Carthage Register*, *The New York Times*, and *The Washington Post*. I wrote checks for each one against the cash in my billfold.

I wanted my relationship with Miranda to be part of history. I didn't need a statue or a museum, but I had loved someone, and we had lived together, and we had plans that never came to pass. We had lived in Carthage, a city that didn't let us show our true selves. To live in a place that does not want you was a sort of hell, but we had made it into something of a paradise.

Leaving was difficult—the smell of the pickle brine, the sound of George coming to work, the tenderness of Henrik holding Miranda's precious head in his hands, even the sound of the cars and trucks passing overhead—my father's statue, Ginny's delusions, the loneliness and grief I had felt here. I had to breathe it in and find a way to carry it forward.

ACKNOWLEDGMENTS

First of all, thank you to the amazing Inlandia staff, including Cati Porter, Janine Gamblin, Shannon Phillips, and Laura Villareal. It was a joy to work with you, and because of you, I'll always be part of Inlandia! And thank you to Carter Kustera for the amazing book cover! It's a work of art for our bookshelves.

The most terrifying part of writing a novel is asking people to read early (or late) drafts, and I had, in addition to my primary writing group, a very kind set of readers who helped me craft and re-craft these pages over the past decade. Thank you to Susan Straight, Nancy Keefe Rhodes, Suchi Rudra, Karien van Ditzhuijzen, Nancy Rawlinson, Sophie Chahinian, Lorraine Adams, Romaine Washington, and Evan Rosen (who gently set me straight about the $100,000 Bar among other critical details).

I can't thank my writing partners Julie Higgins and Kate Anger enough—not only for the countless times they read chapters, drafts, and rewrites—but for their incredible friendship. I wouldn't be the same person without the troves of advice and love they've given me. I love you both.

I did a lot of research for this book, and I could not have done it without the amazing people who have knowledge beyond mere mortals. I thank Gregg Tripoli at the Onondaga Historical Society, the staff at Syracuse University Special Collections Research Center, Joseph Di Mento at UC Irvine, Kate Holmes and Hank for meeting me in Syracuse and being so welcoming, Courtney Rile who made a documentary about the photographs of Marjory Wilkins, Ann and Dale Tussing who met with me at Syracuse University, and Clarence "Junie" Dunham who let me interview him in his home. In addition, I'm grateful to the following authors, books, and films that made up the bulk of my research: Isabel Wilkerson's *The Warmth of Other Suns: The Epic Story of America's Great Migration*, Robert Caro's *The Power Broker: Robert Moses and the Fall of New York*, Anthony Flint's *Wrestling with Moses: How Jane Jacobs Took On New York's Master Builder and Transformed the American City*, and Dag Freyer's film *Breath of Freedom*.

Thank you to Riverside City College for my sabbatical with a full year to work on my novel. Thank you to all my colleagues who continually asked about my work and were always so supportive. I also leaned on and learned from several creative writing programs and publications over the years. Special thanks to Jo Scott Coe for her Inlandia writing classes at the old library and her dear friendship over the years; to the indomitable Sue Mitchell for her "52" exhibition at the Riverside Art Museum; to the AWP Writer to Writer Mentorship Program with its heart and soul, Diane Zinna, and my mentor, Sharon Millar. I'd also like to thank Ursula DeYoung at *Embark: A Literary Journal for Novelists* for editing and publishing part of my first chapter; and GrubStreet for the Muse & the Marketplace, their online classes (especially the one taught by Matthew Salesses), and GrubStreet's founder and my dear friend, Eve Bridburg.

To everyone at Aquamotion, thank you! My time in the pool kept me sane—or somewhat sane—and your conversations and friendships sustained me.

To my kids, Max and Emily, who were always so enthusiastic about my book project, and Ross Carter, my dear husband who always encouraged me to keep writing!

ABOUT THE AUTHOR

THATCHER CARTER was born into a long line of grudge-keepers from Connecticut. Both her parents stopped talking to their siblings for decades, and she grew up trying to understand the mysteries of human relationships. Understandably, she turned to books for comfort and knowledge, and she continues to be an obsessive reader to this day. For twenty-five years, she taught English at Riverside City College. She now lives in Ontario, Canada with her husband and exuberant Springer Spaniel. She has published essays in *Under the Gum Tree*, *Cargo Literary*, *Awake in the World*, and *Writing from Inlandia*.

RAZED is her first novel.

SELECTED INLANDIA BOOKS

Henry L. A. Jekel: Architect of Eastern Skyscrapers and the California Style by Dr. Vincent Moses and Catherine Whitmore

Orangelandia: The Literature of Inland Citrus edited by Gayle Brandeis

While We're Here We Should Sing by The Why Nots

Go to the Living by Micah Chatterton

No Easy Way: Integrating Riverside Schools – A Victory for Community by Arthur L. Littleworth

ABOUT INLANDIA INSTITUTE

The Inlandia Institute is a regional literary non-profit and publishing house. We seek to bring focus to the richness of the literary enterprise that has existed in this region for ages.

The mission of Inlandia Books is to recognize, support, and expand literary activity in Inland Southern California by publishing works which deepen people's awareness, understanding, and appreciation of this unique, complex and creatively vibrant region. The mission is carried out by actively seeking out new works by writers who are affiliated with the region, and also through national literary competitions which elevate Inlandia Books to the national literary stage.

To learn more about the Inlandia Institute, please visit our website at www.InlandiaInstitute.org.